JUNE

SILAS

What do a bunch of hockey players do during the weeks after they've been eliminated after Round 1 of the playoffs? Lay around my apartment to watch more hockey, apparently. Although I really don't mind. These past two years have been crazy, and maybe we all need a breather.

Last season we made it all the way to the finals. It was the ride of a lifetime. And it didn't come easily to me. I'm only twenty-five years old, but already my career has had more ups and downs and bumps than an aging roller coaster.

I'm not one of those guys who rocketed from obscurity to success. There have been moments when I was sure my hockey career was over before it started. There have been terrible disappointments. But now I'm coming off my best season ever.

Though it ended abruptly ten days ago when my defense broke down during overtime and allowed a play that I was helpless to stop. When the puck whistled past my ear and dropped into the corner of the net, nobody even blamed me.

Not much, anyway. But I'm a goalie. You get used to it.

Suddenly, our season was over. We were all on summer break, but you can bet that none of us had planned a vacation.

Who would tempt fate like that—by trying to guess which date in May or June we'd suddenly have a lot of free time? Not this guy.

The first thing I did was fly home to Northern California to spend a few days with my mom. But now I'm back, a little uncertain of how to spend my precious summer weeks.

I'm not the only one, either.

I'm sitting on the center cushion of my sofa, wedged between my old roommate, Leo, and my current roommate, Jason. And Jason's girlfriend, Heidi—who is my roommate now, too—is perched in his lap, so there's four of us on one couch.

At least I have a seat. Our teammate Drake is sprawled out on the rug, and our team captain O'Doul has dragged a kitchen chair into the room for his own use.

We're watching Game 6 of Round 3, between Dallas and Los Angeles. Nobody in this room is rooting for Dallas. Not after last year's overtime loss of the championship. We hate that team. A lot.

I have a good feeling about tonight's game, though. The series is three to two in L.A.'s favor. And L.A. has the momentum. Dallas is going to get a taste of humility tonight. I can't wait to see it happen.

"Who wants to rent a house on the water in early August?" O'Doul asks, poking at his phone. He's surfing AirBnB rentals.

"Sounds like fun," Jason says. "You think you can find something even though it's already June?"

"Dunno," O'Doul grumbles. "Cape Cod and Fire Island are all booked up."

"Of course they are," I mutter. "Shh, you guys! Power play. Gaborova can make this happen."

"L.A. can't win it tonight," Jason says. "They look tired."

"Bullshit!" I argue. "Dallas is playing scared. They lost two in a row. Now they're gonna choke." Ask me how I know.

"You're the only one who thinks L.A. can win tonight," Leo says.

"Really? I think the L.A. fans beg to differ."

"We're just managing our expectations," Heidi says from Jason's lap. "This is *so* stressful. Maybe if someone brought me a drink I could relax." She bats her eyelashes at her boyfriend.

"Great idea. What are we drinking?" Jason asks.

"Hard liquor," his girlfriend says. They grin at each other like a Hallmark movie couple. It's kind of disgusting. Then again, my roommate used to be a grumpy beast, and now he's in a good mood all the time.

Also, Heidi is a really good person, as well as a great cook. Since she feels a little guilty for moving into what was once a bachelor pad, she always makes enough food for three. Tonight she fed me roast salmon over pureed potatoes with wilted garlic-spinach on the side.

So I muddle through somehow.

"What's in your liquor cabinet?" Leo asks from my other side.

"You could go look," I point out. "Don't ask me to get you a drink during the power play."

"L.A. can't capitalize," Leo argues. "Ever since they changed their third line they never score on a power play."

Even as he's saying this, L.A. makes a crummy pass. It lands neatly on a Dallas stick, and I groan.

"Name some towns in the Hamptons, Leo," says O'Doul.

I'm glued to this game, but our captain is trying to find a beach house to rent?

"Southampton, East Hampton, Westhampton," Leo drones.

"Well, duh!" comes the reply. "I tried those first."

"Don't forget Bridgehampton," Heidi says. "Sagaponack. Montauk. And Quogue."

"Quogue?" O'Doul grumbles. "I dunno if I could vacation

somewhere with that name. It sounds like a plumbing product. Unplug your clog with a Quogue."

"Isn't anyone going to watch the—" I break off on a gasp as disaster strikes. A Dallas D-man makes a blind pass to his wing. It never should have worked. But as I stare at the screen in horror, the wing shoots, finding the L.A. goalie's five hole.

Dallas scores in the seventh minute of the game.

"See?" Leo says calmly. "L.A. isn't gonna knock out Dallas tonight."

"Yeah they are!" I argue because I'm in a mood now. "This will fire them up. Just you wait."

"The waiting would be better with beer," Leo prods. "Just saying."

"Fine." I get up, full of nervous energy. "I'll check the fridge." I don't need to watch the Dallas fans celebrate, anyway.

"There's three six-packs in there," Heidi says as I extricate myself from the sofa. "A Brooklyn lager and two ales from... *Whoa!* Silas!"

Heidi's outburst makes everyone turn and look at the screen again. The cameraman is cruising the best seats in the house, and the commentator is pointing out the team owner and various celebrities in the audience.

And—*holy shit*—there it is, the celebrity face that fills my dreams. Delilah Spark, the most celebrated new singer-song-writer in the world, is in the second row at the fucking Dallas game. As I stare at her exquisite face, the commentator says exactly what I'm thinking. *"This is incredible! Who knew that singer-songwriter Delilah Spark was a hockey fan!"*

"Holy moly!" Jason yells. *"Dude!"*

"This is your *chance!*" O'Doul laughs.

Heidi gives a little squeak of excitement. "Now you have something in common! Something besides, you know, mooning over her and playing her music all day and all night."

I can barely hear them, though. I'm still glued to the screen.

"Delilah Spark made the gossip pages last month when she left her on-again-off-again boyfriend, music producer Brett Ferris..." the commentator drones.

My friends all howl. "She's single, man!" Leo yells. "Get in there!" someone else adds.

"Aren't you hilarious," I drawl. And I already saw those headlines about her breakup. But at the moment, it's the furthest thing from my mind. Because I've just noticed something awful. "She's wearing a..." Could it even be true? "A *Dallas* jersey."

The room erupts. Drake howls, and O'Doul throws a paper napkin at the screen. "Ooooh!" Heidi wails. "Plot twist!"

"That is rough, man," Jason says, shaking his head. "So tragic. You think you know a girl." He laughs, because he thinks it's a simple irony.

If only.

Slowly, I walk into the kitchen. I'm suddenly grumpy as fuck. I'm used to taking a lot of flak for my obsession with Delilah Spark, even if my interest in her is slightly less pathetic than everyone assumes.

Slightly.

Still, it's not like I know her. But *Dallas?* It's like a knife to the heart. It also makes no sense. Delilah is a California girl.

I pull out my phone and open Twitter. I follow exactly sixty-seven people on Twitter—teammates, other hockey friends, sports commentators, and Delilah Spark.

Sure enough, she's been tweeting about the Dallas matchup. *My first hockey game! Someone tell me the rules.*

The tweet has 834 likes already, and dozens of replies. *Don't watch the puck, watch the players!* And, *All you need to know is that if the lamp turns red, they scored.* And, *Hockey players are hot!* Etc.

I tweet a reply, even though I doubt she'll see it. *I'm a big fan of yours, but I have to know why you'd support Dallas. Will they even let you back into California after this?*

7

Shoving my phone into my pocket, I don't feel any better. Why couldn't her first hockey game be mine?

I open the fridge. Heidi has stocked us up on beer, just as she said. I take all three six-packs out, grab an opener, and carry the whole lot into the living room. "Nobody better be in my seat," I grumble.

"Wouldn't dream of it," Drake says from the floor.

There's a knock at the door as I'm setting the beer down on the coffee table. "Get that like a good rookie, would you?"

"When am I done being the rookie?" he asks, getting up anyway.

Castro snorts. "The minute there's someone else we can call 'rookie.' You see anybody like that here?"

"No." Drake opens the door to find Georgia, Leo's wife. She's dragging a beanbag chair behind her. And also Bayer, our recently retired teammate.

There's a chorus of happy sounds, because we never see this guy anymore. "He's alive!" someone shouts. "Tell us everything."

"I would, but there's a game on." He kicks the beanbag into place against the wall for Georgia. "Are we ordering pizza?"

"Let's do it," Heidi says. "Who has a phone?"

I unlock mine and hand it to Heidi. Then I open a beer for myself. On the screen, L.A. is looking more alive. "See? They're going to fight for it. Sometimes being down a goal lights your fire."

"Or down a *game*," Jason argues. "We need a bet. Who's with Silas that L.A. can win this thing?"

My teammates prattle on, and I'm trying to watch the game. But now that I know Delilah Spark is sitting just to the left of the Dallas bench, I can't stop looking for her. And every time they cut to a wide shot of the coach chewing his gum behind his players, I get a glimpse. Dark, shiny hair and a smile that knows secrets.

And that green jersey. That's the part I wish I could unsee.

"Everybody owes Silas fifteen bucks," Heidi says, tapping away at a food-delivery app on my phone. "If you don't have change, just make it twenty."

"Did you remember to order one with—" Drake starts.

"Yes," Heidi cuts him off. "You think by now I don't know what everyone likes?"

"My bad," Drake says from the floor, because he's not stupid.

Heidi is a full-time assistant to the team's general manager. Underestimate her at your own peril. "Silas," she says, "your Twitter is blowing up. Here." She hands back my phone.

"Really," I say slowly, taking it from her. Forty-two new notifications. Huh. That can only mean one thing. "Delilah Spark tweeted me back."

"What?" Heidi squeaks. "Let me see!" She grabs the phone before I can read it. "OMG! Listen: *'Can't I be fans of both teams? A Dallas radio station sent me to my first game.'*"

"Wait, you're busting on your idol for wearing a Dallas jersey?" Jason asks, and then everyone else roars.

"I had to *ask*," I say, and it comes out sounding defensive.

My teammates find this hilarious. They laugh so hard that beer comes out of Drake's nose.

"Let me see!" Jason says, and then my phone gets passed around the room, as if we're all in seventh grade again, and a cute girl passed me a note.

"You *have* to reply," Leo says.

"She should wear an L.A. jersey for half the game," Georgia points out, "so she doesn't piss off her hometown fans."

"Ahhh," says the room, because that's a good point. Georgia is a publicist, so she has to think of these things on the regular.

"Who do we know at the game?" Leo asks.

"Well, we know all the guys on the ice," O'Doul says, and I snort. "Can't exactly ask Gaborova to hand the girl his jersey."

"Besides them," Leo argues.

Georgia lets out a little groan and then reaches for her hand-bag. "You guys are going to make me work right now, aren't you?"

"Please?" I beg. "You must know someone in the L.A. office."

"We need an L.A. jersey, right?" she says, poking at her phone. "In a gift bag. And someone to run it down to her?"

"And a note," I say.

"Ooh!" Heidi squeaks and then pokes me in the arm. "What should it say?"

What indeed? "Say... 'This jersey has two purposes. First, it will keep you on the good side of your hometown crew. And you'll also be on the right side of history when L.A. clinches this series in the third period.'"

"They can't clinch tonight," O'Doul argues.

"Just you wait," I snap back.

———

But waiting is hard. I eat too many slices of pizza because I'm nervous. L.A. is fighting for it, but halfway through the second period they're still trailing 2-0. "Come on, come on," I chant on their next possession of the puck. "You can do this. Dallas is getting complacent."

"For a reason," Jason whispers.

"You shut up."

The stress of the game is compounded by Delilah Spark's frequent appearance on our screen. The TV camera loves her almost as much as I do. She's still wearing that godawful jersey, though. I'm trying hard not to see it as some kind of jinx.

But then L.A. calls a time out, and while they enjoy their sixty seconds of togetherness, the camera cuts once again to Delilah. And—holy shit—someone wearing an L.A. jacket is trying to hand her a bag. After a moment's negotiation with a burly-looking bodyguard, the bag is in her hands.

"Did it!" Georgia yells. She gets up off the beanbag chair and pumps her fist.

"You are such a babe!" Leo says, getting up to high-five his wife. He blocks my view of the screen for a second, and when I look again, Delilah is pulling a black garment out of the bag.

"What's this?" a commentator asks. "Delilah Spark is getting a gift at her first hockey game. It's..." Delilah reveals the L.A. logo on the jersey.

The crew in our living room goes wild.

"This is hilarious," Jason says beside me. "Even if Dallas wins—"

"Bite your goddamn tongue."

"Wasn't there a note?" Heidi asks. "Did she see it?"

We don't find out, because the camera cuts away again to set up the faceoff.

Bummer.

"You have to tweet her again," Heidi says. "She needs to know it's from you."

"No, she doesn't." It really doesn't matter one way or the other.

"But what if the note fell on the floor?" Heidi presses, and there's a worried line between her eyebrows.

"Then it fell on the floor," I say. There are worse accidents of fate. Ask me how I know.

"Let me see your phone," Heidi says.

"No way."

"I just want to see if she replies."

"Tweet something and die," I threaten, handing it over.

"Power play!" Drake yells, and my attention goes right back where it should be—on the game.

"L.A. can't capitalize," Leo grumbles.

But they do! Dallas gives up a goal twenty-seven seconds into the penalty period. And then Dallas has a meltdown, tripping an L.A. player right in front of the ref and drawing a second penalty.

The room goes silent. All eyes are finally on the screen. Forty seconds later, L.A.'s Gaborova scores again, tying up the game.

The Slovak player pumps his fist, and my living room erupts with excitement.

"Told you they could do it!" Leo says, earning a punch from me. "Ow. Kidding!"

"Boys!" Georgia says. "Look."

The camera pans wide, and there's my girl again. Now she's wearing a black jersey and laughing. She takes her phone from the woman sitting beside her, and taps something on the screen.

"This is her tweet!" Heidi says a moment later. "*'Apparently I'm magic,'* it says. *'Who knew?'* Now her feed is going to be full of Dallas fans begging her to change back into the other jersey."

"She can't!" O'Doul yells at the screen. "This is finally getting interesting."

Heidi nudges me with her elbow. "Look, Silas. She thanked you."

I grab that phone so fast that I hear laughter.

@SilasKellyGoalie Thank you for the jersey. It seems to be working.

I type back quickly. *@DelilahSpark Had to be done. If you could leave it on until the end of the game, it would be much appreciated.*

"Oh, my heart!" Heidi coos. "Silas is flirting with a rock star on Twitter."

"L.A. still probably can't win," O'Doul says, just to infuriate me. "They've switched up the lines to rest Myerson. That tendon of his isn't gonna magically heal before the buzzer."

Unfortunately, he has a point.

The next forty minutes are brutal. When there's just five

minutes left—and still a tie score—I'm as tense and exhausted as if I'd played the game myself.

I don't know much about hockey, tweets Delilah Spark during the Dallas time out. *But five minutes isn't long, right? What happens if they tie?*

"The poor girl doesn't know the rules," Heidi says. "She needs private hockey instruction from you, Silas."

"Yeah," Jason says with an evil grin. "That's what Silas wants to give her. Private instruction in *hockey*." He takes the phone out of his girlfriend's hands.

And here's where I make a big mistake. I look away, watching the faceoff instead of watching Jason. It isn't until after the play travels down the ice and into a corner that I notice he's typing something on my phone.

"Hey!" I lunge for it, but he holds it out of my way. "What are you doing?"

"I'm helping you," Jason says, cocking an eyebrow. "This is what you should say next—*'Let's make a bet, Delilah. If L.A. scores in the next five minutes, you'll go out on a date with me.'*"

"No," I say calmly, measuring the short distance between me and my phone. The only problem is that Heidi's in the way. I need to get it back without clocking her in the struggle.

"This is a great idea," Jason says, his grin devilish. "You'll thank me later."

"Dude, yes!" Leo agrees. "Let's vote. Who wants Silas to ask Delilah out?"

Everyone in the whole goddamn room raises his hand.

"Not funny," I say through clenched teeth. I glance away, but it's just a fake-out. Quickly, I turn back toward Jason as I shoot to my feet.

It should have worked, but when you tussle with professional athletes, anything can happen. Jason and I are well-matched for both strength and sharp reflexes. My hand darts toward the phone, but he anticipates me, his fingers closing around the screen.

Where the SEND button is.

"Did you just hit Send?" I demand.

"I... Um... Let's see." Jason looks at the phone in his hand and lets out a nervous laugh. "I'm afraid to look."

"Oh dear," Heidi whispers.

I lunge for the phone.

THREE YEARS EARLIER

SILAS

It's four o'clock, and there's nobody sitting at the bar. The outdoor tables will be filled to the gills all day and night, and the dining room will start its dinner rush in another ninety minutes.

But since it's summertime, the dimly lit bar area will be dead until later. I use the quiet time wisely—cutting up lemon and lime wedges before the happy-hour rush. Restocking the beer and wine.

Oh, and kicking myself for recent disastrous events in Ontario.

When I was still in college, Toronto chose me as their second-round draft pick. Early-round draft picks always find a spot—even if it's on the team's minor league affiliate. This past May I graduated. Which means that four weeks ago I was living the dream—skating with the pros at a Toronto training camp.

My agent told me their contract offer was forthcoming. This was my moment. I was ready to conquer the league.

Or not, as it turns out. The pressure got to me, and I choked in Ontario.

The contract never arrived. Toronto's new goalie lineup did

not include me — either at the NHL level or on the affiliate team. And they released me, unsigned.

Now I'm back behind the bar at Roadie Joe's Bar and Grill, cutting up limes to shove inside bottles of Mexican beer.

The fact that Mr. Dirello gave me a summer job is a blessing. It wasn't charity on his part, though. Darlington Beach is a fancy town and host to a six-week-long music festival from August into September. It's the busiest time of the year for Roadie Joe's.

It's not the Ritz, but at least I'm employed. And I can live with my mom. (Like only a loser does.)

I'm right in the middle of this private pity party when I become aware that someone is now seated on a bar stool in front of me. I glance up, and my gaze collides with the most arresting young woman I've ever seen.

The girl's eyes are dark brown and almost too large for her face. They're round and doe-like with long lashes. They ought to look innocent. Except they're framed by a pair of arched eyebrows that lend her a mistrusting expression.

And there's just something about that gaze that makes it difficult to breathe. "Hi," I wheeze.

"Hi," she says. And her voice catches me off guard all over again. I'm so startled by its unexpected texture that the knife I'd been using actually slips off the lime, nicking my thumb and my fingernail.

"Shit," I hiss. "I'm sorry. What did you need?"

A few seconds tick by, while she's trying to figure out if I'm sane. "Is the bar open for business right now?" Her voice has more depth than a person that size usually has. And there's a grit to her tone that's almost as captivating as her face. "Because if it's not, I need to know that. Please." She taps a large watch on her slim wrist. "I'm on a schedule here."

"Sorry. Yes. Sorry," I stammer. And then I look down to see blood running off my thumb and onto the cutting board.

"Ouch," she says, her voice softening. "Better take care of that first."

There is no end to life's petty humiliations. "Better not order a margarita, I guess." I tilt the contents of the cutting board into the trash, then dump the board and the knife into the sink. I run water over my cut and then grab a paper towel and squeeze it around my thumb to stop the bleeding.

"I only wanted a beer, anyway," she says. "A really cold one, preferably a lager. And it has to cost less than eight dollars including tax and tip because that's exactly how much I have."

"I can work with that." With my good hand I aim for the reach-in, plucking a bottle of von Trapp Vienna from deep down in the bed of ice, and setting it on the bar.

"No glass," she says as I reach for one. "I'll take it from the bottle."

"Sure." Another brilliant utterance from me. I make a move to open it, but she stops me with a raised hand.

"I'm sorry. I know this is weird, but I need to open it myself." She holds up her key chain. It has a church key on it.

"Okay," I say slowly. I can't stop staring at her. She has dark, wavy hair and delicate features. But there's nothing delicate about her bearing.

"It's just my odd little habit." Her gaze challenges me to argue with her.

"Go for it." I hand over the bottle, and she pops off the top.

"Thank you," she says. "Is your thumb okay?"

"Absolutely," I lie. But I don't want to talk about how distracting I find her, even now.

She leans an elbow on the bar and inspects the place, starting with the garage-door-style windows that stretch from floor to ceiling, then taking in the beer taps and the liquor shelf.

And then me. When those big eyes sweep all the parts of me that she can see, I feel weirdly electrified.

"Thank you —" She focuses on my name tag. "— Ralph."

"N-no problem." My hand covers the name tag before I realize what I'm doing. So I drop it again.

I spend a half second wondering if I should explain that Ralph isn't really my name. The tag is a joke. I went to high school with the owner's son — Danny Dirello. And Ralph is the nickname he gave me junior year when I ralphed all over a parking lot after my first kegger.

But you just don't tell the most stunning girl you've ever seen that your nametag is a vestigial reminder of the time you puked in front of all your friends.

And anyway, she has her drink, and my work here is done. I need to find something else to do with my hands and maybe also my brain. Otherwise, I'm just going to stare at her and measure all the ways that she's beautiful.

It's not easy to look away, though. Even as I locate a Band-Aid and slap it over the gash on my thumb, I'm stealing little glances at her. She's lanky, with long arms and a smooth neck that I study as she lifts her beer and takes a swig. But her edges are softened somewhat by waves of thick, dark hair.

She's wearing a simple black T-shirt that says, *Kind of a Big Deal.* And it makes me smile.

"What?" she demands, putting down the beer, and proving that I've completely lost my ability to be subtle.

"Nothing. Just amused by your shirt."

She glances down and frowns, as if she's never seen it before. "You have to laugh at yourself in this town, right?" She looks up again and pins me with a gaze that stops my blood from circulating. "Everyone takes themselves so seriously. I thought Northern California was supposed to be laid back."

"Oh, we are," I promise. "I go surfing whenever I get a day off. You can't surf and be uptight. They'll run you right out of town." I hear myself babbling, and I don't even care. So long as she keeps looking at me. "Unless you're here with the music festival people. They turn this place into a different planet during the summer."

"So you're saying I'm here with the wrong crowd?"

"Um…" She takes another sip of beer, and I watch helplessly as her elegant throat swallows. "Maybe. Not a lot of music executives on surfboards. Just saying."

She smiles at me, and her expression is wicked. "They might get their Rolexes wet."

"Those are actually waterproof," I say pointlessly.

"Figures." She rolls her eyes. "Well, Ralph, you've been very enlightening. The fact that I'm working every day for slave's wages kind of proves your point."

I pick up a rag and wipe down a bar that doesn't need wiping. "What do you do for the festival?"

"Well…" She chuckles. "I play whenever they'll let me. I'm background music at some very fancy catered lunches, and I'm given slots on the main stages at awkward hours."

"No way." She's a performer. I hadn't expected that, probably because she looks so young. Early twenties, I think. "That still sounds fun."

"Oh, it is. I would be loving every second of it. But the point of playing all those little gigs is to try to get important people to notice me. So that's stressful. And my manager wants to talk shop all day and all night." She rolls her eyes. "I just need a lucky break. And maybe a day off."

"Well…" I'm about to offer a hand with that, but I don't get the chance.

"Ralph!" my buddy Danny calls from the kitchen. "Bring us some wine for the coq au vin!"

Seriously? He can't just come out here and get it himself? "Oui monsieur!" I yell back. "Does sir require anything else? A fresh drink? A foot massage, maybe?"

A hand appears in the passthrough window between the kitchen and the bar. It gives me the finger.

The most gorgeous girl in the world laughs.

"I'll be right back," I tell her. As if she cares. Then I grab a bottle of pinot noir and duck around the back of the bar where a door leads to the kitchen.

Danny is stirring a giant pot with a wooden spatula as long as a Louisville Slugger. He studied hospitality management in college and seems to be settling in to work with his dad. "Having fun today?" he asks me with a smirk.

I drop my voice to a whisper. "You're a giant dick."

"Maybe." He chuckles. "But I still need the wine. Open 'er up and let her rip."

I pull a corkscrew out of my pocket before he's even finished speaking. The faster I get this done, the faster I can go back to her.

"Date tonight?" he asks as I work the cork out of the bottle.

"We'll see," I mutter.

Danny grins. He grabs the bottle and unceremoniously starts pouring it into the pot. "Better get back to it, then," he says. "I'm pulling for you."

"Yeah, I'll bet."

But now a new voice comes through the pass-through window. A loud one.

"Don't tell me they don't like the cover in Germany! It's a great fucking cover, and I used their photographer. They can bite me. That cover tested well in two quadrants, and we're never pulling women over thirty-four for that artist anyway."

Danny and I both turn around at the same time and bend over just far enough to look through the window. "Fuck," he whispers.

We both see a blond, preppy guy wearing shades and a crisp shirt, Bluetooth in his ear, chattering away at top volume, like the asshole that he is. Anyone would take one look at him and guess: *he's probably a superdick.*

But I don't have to guess. I already know this particular

superdick. He is—without exaggeration—my least favorite person in the world. And that's saying something, considering my violent father is serving prison time for assault.

Brett Fucking Ferris. It's my first time seeing him since I landed back in Darlington Beach. His family owns this town. And his mother runs the music festival. I'm tending bar at one of the busiest restaurants in town.

Seeing him was inevitable. But that don't make it right.

"Easy," Danny whispers. "You want me to take his order?"

"No," I grunt. "You really think I can't control myself when that asshole comes in here? Like I didn't already learn that lesson?"

"I didn't say that," my oldest friend says. "But he won't make it easy."

He's probably right. But it doesn't make sense for me to change a single minute of my day for that prick. And at least I don't have to see his mug every day, like I did when we attended the same private school.

I was there on a tennis scholarship, although hockey was really my sport of choice. But this is California, and the prep schools will give you tuition money to beat the other prep schools at tennis, not hockey.

So I did both—captaining the tennis team and minding the net for the best club hockey team in Northern California. Because diving for flying objects is my forte, whether I'm in white shoes or black skates.

Brett Ferris had also played varsity tennis. He fancied himself a star and that meant he'd hated me from the second my scholarship ass walked through the door. I didn't worry about it, though.

But I should have.

In the stockroom, I grab the case of Dos Equis that I need to restock and then reenter the bar. Ferris doesn't even look up. Not that I'm surprised.

What's more surprising is the way he snaps at the lovely creature drinking her beer on the barstool. "Been looking everywhere for you. Let's go."

And just like that, my blood boils. I think I hear Danny groan from the kitchen.

But my girl just lifts her bottle and takes a leisurely sip of her beer, as if he hadn't said anything at all.

Not that many people ignore Brett Ferris, so I laugh.

That's when he notices me, his expression turning to distaste, and his eyes narrowing. He's still on the phone. "Did you hear back from the Aussies?" he asks the unfortunate soul on the other end of the line. "Well, wake them up! Jesus. I need those numbers by Friday. Gotta run." He taps the screen and then turns to her. "Let's roll."

She does not seem the least bit put off by his rudeness. "I need a minute," she says to him. Then she waves a hand toward the door, as if to nudge him outside.

But he doesn't budge, frowning down at her T-shirt instead. "*That's* what you're wearing tonight?"

A flash of irritation sparks in her giant eyes. "It's funny! God." She shakes her head. "I'll follow you outside. Ralph, here, doesn't need to listen to your calls."

"Ralph, the bartender." Brett smirks at me. "Nice career choice."

"It's *honest* work," I say. Note the emphasis. But that's as far as I'll let myself go, even if he's already killed every happy thought in my head. Not like that's difficult these days.

"You two know each other?" she asks.

I am spared hearing Brett's answer, because his phone squeals again. It practically splits my eardrums. I didn't even know you could set a ringer that loud.

She winces and then points at the door. "Outside with that. Let me finish this in peace."

"Hurry up," he says. As he turns around, I notice that he's

wearing the biggest, shiniest gold Rolex ever made. Of course he is.

No wonder this girl is having a rough summer, if she has to spend it with that tool. His phone rings again, but mercifully he answers it. All we can hear is his barking as he recedes toward the door.

"High school," I say to answer her questioning gaze. "He didn't like me very much."

"Competition?" she guesses.

"Something like that." Yeah, it was *exactly* like that. But I don't want to tell her my sob story. "His family runs this town," I say instead. "And his mother created the music festival."

"So I heard," she says. "I've been following him around like a baby duck because he can introduce me to all the people that matter."

"I'm sure that's true," I say, my mood plummeting even further.

She takes her final swig of beer. "Gotta hop." She reaches into her pocket, pulls out exactly eight dollars and slaps it on the bar.

She's on her feet by the time I can even pick it up. "Wait! Here's some change." Even with the tip the beer isn't eight bucks. That's why people come to Roadie Joe's.

"Keep it!" She grins at me. "You're a good man, Ralph."

I push two dollars in her direction. "Tell you what. Give me your number instead."

Her eyes widen. "I…" She hesitates. "I'd better not."

Crash and burn. Wow. "Have a good gig, tonight," I say, wondering how my life got to this point. One more little disappointment in a pretty brutal streak.

And I must not be very good at hiding it, either. "Thank you." She bites her lip, turns around, and then leaves. The singles are still on the bar.

I didn't even get her name.

SILAS

Not three days later I see her again.

I'm coming out of the gym after a brutal workout. My legs are shaking from the squats I just did. It's hard to say why I'm still pushing myself like this. My athletic career is probably over. But I'm not ready to accept it.

Anyway, I step out onto Main Street, wondering which protein shake to order, when I see those dark, expressive eyes looking out at me from a poster on a kiosk. And—this is embarrassing—I'm so startled that I actually trip over my own feet. One sneaker catches on the other one, and I briefly lose my balance and nearly go down.

Thank God only her photograph is there to see it.

Once I regain my balance, I move in for a closer look. *Friday, nine p.m. at the Coconut Club. Singer-songwriter Delilah Spark.*

Delilah. Now I know her name. And it looks like she finally scored a decent time slot at one of the bigger music clubs. Standing there on the street, looking at a poster, my smile is as bright as the sun.

"She sure is a looker," rasps a voice beside me.

I jerk my chin to the left to see a red-faced older man chuckling to himself. Immediately, my blood flashes hot with irritation. I can't stand the sound of his laugh or the leer in his eye.

Easy, I coach myself. I'm not used to having such a strong reaction to anyone. I turn away and amble down the sidewalk, knowing I'm the worst kind of hypocrite. Whatever Delilah does to that guy, she does to me, too. Times ten.

The difference between us, though, is that on Friday night I actually show up to hear her at the Coconut Club. I pay the bouncer a twenty-dollar cover that I really can't afford, and I take up a position on the wall. The place is packed. Every table is filled, and every barstool.

There's a band onstage already. A decal on their bass drum gives the band's name: Pebble Yell. It's the dumbest name I've ever heard, but the band is better than its name. Much better. They have a warm, nineties grunge sound that has the whole club in their thrall. The lead singer looks like a young Eddie Vedder, but sings with a silkier voice. And their lead guitar is a wizard.

And Delilah has to follow this act?

That's when I feel my first frisson of nerves for her. And where is she? I scan the eager faces in the audience and find Delilah. She's leaning against the opposite wall, down near the stage, a bottle of water in one hand and a guitar case in the other. She looks completely calm—like she doesn't know she's going to have to sound like *that* to keep these people in the room.

An all too familiar emotion rolls through me—a cocktail of excitement and dread. It doesn't matter how talented you are or how much you deserve a chance. Sometimes the odds are stacked against you. I have the weirdest urge to cross the room and stand beside Delilah. To shore her up.

But I stay put, because that would just be weird.

Meanwhile, the audience is loving Pebble Yell. The people seated at tables are all leaning forward in their chairs. And the back of the club is so packed full of fans that the cocktail wait-resses can hardly get through to hustle drinks. When the last, rich chord finally reverberates through the amp, nobody is ready for it to end.

The applause is like thunder, and half the room stands up.

Now I'm sweating. I don't even know Delilah, but what if she bombs? What if the audience wants more of the grunge band and not the quieter tones of a female vocalist? Or—worse—what if Delilah sucks? What if she can't carry a tune in a bucket?

That's when I notice that about a quarter of the audience has decided that the party's over. People are gathering their things and streaming for the exits. A fresh wave of unease rolls through me, as if I'm the one who has to get up on that stage and sing.

How do people do that, anyway? And why did showing up here tonight seem like a good idea? I could have spent that twenty bucks on fish tacos and beer. I could be lighting up a joint on the beach right now, walking in the moonlight. There's enough failure in my life already. Who wants to watch a pretty girl go down in flames?

Not me, that's for sure.

Speaking of failure—at this very moment there's a voicemail on my phone from my agent. I'm avoiding listening to it, because I know it's bad news. If she had good news, there'd be four calls and several text messages, not just the one call.

Listening to her message is unnecessary, because I already know what it will say. *"Listen, Silas, if you just wait a few months, we might find a minor league team that's struggling with its goalie lineup. And if that doesn't work out, I could find a spot for you overseas. Germany or Russia, maybe."*

But that's where the washed up hockey players go. I'm not ready to be a has-been at twenty-two.

Grumpy now, I eye Delilah's audience with suspicion.

People who were stuck in back before are filling in the empty tables. So at least that's something. But they aren't even looking at Delilah. They're texting and drinking. One guy is feeling up his date, who looks annoyed. And another couple is fighting. They're right in front of me, hissing at each other with angry eyes. Then the dude actually stands up so fast his chair tips over with a bang. He stomps away, while the woman sits there looking uncomfortable as we all stare.

She leans down and picks up the chair, shell-shocked.

Delilah doesn't notice. She's already seated herself on a stool in the middle of the stage. She's adjusting her microphone. A single circle of light picks her out of the inky blackness. It glows brightly, giving her dark hair an ethereal purple sheen.

A man jumps up on the stage. He grabs the mic that Delilah has just taken pains to adjust and says—in a voice that sounds super-bored—"Let's give it up for new talent, Delilah Spark."

Then? He hops down even as he slips a cigarette out of the package in his fingers, as if to say Delilah's set is the perfect time to step out for a smoke.

I want to kick him in the teeth, I really do.

Delilah looks entirely placid up there, though. She readjusts the mic and then tunes her guitar. From the expression on her face, she might be sitting in the middle of her own living room, calmly adjusting each pin and then plucking quietly.

Don't singers warm up beforehand? Christ. This is going to go badly. A drop of sweat rolls down my back.

Some of the conversation stops but not all of it. I stare pointedly at a woman who's yapping into her cell phone right now. "You're where? At that place on the beach?" She doesn't even notice my irritation.

And then some drunk near the front yells, "Bring the band back! They were fucking great."

My hands ball into fists.

Delilah silences her guitar strings with her palm, and looks right at him. "You mean bring back the dudes, right? You think only a penis can rock?"

The crowd laughs uneasily.

"You know what I mean," the drunk grumbles. "A girl and a guitar. It's not the same."

She adjusts the mic one more time, not even bothering to glance back at him again. "You, sir, are why I write music. You go ahead and say whatever you want, because I enjoy it when people underestimate me."

The room is *silent* now as Delilah begins to strum her guitar strings in a pronounced rhythm. It takes me a second to realize that she's already got everyone's attention, and she didn't even need a decent introduction to get it.

Her fingers pick up speed on the fretboard. The chord progression isn't complicated, but goosebumps climb up my spine. What's she playing? It's familiar, but I can't place it until she opens her mouth and starts to sing.

That's when I experience a full-body shiver. Because that *voice*. It's husky and full of texture. It vibrates through all the empty parts of my chest. Delilah is covering "Black" by Pearl Jam. Maybe she picked it as a great segue from the last band's nineties sound. Or maybe she always opens with this song, because in her voice the lyrics are even more interesting than in Eddie Vedder's.

I mean—goddamn. You can't hear that and keep up your conversation at the bar. You can't text your mom or grope your girlfriend or scratch your nuts anymore, because that smoky, wild voice is crawling through your soul and you have no choice but to listen.

The music washes over me in waves. Every line is ecstasy. If I wasn't already fascinated with Delilah after a short conversation at the bar, I would be right now. Note by note she takes the room apart with a song about anguish and a lost love.

Man down. Seriously. She's magic.

And it doesn't let up. After she wrings the whole room out with Pearl Jam, she goes on to cover Bonnie Raitt. "I guess it's a nineties kind of night," she whispers into the microphone after her second song.

The audience laughs warmly, as if they're old friends of hers. And by now I guess they are. That's her gift, apparently. I'm surely not the only one in the room who feels a strange connection to the amazing woman on the stage.

Crowds are part of my world, too. When the fans are on your side at a game, there's nothing like that roar of support. It's like the best hug you ever got, coupled with a high-five from God himself. It feeds your soul. I feel the most alive when I'm having a good game in front of a good crowd.

Or I used to. I feel pretty fucking alive right now, too.

"Now this is a little song I wrote for some of the women in my life. You know who you are," Delilah says. She's strumming her guitar gently, and the expression on her face is almost private—as though she's playing this for herself. As if the audience is just an afterthought. She lifts her face and closes her eyes. Then she begins to sing.

You shouldn't wait around for him
Men don't have a lock on praise
Show me how you lift your chin
Show me how you own this place
Sparkle on, honey, sparkle on...

She takes a breath, and I realize I'm holding mine.

Don't let him tell you lies
He doesn't get to write your story
You're not his to minimize
Own your flaws and mine your glory
Sparkle on, honey, sparkle on...

The song weaves the tale of a woman who's lost herself. But at the end of every heartbreaking stanza, Delilah looks up and tells the audience to sparkle on.

She's the one who shines, though. The room is still so quiet that I can hear the scrape of Delilah's guitar pick against the strings. I scan the crowd, and all their faces are rapt. Drinks are forgotten on the table. My gaze lands on the woman in front of me—the one whose boyfriend left in a huff. She's wiping a tear from the corner of her eye.

Delilah has been playing that guitar for less than fifteen minutes. And she's already made someone cry.

Now that's power. Jesus. What a total babe.

The song ends way too soon. But at least there's more. The tempo picks up as Delilah swings into another original song. She does this thing with her hand—slapping the body of her guitar to beat out a rhythm. It gives her a bigger sound, and gets the whole room moving subtly with the beat.

I can't help wonder what she'd sound like with a band behind her. Amazing, probably.

The club is packed again. Every chair is taken, and it's standing-room only at the bar, hundreds of people leaning forward to get a little closer to the little girl with the big sound.

Then it's over. Before I'm ready, she's rising from the stool and saying goodnight while the audience hollers their approval. I'm still standing there clapping, mouth open, cycling through every possible human emotion as she's stepping off the stage.

That's when Brett Ferris comes out of the shadows to claim her. He throws a victorious arm around her while the audience still applauds.

Then he pulls her into a hard kiss. It's a caveman move.

And I am... Crushed isn't even a big enough word. Horrified. Defeated. Pick one. The idea of *him* touching her makes me want to barf.

And that was such a Brett thing to do—homing in on her moment. Claiming it as his own.

It's barely any consolation that she looks annoyed, too.

That's when I have to tap out. I push off the wall and slip toward the back door, dodging bodies to get to the exit.

Outside, the breeze smells like the ocean. The door closes behind me, muting the sound of applause and laughter. I take a deep breath and head toward the beach. I need the sand and the fresh air. I need the sound of crashing waves to drown out the drum beat of my own rage.

Jogging toward the sound of the water, I have the strangest urge to howl at the sky. I don't even know that girl. Not really. But I want to. And I can't shake the feeling that the Bretts of the world get more and more of what's good. While the Ralphs of the world serve them ice-cold champagne and light their cigars.

Delilah, though. She could go places. I hope like hell that someone other than Brett takes her there. I know nothing about the music industry. But I know in my gut that she could be a star.

I walk a long way on the beach. There are very few people out here with me, and none at all with their feet in the wet sand, trudging along alone.

The voicemail in my pocket mocks me. When I finally listen to it hours later, it says exactly what I expected it to.

JUNE

DELILAH

"Omigod, Delilah!" My publicist, Becky—and best friend—has to shout over the roar of the stadium crowd.

"What?" I'm not listening, though, because the players are whipping past us on the ice at breathtaking speed. And then they do that thing where they swap players really fast—two of them piling back through the little doorway while two others vault over the wall and skate toward the action. "How do they know when it's their turn, anyway?"

"The coach gives them a signal. Like I'm trying to do right now." Becky snaps her fingers. "Listen. A cute boy wants to go on a date with you. And Twitter is amused."

"A cute boy? What is he, twelve? And you're the one who tells me never to respond to the pervs on Twitter."

"This time it's different."

"Uh-huh." I tune her out again, because they're fighting for the puck *right* in front of me. And it's thrilling. "Hockey players have muscular asses. I guess that makes sense to me. But why do they all have beards? Is it, like, in their contract?"

"They don't shave during the playoffs," Becky says, still squinting at my phone. "You like beards?"

"So what if I do?" My ex was as clean shaven as a baby's behind, to the point of being prissy about it. And he was the biggest mistake of my adult life, so obviously I need to branch out a little.

Although. I was once attracted to a bearded guy. A really nice one. And that went nowhere.

"You think hockey players are pretty cute, huh?" Becky says. There's coyness in her voice.

"Cute isn't the right word. They're so..." I let out a sigh. "Rugged, I guess." It's not like I can easily see their faces, what with the helmets and the eye-shields. But I get glimpses of cut, masculine jaws and strong chins. Flashing eyes, bent on victory.

It's very sexy. Although maybe I do need to get out more.

"You need to get out more," Becky says, echoing my thoughts. "And what if I told you the guy who wants a date *is* a hockey player. Look." Becky elbows me.

"This better be good," I grumble as I lean over her phone. "I'm missing some serious hockey action right now."

"First game, and you're already a fan?" She laughs. "This is the guy asking you out on Twitter. He's the one who had the jersey delivered to you."

I look down at the black jersey I'm currently wearing. "Is he *here?*"

"No! That's why he's tweeted it. See?"

I finally read the tweet. *If L.A. clinches before the buzzer, will you go on a date with me?*

Okay, that's kind of cute. "He's asking me out, but it's also a bet?"

"Basically. Yeah." Becky is practically bouncing in her seat.

"Who is this guy?"

"He's a goalie on the Brooklyn team that already got knocked out of the playoffs. Apparently he hates Dallas. I think Dallas beat them in the finals last season."

That's as good a reason to hold a grudge as any. But I'm not in the market for a date. Or anything else to do with men. Possibly forever. "Show me a photo," I say anyway. Because I never was very smart.

Becky taps my phone for a couple seconds. "Oh, he's cute!"

She turns the phone to show me, and I laugh. "Becky! How would you know? He's wearing a full face mask!" When I look out across the ice at the L.A. goalie, I see the same thing—a cage over the guy's face.

"That jaw, though. The part we can see is cute. Besides, look at how bendy goalies are."

We both watch the on-ice action for a few contemplative moments as the goalie scissors his body to make one save and then another. And a couple months of celibacy are really screwing with my libido. The raw masculine power I'm witnessing tonight really speaks to my inner cavewoman.

These men are like warriors. Bendy, bearded warriors.

And the goalie is always in motion. And I love the way his awareness of the play around him is dialed up to eleven. It would feel pretty incredible to have that kind of focus directed at me.

"I see the potential," I admit.

"And it's just a date—with a professional athlete who says he's a fan of yours. He follows you."

"Him and two million other people. You're going to make this whole thing into a PR moment, aren't you?"

"It already *is* a PR moment," Becky insists. "Besides, I doubt L.A. can clinch in the next four minutes. If you say yes, you still might not ever meet him. But Twitter will swoon if you take the bet."

"And I live to make Twitter swoon."

"Maybe you don't, but I do." Becky blinks at me with wide blue eyes. We're such opposites. She's trusting and open, and I'm...not. But maybe that's why we get along so well.

"Type up a reply..." I say.

She gives a squeak of joy.

"But don't send it yet! Jesus. I'm still thinking."

"What?" Becky pouts. "Come *on*. Make Twitter swoon."

"I'm thinking, okay? What if Mr. Muscles wants to frisk the guy or something."

Becky looks over her shoulder, checking the whereabouts of my bodyguard before we talk about him. "You're allowed to have a life. And if you do go out with this guy, we can clear him in advance. He's a public figure, Delilah. Not some rando." She's already tapping on her phone, trying to figure out how to phrase our reply.

Tweeting for me is literally Becky's job. A good day at work for her is a bunch of new Twitter followers and a few new photos for Instagram where I don't blink at just the wrong time.

Those apps are on my phone, too, but I rarely look at them. People are horrible to me on the internet. To be fair, people are also lovely to me on the internet. It's just that if I hear a hundred bits of praise and two nasty comments, it's the nasty ones that sink into my soul.

It doesn't make any sense, but there you go.

"Okay," she says. "My finger is on the trigger."

"What did you write?" I ask. But then I lose focus for a moment as Dallas gains the puck. Two of their players pass it rapidly down the ice, and I find myself leaning forward in my seat and holding my breath.

The whole date thing is moot if Dallas scores right now. And why am I strangely disappointed?

The Dallas player makes his charge. I see him swing his stick, and the bendy goalie is already in motion —

"A glove save!" Becky screams. "Whoa!" Play halts for a moment, and my heart is beating faster than it has in a while.

Honestly, this is the first time I've ever understood why people watch sports. Staring at the game on a screen seems like a waste of time. I can never sit still long enough to watch TV. But a live hockey game is much more fun than I expected.

Furthermore, twenty thousand other people dressed in green or black agree. I consider myself a connoisseur of crowds at this point. And this stadium is *rocking*.

The players line up again, and the ref drops the puck between two them. They pounce like hungry tigers. You can feel the tension in the room as the clock ticks down. There's fewer than four minutes left.

The puck flies in our direction, and then a Dallas player slams an L.A. player against the plexiglass right in front of me. The first time they did that, I actually jumped like a frightened kitten. But this time I'm ready. The player is so close to me that I can see the beads of sweat on his eyelashes. That really shouldn't be sexy, but it is.

Professional athletes. Who knew?

Come on, L.A., I find myself thinking. Now that I might meet a hockey player, I am even more invested. Although it's looking increasingly unlikely. Four minutes become three. "What happens if it's a tie?" I ask suddenly.

"They go into overtime. They put another twenty minutes up on the clock. The first team to score during that period wins. Rinse and repeat."

"Oh. But the dating goalie thinks L.A. can win inside of three minutes?"

"That's what he said. But it seems unlikely."

I guess it doesn't matter what I do, then. So I take the phone from Becky and erase her reply.

"What are you doing?"

"I'm rewording it." *Sure, if L.A. wins in the next three minutes, I'll go out on a date with you. I'll put the green jersey back on, though, just to keep this interesting.*

"Delilah! That's bitchy."

"It's a *shirt*, Beck." I hit Send. "No shirt ever changed the outcome of a game. Where's the green one?"

She blinks at me. "I'm not giving it to you."

"Why not? I'm being fun."

"No, you're sabotaging yourself. It's like you don't even want to meet a nice man. I'm worried about you."

"I would love to meet a nice man," I tell her. "Except those don't really exist."

"See?" she sputters. "That's not true."

"Name one. A *real* one. Not a guy from one of your books."

She bites her lip. "Okay, just because we meet a lot of assholes in the music business doesn't mean nice guys don't exist."

"Really? Between us, we have fifty years of experience meeting boys. And not one nice boyfriend to show for it."

"I had a *very* nice boyfriend," she argues. "It's just that he now also has a very nice boyfriend."

"Well…" I have to admit that her ex is a good guy. "Whatever. There aren't many. And you're stalling. Hand over the Dallas jersey."

"You'll have to kill me first," she says crisply. "One of us is going on a fun date, damn it." She checks her phone.

"What did he say?" I find myself asking.

"Nothing at all." She stashes her phone. "He's glued to the game, I'll bet. That's why I want you to meet him. He's interested in you, but he has his own life. Not like Ferris, the bloodsucking vampire."

"I thought we weren't talking about him tonight."

"Fine. Two minutes," Becky says, leaning forward in her seat. "The suspense is killing me."

I have to admit it's killing me, too. The puck is in the far corner now, with players fighting over it. I can almost feel the clock ticking down in my gut. Then L.A. flips it loose, and the chase is on.

"He replied!" Becky says, her phone in her hand again. "He says: *Even if you wear the Dallas jersey, this is totally happening. You look pretty great in black, though. Just saying.*"

It ought to seem a little creepy that he can see me when I can't see him. But for some reason the compliment spreads warmth across my face, anyway.

"Aw! See how cute he is?" Becky gasps. "You two can tell this story to your children."

"Oh stop." My cheeks are on fire, and it makes no sense. Besides, there's only ninety seconds on the clock now.

"Come on L.A.!" Becky hollers. "Let's make some opportunities!"

The players' speed is almost dizzying. I guess it would light a fire under my ass, too, if I knew this could head into infinite overtime. It's a blur of black and green and sheer ambition. I lose track of the puck near the Dallas goal. "What's happening?" I ask pointlessly.

"SHOOT!" Becky screams.

And then twenty thousand people stand up for a better look as the Dallas goalie dives.

I stop breathing. And then the crowd makes a deafening roar as the lamp lights behind the Dallas goal.

"OMG!" Becky squeaks. "L.A. scored!"

"There's still another minute on the clock," I say slowly.

She cackles. "What are the odds? I think you're going on a date."

I take the phone out of her hand. *So, um, where do you live?* I reply to the goalie.

It looks like I'm going to meet him after all.

THREE YEARS EARLIER

DELILAH

My set at the Coconut Club sets off a flurry of meetings with record labels. For a few days, it's wildly exciting. Although nobody offers me a contract.

"*Yet*," Brett corrects me when I point this out after one of the meetings. His brand-new pair of mirrored sunglasses shine in the California sunlight, and he flashes me a smile full of perfectly whitened teeth.

I want to believe him so badly. But I can't shake the feeling that I'm just one more shiny thing in his life that he'll discard when a newer model comes along.

"We're not taking the first offer that comes, anyway," he adds. "I'm going to play hardball."

Brett is fond of using sports analogies. Just an hour ago he said that if nobody signs me he'll throw a "Hail Mary pass" and record the album himself.

I had to Google it, because I don't follow sportsball. But a Hail Mary pass is something you do in football if you're running out of options.

This is life in the arts. You have these little moments of glory when the applause is loud, and it feels like you might finally take things to a whole new level. But then the glow wears off and you realize nothing has changed.

"I think I'll go off in a corner somewhere and do some writing," I tell him. "Get my mind off it."

"You do that." I get another blinding smile. He puts a possessive hand on the back of my neck and gives me an appreciative look.

It would be so easy right now to lean in and let him kiss me. I don't do it. But I don't hate that look he's giving me—like I'm fascinating. Sometimes I make bad decisions when men look at me like that.

But not today. I ease back, disappointing him. He doesn't force the issue, though, especially after the earful I gave him after that obnoxious kiss in front of the Coconut Club crowd.

"We are not a couple," I'd reminded him. *Not yet, anyway.*

"I was just overwhelmed," he'd said. "You were so amazing. I lost my head."

He said it wouldn't happen again. And it can't. If I give in to this man, he'll take me for granted. I need him to find me a record deal more than I need a man in my bed. Even if he is objectively attractive and successful.

"Chin up, girl," he tells me now. "You have what it takes. I'm going to make sure everybody knows. There will be more meetings."

"I know." I plaster a smile on my face and make plans to meet him later. Then we part ways. I walk down Main Street, glancing into shop windows, taking my time.

Darlington Beach reminds me of the Colorado town where I went to high school. There were mountains there instead of the ocean. But the vibe is the same, as is the string of expensive shops.

There isn't a single thing in these window displays that I could ever afford—then or now. I really don't understand how they stay in business selling artisanal pottery. Only one of the pieces in the window has its price tag showing—probably in error. It's a $160 bowl. And it's not even large.

When I was sixteen, I was placed in my seventh foster home. The couple were both pastors at a pretty stone church. Taking in foster kids was part of their calling, they said.

They were okay. I have no horror stories about them, other than his laugh sounded like a drunk hyena's. But the school was a disaster for me in my second-hand clothes and off-brand jacket. I didn't wear North Face or play a sport or snowboard.

I spent a lot of time alone, scribbling poetry into notebooks and practicing the beat-up guitar that I'd literally found on a curb on trash day.

My foster parents tried to get me to play during their church service, but I wouldn't do it. I didn't need one more way to look weird in front of my peers.

The high school music teacher tried to help me, though. Mrs. Hernandez was a taskmaster, but she cared. She paid for new strings for my guitar out of her own pocket and had one of the tuning keys fixed.

"It sounds like a new instrument," I'd said in a hushed voice when she handed it back to me.

"You keep practicing those arpeggios," she'd said in her clipped voice. "Music builds character, and it's good brain work."

I just liked the way I felt when the chords hummed against my body. Calmer.

Then the high school held a fundraiser, and Mrs. Hernandez —whose practice rooms I'd been using after school—paired me up with Travis Baker. "Guitar and piano, guys. Pick a piece and perform it. I don't care what you pick as long as its inoffensive and under eight minutes."

Travis Baker. He had strong-looking arms and a slow smile that I'd been admiring from a distance ever since I landed at Cottonwood High. He was also wildly popular with the girls who ran the school. He had a shiny, black Jeep—a Wrangler—the cool kind made for adventure—and I never saw him in it alone. The glossy ponytails of various girls were always visible beside him.

"Heartbreaker," was the word I'd most often heard in reference to him.

We'd never spoken before. But spending hours alone in a practice room has a way of bringing people together. Travis dropped his cool-guy facade pretty fast when it was just the two of us.

I couldn't believe my own luck. Not only was it fun to have someone else to play with, he was *good*. I let him choose the music. He brought in sheet music for an Eagles medley.

Don Henley doesn't really do it for me, but at least the hottie hadn't chosen a bad piano arrangement of Metallica.

I still wouldn't have argued, though. I was deep in lust before we ever sat down to play together. Rehearsals were heaven. I got to watch those muscular arms move up and down the keyboard.

And all musicians have a music face. It's an expression that's out of your control, because you're concentrating on the sound and forgetting yourself. Everyone's music face is different. Some people look dreamy. Some look constipated.

Travis looked...serene. Everything felt softer inside me while I watched him play. And whenever we finished a part, he'd look up at me and smile. "Not bad, right?"

I swear to God, it was the first time in my whole young life I'd ever felt *seen*.

So when he leaned over and kissed me one afternoon, I was less shocked than I should have been.

After that, our remaining rehearsals were half spent on music, and half on fooling around. One practice room had a lock on the door, since it was once a teacher's office. Travis made sure to grab that one, I noticed. After a run-through of our material, he'd pull me into his lap and put his hands up my shirt. And my hand down his pants.

One inevitable afternoon he forgot to lock the door. I heard a click followed by a sharp intake of breath. Then the yelling started.

Even as Travis zipped up his pants, Mrs. Hernandez was shrieking, "Idiot! Are you crazy? Are you *stupid?* Do you not know how this works? You make good choices—you could go to college and *be something*. I tried to help you! And you do this? Stupid little slut."

She yelled only at me. Travis snuck out of there unscathed. Six years later I still cringe when I remember all the awful things Mrs. Hernandez said. She also canceled our duet.

But that's not what hurt the most. Travis never spoke to me again. Unfortunately, he spoke *about* me. There were whispers and pointed fingers the very next day.

Slut. Trailer trash. Those are just a few of the choice words I heard about myself. That's my most indelible memory of high school. And I've been a mistrustful person pretty much ever since. People who appear to appreciate you can turn their backs in an instant.

That's why I've kept my distance from Brett Ferris. He may well be the grown-up version of Travis. A rich guy with big plans and plenty of options.

I'm still the poor kid toiling in obscurity. But if I'm careful and patient, I can put my career first. And if Brett Ferris still wants me after I don't really need him anymore, then maybe we are a good fit.

Maybe. I'm not ready to trust it.

Today I'm too far inside my own head. Any songwriting I do will come out broody and self-conscious.

So I don't take my notebook to the park near the beach and find an isolated spot in the shade. My feet lead me somewhere else entirely. The fine shops on Main Street eventually give way to a gas station and a nondescript post office.

Past that is my true destination: Roadie Joe's.

Just like the last time I was here, the outdoor tables facing the beach are all occupied. But as I pause at the side window and peer into the darkened bar, I see only one person.

Ralph is there, just like last time.

I pause for a moment, taking him in. He's chopping something with those strong hands. I have a thing for men's hands, apparently.

The rest of him is pretty great, too. There's something sexy about the way he moves. And the trimmed beard works well on him. It makes him more rugged than beautiful. Except for those kind eyes. They're special—a green-blue color, rimmed with dark brown lashes.

Still, California is full of attractive men. Standing here, gazing through the window, I still can't figure out why he's so fascinating to me. But he is.

So I open the door and step inside. There's some music playing at low volume and kitchen sounds, too. Ralph doesn't hear me as I cross the room to the bar. The stool slides noiselessly when I pull it out. I sit down, still unnoticed.

Then, as he twists to reach for a pitcher, he finally spots me. He's startled, pausing midstep. Then something goes very wrong. One moment we've locked eyes, and the next moment he disappears from view, falling violently to the floor with a horrible crash and a thump.

"Omigod are you okay?" I squeak. "Ralph?"

"Fine!" He lets out a frustrated groan and climbs to his feet. "I slipped. My buddy took the rubber mats outside and..." He shakes his head, then rubs the side of it. I suspect he whacked it against something. "What are you, part ninja? At least nobody else saw that."

"Dude, are you okay?" another voice asks. A young guy in

an apron appears, carrying a black rubber mat behind the bar area. "That looked rough."

Ralph rolls his eyes. "Looked worse than it was," he lies, trying to save his dignity. "And it's *your* fault, anyway."

The guy laughs. "Let's put these back down before I'm responsible for your death."

Ralph ignores him. "Would you like a beer?" he asks me.

I glance at the pile of mint leaves on his cutting board and hesitate. "Sure," I say. But the mint looks so fresh and pretty.

"I could make you something different."

"Beer is great. A cold..."

" —lager," he finishes. "No glass, no opener."

When I look up to flash him a smile, my heart does a little somersault. Those kind eyes are smiling at me, too. "Thank you," I whisper.

"It's really no problem." He turns toward the beer cooler. "You're an easy customer, trust me."

But I really meant—*thank you for remembering.* As he leans down to grab a bottle for me, I find myself admiring the strong muscles in his back. *Stop it,* I admonish myself. It only gets worse when he turns around and places the bottle in front of me. I've never seen hands like his. I didn't even know wrists could look muscular.

Even so. Ogling him is not why I came here. I pull out my keychain opener and remove the cap from my beer.

Ralph discards it, gives me another pleasant smile and then picks up his paring knife again.

I take a sip, wondering when he's going to mention my show at the Coconut Club. He was there. I saw him.

He separates some mint leaves from their stems and says nothing.

I last about seventeen seconds. "Well?"

"Well?" He looks up. "Sorry?"

"Jesus lord." I close my eyes and then open them again. This is not going how I'd hoped it would. "What did you *think?*"

"Of...?" His amazing eyes are studying me.

"Forget I asked." I take a swig of beer.

"Think about what?" He pushes the cutting board aside, and his smile turns knowing.

"My set at the Coconut Club! I saw you holding up that wall in the back. Don't lie."

He tips his head back and lets out a sudden laugh. "I'm so busted. I loved your show, but I didn't expect you to spot me."

"You loved it so much you weren't going to say anything?" The sentence sounds crazy to my own ears. I put down the beer. "You know what? Never mind. I'm just being psycho right now. This town is getting into my head."

"Listen, girly." He braces both (muscular!) hands on the bar and looks me right in the eye. "I loved it so much that I don't even know what to say about it. From that moment at the beginning—when you shut that asshole's maw? To the part where you made a lady *cry*." He shakes his head. "I couldn't look away. And I never wanted it to end."

I give him a slow blink, just trying to take that in. It's so much more than I was even hoping to hear.

"Shit, Delilah. If that set doesn't win you whatever contract you're looking for, they don't even deserve you."

Something warm and unfamiliar settles into the center of my belly. "That might be the nicest thing anyone ever said to me. Which only means you're still trying to get my phone number."

He laughs immediately. "Can't both things be true? Both my musical assessment and my interest in your evening plans?"

"Because you know so much about music." I flip my hair and take another sip of beer.

"Look. I don't know shit about music. But I know plenty about talent." He leans down on a set of forearms I shouldn't be noticing. "I know that talent sometimes takes a nap at just the wrong moment, but it never stays asleep for long. I also know that luck matters, too. If they don't give you what you want, it won't be your fucking fault."

"Thank you," I say quietly.

But he's not done. "I saw something else valuable the other night. You're good in the clinch. And that counts for double, I swear to God."

"The clinch?"

"Yeah. You're not just good at practice." He pauses, wrinkling up his interesting nose. "What word would a musician use? Okay—you're not a *rehearsal* musician, Delilah. That stage was like your home. Either that or you fake it really well. That's going to pay your rent someday, I promise."

"Wow." It's like he looked right into my terrified little soul and found the very thing I needed to hear. Those beautiful eyes of his are practically burning me right now, so I have to look away. "Thank you, Ralph. Really. I really needed that pep talk."

I make the mistake of looking up at him again, and, for a split second, I see pure yearning. It's like our souls vibrate at exactly the same frequency. And I have no idea what to do with that.

Ralph doesn't either, apparently. He sighs quietly and goes back to work, adding mint leaves to a pitcher where limes and sugar are muddling together.

"Is that a pitcher of mojitos?" I ask. I inhale deeply and take in the scent of mint and lime. "Wow, I miss those."

"Want one?" he asks me. "I could make an extra." He reaches for a glass, but I'm already shaking my head.

"No thank you. I had a bad experience once. It was here at the festival last year, actually."

His hand freezes on its way to the glass. "Wait. You were here last year, too?"

"Yes and no. I came by myself to try to do some networking. I had to wait tables just to afford to hang around for six weeks.

I worked at Pizza Palace, trying to upsell wings at every table. This is where I met Brett Ferris."

"At the Pizza Palace?" He snorts. "Unlikely."

"No!" I laugh. Because Brett wouldn't be caught dead in there. "I mean here in Darlington Beach. I introduced myself to him after another artist's set, and after I talked his ear off for a while about song-writing, he agreed to let me audition for him."

"As if that would be a hardship," he mutters under his breath.

I reach across the bar and poke him in the arm. "It was business, Ralph. I didn't show him my tits to get the audition."

He flinches. "I'm sorry. I didn't mean to suggest you did. It's just…" He clears his throat. "You're a couple now?"

"No," I say immediately.

He raises his eyebrows, disbelieving. The whole freaking town watched Brett plant that kiss on me. I knew it.

"It's complicated with him," I admit.

Ralph goes back to his work, not saying anything. Where Brett lacks discretion, this guy has it in spades.

And when I said it was complicated, I meant it in the most literal way. I've been corresponding with Brett about music for a year. And I've seen him at various music festivals, where we're all business.

But when I came to Darlington Beach a couple of weeks ago, he offered me the guesthouse at his parents' place. I accepted because—hello, free room. But he also made it clear that he wants us to be a couple. And I don't know what to think or do about it. I'm on the one-day-at-a-time plan.

"You're not sure about him, then?" Ralph finally asks. There's something in his delivery that sounds hopeful. And maybe a little smug.

And he's right. I'm not at all sure about him. "People say awful things about women who date powerful men."

"So that's another vote in my favor." Ralph spreads his

strong arms in a gesture of greatness. "Pick me, and nobody can ever claim you were using me. I'm as washed up as they come."

I laugh suddenly, and so does he. And I swear it's the most relaxed I've been in weeks.

Ralph goes back to his pitcher of mojitos, finishing it off with ice and soda, then passing it to a harried waitress who runs in from the patio.

"Better start another one," the young woman says. "I got a feeling that table will be here a while."

"Sure," he says, reaching for the mint.

I take a deep breath as he begins to chop. Without missing a beat, he hands me a sprig. I pluck off a leaf and roll it between my fingers. "So what's your story?"

"What do you mean?"

"I can sense bitterness in people, Ralph. It's my super power. You're a good bartender, but you don't love it. Plus, you just gave me a big speech about talent. What's yours?"

He glances up at me, and I see him thinking hard. "I don't think I'd enjoy telling a pretty girl about all my failures. And I'm sure I'll figure my shit out eventually. My plans for after graduation didn't work out. Suddenly, I'm in need of a Plan B. But I never made a Plan B, and now I'm regretting that choice."

Wow, I know this song so well I could have written it myself. "You didn't make a Plan B, because that felt like cheating on plan A," I tell him. "You thought that if you made a Plan B, then it would mean that you doubted yourself. And the universe would make sure that Plan A never happened." Source: all my life choices.

"You seem to know a lot about this," he says, reaching for the limes.

"I'm a girl without a Plan B. Plan A is taking so much longer than I thought."

He glances up at me, and the kindness in his expression hits me like a wave all over again. "People say the music industry eats its young."

"That's true," I agree. "With gusto. And extra hot sauce. At least you have a college degree. I don't even have that. And I don't have any family to fall back on. Not that I want to give up, but I bet everything at this roulette table, and I still don't know how it's going to work out."

He studies me for a moment with serious eyes. "Don't give up, Delilah. Not yet. Promise?"

Something passes between us again that's bigger than flirting. For a songwriter, I'm a pretty cynical girl. I don't look for love stories on every street corner. But Ralph has the strangest effect on me. When he smiles, it makes me want to write sappy songs and believe things that I don't usually believe.

"I promise," I say, sounding like a soap opera character.

Ralph gives me a smile that I feel everywhere. Then he goes back to work.

I pull out my notebook and flip through my songs in progress. I appreciate how empty the bar is. Ralph is busy making drinks for patrons out on the patio, but there is literally nobody on either side of me. It's like I'm at a library that serves beer.

Wait. There should be libraries that serve beer! I scribble that down on my notebook page to think about later. You never know where you're going to get an idea for a song.

A lovely hour passes this way. When my beer is drained, Ralph asks me if I want another.

I shake my head.

"Glass of water?" he asks.

"Well…" I'm embarrassed to tell him how deeply my phobia runs. "No thank you."

He puts an empty glass on the bar. Then offers me the soda gun. "Are you sure?"

This guy. I take the gun and point it into the glass. One of the buttons is labeled "water," so I press it, quickly filling the glass. "Thank you," I say, feeling ridiculous. I already know this man isn't going to slip anything into my drink. And yet I can't bring myself to let anyone serve me.

So I tease him, instead. I reach over and press the button again as I'm handing it back to him, drenching the back of his hand.

"Now you've done it," he says, grabbing my wrist and wielding the soda gun like a weapon.

Caught, I let out a high-pitched shriek that I'll probably be embarrassed about later.

But he doesn't spray me. He just lets go of my hand and laughs. "You're lucky you have that notebook, girly. I don't want to wreck the next Grammy-winning song."

That shuts me up, because it's rare for anyone to show so much faith in me. Except for Brett, of course. He's the first man who ever said, "I think you could go all the way with your music."

And speak of the devil. His voice is somewhere behind me now and getting louder. "The tracks are good, Arnie!" he barks in a voice that's too loud. But that's Brett for you. "You get them in front of Chet by next week, or I'm taking them somewhere else!"

The whole world suddenly hopes that Arnie gets the tracks in front of Chet just to save our eardrums.

He strides up next to me, still yapping into his Bluetooth. And he actually snaps his fingers at me, the way you'd summon a dog.

Okay, that's mortifying. When Brett and I are alone together, he seems driven and a little eccentric. Out in the world, he just comes off as rude. "I have five more minutes," I point out calmly. Even though Brett is pretty much in charge of everything that happens with my nascent career, I make a point to never take any shit from him. "I need to finish my water."

Scowling, he checks his gold watch.

"Go outside," I insist, reaching out to give him a gentle shove on his khaki-clad hip. "I'll be there in a minute."

"Chet needs to hear these sooner rather than later," he bellows. But at least he turns toward the door.

I don't glance up at Ralph until he's gone. My bartender doesn't say anything, but it's so obvious he'd like to.

"You don't like him," I say pointlessly.

"Maybe I'm just jealous." Ralph wipes down the bar where I splashed the water.

"No," I press. "You think he's an arrogant, entitled asshole."

"Well, now that you mention it." He grins down at the shiny wooden surface.

And I have to laugh. "He's really not that bad. And he's a bulldog for his artists. I need someone like that who's willing to browbeat the label into giving me a chance."

"His artists," he says slowly. "You know he's only one year out of college, right?" Those green eyes lock on mine. "He's well-connected, thanks to his parents. But still."

"How well do you know the Ferris family?"

Ralph looks uncomfortable. "Brett and I were the same year in school, but I took a gap year before college."

I wait, but he doesn't volunteer more. "And...you guys hated each other?"

"Well, we were competitors," he says slowly. "Brett was used to dominating everything from the student council to the tennis courts. And..." He shakes his head.

"And what?" I wait. "I might sign a contract with him. I need to know the dirt."

Ralph chews his lip. "You won't tell him I said this?"

"No! I swear."

"He's a cheater." He leans on the bar and looks down at me.

"On women?"

"Oh—not what I meant." He shakes his head. "He's a

cheater at *life*. If he sees something he wants, he takes it. Doesn't matter if it's not his."

I consider this and wonder why I'm not more afraid. Probably because I'm desperate to break through. I've seen enough of the music industry to know that sitting quietly in the corner doesn't work. "Even so," I say quietly. "Brett was the first one to tell me that I had something special."

"That can't possibly be true," Ralph says, tossing down his rag. "And even if he was, he won't be the last."

"Maybe. But he was the first one who could do something about it," I admit.

"Ah, well." Ralph props his chin in his hand, and we're eye to eye. "I understand the appeal, I guess. But you could give me your phone number anyway." He gives me a sneaky smile. "Don't put all your eggs in one basket."

"Oh, Ralph." I return his smile, but it's meant to cushion the blow. "You are the nicest guy I've met in... Okay, *ever*. But did you consider what would happen if I said yes? I'd get to date you for *maybe* three weeks."

"Three spectacular weeks," he interjects.

I laugh. "Three *earth-moving* weeks, sure. But it will piss him off." I jerk a thumb toward the man just outside the door. "Then I'll still have to go back to L.A. and work with that guy. He's going to figure out how to get my record made. And if that fails, he's going to make it himself."

"Well, Delilah." Ralph's expression turns resigned. "You're definitely in the right line of work."

"Why?" I demand, and it comes out sounding bitchy. "You think I'm mercenary? That I'll do anything to get ahead?" *You might be right.*

"Back up, buttercup. All I meant is that you broke my heart in two minutes flat." He stands up straight and starts wiping again. "That's a songwriter's mission, isn't it?"

This guy. "Stop being so great, okay? It's really hard to turn you down." I drain the water and push the glass toward him.

"Leave me your number anyway," he says, pushing a cocktail napkin toward me. "We can be friends."

"Uh-huh," I say, ignoring the napkin. "Seeing as I have very poor impulse control, that's not a great plan." I take out some cash to pay for my beer. Then I gather up the bits of mint I've torn apart and place them on the napkin.

"Hey," he says as he makes change for my twenty-dollar bill. "What did you mean before when you said you had a bad experience with mojitos?"

"Oh." I frown, because I *never* talk about this. "Not mojitos —no mojito ever did me wrong. But last summer I had a mixed drink at a party, and..." I fight off a shudder. "Well, I got roofied. Didn't regain consciousness for fourteen hours." Somehow I say this in an almost normal voice. But it freaks me out even to this day.

Apparently, I'm not the only one. The spoon rattles out of Ralph's hand, hitting the bar and then the floor somewhere below him. "Jesus Christ," he whispers, gaping at me from across the bar.

Now I'm sorry that I told him. He's actually turned white.

"Hey," I say quietly. "It isn't what you're thinking. I woke up among friends in a safe place. But I couldn't remember *anything* about the night before. So..." I clear my throat. "It could have been a whole lot worse. And before you judge *him* too harshly." I nod toward the man outside. "He does actually have a knack for turning up when I need him most."

Ralph's eyes travel to Brett's blond head, just visible in the window. "Still," he says, almost gagging on the word. "That sounds horrible."

"It was," I admit, sliding off the barstool. "It wasn't like being asleep. You lose time." I shiver. "And I'm phobic about drinks now. I'm sure you've noticed."

"I'll bet you are. Hey!" He snaps his fingers. "Do you want to make your own cocktail? Some afternoon when it's quiet, you can come behind the bar and make a mojito. Or whatever you want. I'll let you open a fresh bottle of rum and everything."

"Oh, wow." I feel my face heat. "That is a really nice offer."

"Think it over," he says gruffly, pushing my change toward me. "Now go on before Music Man starts barking at us again."

"Later, Ralph," I say softly, hoping he'll give me one more smile.

"Later, girly," he says with a resigned sigh.

I have to leave before I get my smile.

DELILAH

The next two weeks go by at lightning speed. And nothing changes.

I still don't have a recording contract. I'm still playing for whichever crowds Brett can find me. Still taking any meeting I can get. Still avoiding being alone with Brett, so I don't have to make the decision about whether I'm going to give in and sleep with him or not.

Meanwhile, Ralph asks me every day for my phone number. But it's our little joke now, and he smiles when he asks me, and he always gives me another friendly smile after I say no.

In fact, Ralph and I have settled into a rhythm that resembles an old-time comedy routine. Every day I come in to Roadie Joe's before the happy-hour rush to enjoy a quiet hour of sitting and scribbling in my notebook while watching him mix drinks with those strong hands.

It's my favorite hour of the day. No contest.

Brett hates that I come here. In fact, I think he tries to schedule things for late afternoon now just to foil my chill session at the bar.

Ralph, on the other hand, has gotten used to me showing

up. He no longer cuts himself or falls down when I appear on a barstool. He just brings me a beer in a bottle — unopened — and gives me a smile.

God, that smile.

My notebook is nearly full of lyrics, but Ralph knows he's not allowed to read them. One time last week I forgot my notebook and ended up writing lyrics on a napkin. Those were pretty good lyrics, too. Ralph didn't say a word. He only offered me more napkins.

"Most of what I jot down is pure trash," I've explained. "But once in a while something clicks."

"That seems like a pretty good description of my life right now," he said.

"Mine, too."

"So we have that in common." He winked and washed up some celery for Bloody Marys.

It's another beautiful September afternoon, and the outdoor tables must be jammed because Ralph is neck-deep in orders. I glance up from my notebook to watch him sometimes, but we don't get much time to talk.

Business finally dies down, and he wipes down the bar, eyeing me as I tap out a rhythm with my pencil eraser. The song I'm working on relies upon syncopation. I can hear it so clearly in my head, but I just don't *quite* have the lyric.

Ralph is watching me. I like it, but he's not allowed to know that. "Omigod, what?" I demand, looking up. "You're staring."

"I was just wondering when you're going to give me your phone number."

This is our fun little game, but the music festival closes in a few more days, and once I leave town, that's it. Bye, Ralph. There's no telling whether I'll ever come back here.

That makes me a whole lot sadder than I'm ready to let on.

"Is never good for you?" I give him a cheeky smile. "Oh my

God, that's a good song title!" I flip open my notebook to scribble it onto the inside cover.

"Wow. Please write a song about my heartbreak. That's not cruel at all."

"I'll dedicate it to you. This one goes out to Ralph the bartender."

"Write quickly. Because I'm all set up back here for you to make your own mojito."

I sit up straight on the barstool. "Really?" Damn, I really want a mojito. Or anything that is fresh and minty and not straight out of a beer bottle.

"Would I lie about a thing like this? Get back here before the happy-hour orders start rolling in. Quick!"

I've probably never moved so fast. A couple seconds later I'm standing beside him. "Are you going to get in trouble for this?"

"Nah. Let's do this. First step—cut up this lime." He places it on the cutting board in front of me.

I know better than to waste time. I pick up the paring knife and start slicing the lime into discs.

"Toss the slices in here." He sets a pint glass down in front of me. "Then use the spoon and smash them up a little bit. That's right," he says as I work. "Now add this." He unfolds a sheaf of wax paper, revealing a bunch of mint he's already prepped for me.

My heart gives a gratuitous little flip.

"Thank you." I drop the mint leaves into the glass, then pick up the wooden spoon and crush the leaves against the sides.

"There you go. Isn't it therapeutic? When you're done, you need these." He pushes a couple of sugar packets in my direction.

I've been watching him too long to think that's right. "Don't you use that fine stuff, so the sugar melts?"

"Well…" He pulls the canister of superfine sugar off a shelf. "This stuff isn't in a sealed packet. But it does work better."

I put down the spoon and turn to face him. Suddenly, we're standing so close that I forget to breathe. And when I look up into his pretty eyes, I see my own foolish attraction reflected right back at me. "You are a prince, Ralph," I whisper. "I hope you know that."

"That's what all the girls say," he teases quietly.

Inside I'm dying. The feeling I get when he's kind to me is so new and unfamiliar. He's sexy as hell. But he's also sweet. I didn't even know that combination was possible in a man.

Just standing close to him makes my body run hot. And I want to know what he'd be like in bed. I'm curious on a gut level.

The universe doesn't care, though. I'm going back to Southern California in less than a week. And Ralph isn't. We are two people at two different crossroads.

Every day I think about actually giving him my phone number. And every day I don't go through with it. Texting with him a week from now? It will only ruin the memory of sitting in this bar every day in his quiet company.

Some memories are sweeter if you don't ruin them by hanging on too tightly.

Carefully, I turn around. I go back to muddling my limes. I open the superfine sugar canister and measure out a portion with the spoon Ralph hands me. I can't stop my awareness of how near he is. And how good he smells—like soap and limes and summer near the ocean.

"Now what?" I ask, leaning over the glass to inhale mint. "This smells so good." *As do you.*

"Here." He hands me the ice scoop. "Fill the glass to the top."

Gleefully, I plunge it into the ice bin and noisily fill the glass.

"This is fun. And good practice for the jobs I'll get after I bomb out of the music industry."

"Never gonna happen," he says. "Now this." He hands me a bottle of Bacardi that's never been opened.

I break the seal and remove the cap.

"You can eyeball it, or you can measure it with this." He nudges a shot glass towards me.

"I'd better measure. I'm supposed to meet some other song-writers later. I should probably stay lucid."

"If you're into that." His chuckle resonates in my belly. "Last step," he says, handing me the soda gun. "Just a splash of club soda and you're done."

"Thank you," I say as I finish making the perfect summer cocktail. "You're the best. And I swear I'm not phobic about anything else. I don't mind tight spaces or spiders."

He grunts. "I'm not a big fan of tight spaces. And you come by your phobia pretty honestly."

"I'd rather have come by it dishonestly," I point out, stirring my drink with a straw. I lift the glass and peer at the minty ice swirling inside. "That is beautiful." I take a sniff and sigh.

He waits, maybe wondering if I'll be able to drink it.

But it's no problem at all. I take a gleeful gulp. "*God.*" I take another. "This is even better than I remember. Taste?" I offer him the glass.

He takes it from me and takes a quick sip.

What I really want is to sit down somewhere and drink a pitcher of mojitos with him. I want to lounge on a beach in the sunshine and watch the wind tousle his hair. In this fantasy, he's shirtless, of course.

"Good stuff," he says, handing it back.

"Ralph!" shouts the owner from the kitchen. "How many cases of Malbec do we have? I got the distributor on the phone."

"One sec!" he calls. He disappears into the stockroom. A

few seconds later, his head pops around the corner. "Six!" he yells.

"Good man."

I'm still standing here behind the bar, and now he has to go back to work. But I didn't thank him properly, so I walk around the corner to find him. The stockroom is narrow and dim. One wall has all the beer keg hookups, and the other is stacked to the ceiling with cases of wine, beer, and spirits. Ralph is rearranging a couple of them.

"Hey. I just wanted to thank you for this."

He straightens up. "You know it's my pleasure."

I put a hand on his shoulder and rise up on my toes, because he's tall. I aim my kiss at his cheek.

But in a move so smooth that it deserves some kind of award, Ralph turns his head. My kiss lands on the corner of his mouth instead. He catches me around the waist and pulls me in.

I swear my heart stops beating as he changes the angle and kisses me for real. Soft lips. Hard body. Mint and lime juice. Heat. *Hell yes.* I don't even pretend to be surprised. His kiss is every bit as good as I knew it would be.

He smiles against my mouth, his beard tickling my chin. I feel it like a beam of sunshine on a cold day. Then he sets me back onto my heels. "You're welcome for that, too," he says.

It's an infuriating thing to say. But only because he's right. Both the kiss and the drink are the most fun I've had in a long time. I open my mouth to tell him so, but nothing comes out. I feel flushed and a little off-kilter.

He pats my hip. "Skedaddle back onto your side of the bar, miss, before Mr. Dirello happens to walk through here."

No witty comment presents itself to me. No cynical backtalk. I retreat back to my usual spot. He tidies up again while I sip my perfect cocktail and try to get my head on straight again.

"How's the mojito?" he asks without looking me in the eye.

"You know it's *good*. You're just fishing for compliments." We're not talking only about the drink, either.

"Uh-huh." He gives me a smile. "Write anything good today?"

"It's getting there." I glance down at my notes and try to remember what I was thinking about fifteen minutes ago. "Some songs come easy, and some of them are like pulling teeth."

"Which kind was 'Sparkle On'?"

I blink at him for a second, because I'm surprised he remembers the title of my favorite song. "That one was easy. I wrote it in an hour. I mean—I tweaked the lyrics afterward. But the guts of it came out of my guitar, fully formed. Why?"

"Someday..." He shakes his head. "Someday I'm going to hear that song everywhere. I'll be walking down the beach and hear it blaring out of three different radios at once."

For a split second—before I can rein it in—I let the pure joy I'm feeling break across my face. God, I want that so badly. But it doesn't do any good to think like that. "That's your pick, huh? 'Sparkle On.' I would've taken you for more of an uptempo guy. 'Sparkle On' is my girliest song.

"It's not my usual sound," he admits. "But it's *your* sound. And you made a woman *cry*." He tosses the rag in the sink. "I think maybe the world needs 'Sparkle On.'"

Oh my. I just sit with that for a second. Every artist loves praise. If she says she doesn't, she's a liar. But the quality of that praise is so unlike anything I've heard before, that I need a moment just to appreciate it.

When Brett talks about my music, he uses words like *demographic* and *market potential*. But Ralph *felt* my song.

My poor little heart creaks again.

"Besides," Ralph says, lightening the mood. "Can a dude not want to sparkle on? Are you insulting my manhood right now?"

"Maybe just a tiny little bit," I say with an evil smile.

"Don't ever use 'tiny little' when we're discussing my manhood, okay?"

I actually giggle, which never happens. It sounds all wrong on me. I take another sip and change the subject. "Enough about me. Have you made any progress on your Plan B?"

"A little," he admits. "It's still not my favorite topic. But I've been looking at some masters programs in education."

"Whoa!" I can totally picture this. "High school teacher? The girls will all stay after class every day just for a few extra minutes of your time."

"Nah." He rolls his eyes. "Besides—the only girl I want is the one in front of me."

Oh.

We're both quiet for a second after that little truth bomb. "What will you teach?" I finally ask.

"History, maybe." He rubs his fingertips through his beard. "And I want to coach."

"Coach what?" I hold up a hand. "Wait, don't tell me. The surfing team."

"Surfing team? Is that a thing?" He laughs.

"I don't know. You're the Californian. Didn't you offer to teach me how to surf?"

"Yeah, but you always say no." We have this conversation almost as often as we discuss my phone number. "Any day, anytime. I'm totally serious."

"How about Friday?" I hear myself ask.

"Done," he says immediately.

Uh-oh. What did I just do? "Can you get Friday afternoon off from the bar?"

"Mr. Dirello!" he hollers immediately. "I need Friday after-noon off. I can be back by the dinner rush."

"What for?" an older man's voice barks from somewhere in the kitchen.

"I'm teaching a surfing lesson."

"You're moonlighting?"

"No, it's for a friend."

"She pretty?"

"Devastating," he says, looking me right in the eyes. There's a beat of silence while Ralph and I stare at each other.

I can't believe I finally agreed to hang out with him, and right before I'm scheduled to leave town. It's either a brilliant idea or heartbreaking.

But the restaurateur seals the deal. "Eh, okay, kid. After the lunch rush is done. And you come back at sunset."

"Thanks, man."

Well. I guess I'm going surfing on Friday. "Wow, okay. What do I need to bring?"

"Not a thing," he says. "Just wear a bikini. The smaller the better. It's more aerodynamic."

"Ralph."

"Kidding! I'll bring you a rash guard as well as a board. This is going to be great." He looks thrilled, honestly.

"There will be a couple of rules," I say slowly. "Don't stand me up."

"That's an easy one. I would never."

"And you won't get me into bed. So don't try."

His smile says, *Oh, I'll try*. But he jerks a thumb toward the kitchen. "You heard the man. I have to come back to work."

"And promise you won't let me drown."

His smile fades. "You'll be absolutely safe. I'll bring you a life vest so you don't have to even think about it."

"Do you think I can do this? I'm not very coordinated."

"You can totally do this. It's going to be so much fun..." But then his face falls. "Heads up. Your jailer has arrived."

"Oh, brother." I flip my notebook shut. Brett seems to fetch me from this place a little earlier every day.

"Delilah!" he barks. "Time to go. What the hell are you drinking? Don't you *learn?*"

Across from me, Ralph goes pale.

"*Hey!*" I snap. "I made this drink myself."

"With the professional bartender's help?" He gives Ralph a cutting look. I don't know what passed between these two in high school, but it couldn't have been good.

"You think I can't mix a drink for myself?" I ask, feeling tired. "He's not my bartender. He's my surfing instructor."

"Your — ?" He scowls. "Let's just go. Don't keep other song-writers waiting."

"Wouldn't want to be *rude* or anything." I give Ralph a wink. "Bye, Ralph."

"Don't forget about your lesson!" he calls after me. "Friday. Three o'clock."

I stop, shaking off Brett's hand. "Wait. Where do I meet you?"

"Darlington Beach, beside the lifeguard station."

I give him a giant smile, because that sounds like so much fun. "I'll be there."

Brett makes an ornery sound beside me. But I ignore it.

———

As it happens, I do wear a bikini on Friday. A little one. A last-minute fling with Ralph is probably a terrible idea, but he's *so* wonderful. Almost too good to be true.

And I'm not the most disciplined girl. Sue me.

Friday is another beautiful California beach day. The sky is so blue it hurts my eyes. I bring a towel from Brett's guest-house. I feel weird about staying there all summer for free. Maybe he expected us to have a lot of sex in the guest bed.

He still wants to, but he doesn't seem mad about it. If anything, he just seems more determined. Brett is a puzzle in my life that I can't solve. It's clear that he wants me. But he also wants my music.

Which thing does he want more?

I'm sure not here to think about Brett, though. I find the lifeguard station, and I put my towel down just a couple of yards away. And I wait for Ralph. There are a couple of surfers in the water already. From this distance it's not easy to tell, but I don't think he's one of them.

So I turn around and watch the pathway where people emerge from the parking lot. I don't see a guy carrying a surfboard. Or two surfboards.

Maybe I should have met him in the parking lot, instead?

I stay on my towel and wait. Three o'clock comes and goes. I try not to worry, because if there was a rush of drink orders, he would have to help out.

It's three thirty suddenly. And then four.

Still, I don't leave. Ralph isn't the kind of guy to ask me out all summer and then bail. There must be a problem.

The sun sinks lower and lower in the sky, and my heart sinks, too.

He's not coming. He forgot all about me, I think. Who does that?

You never gave him your phone number, my conscience reminds me. *He can't call and explain.*

But really—how hard could it be to ask a bus boy to run down and tell me he's not coming? I'm, like, two blocks from the bar right now.

I know I shouldn't take it hard, but I do anyway. As I sit here on the towel, my insecurities multiply like bunny rabbits. I'm a fool. I came here to focus on music, not men. I'm too distracted. I'm too flighty. I'm too selfish. Maybe that's why nothing ever pans out for me.

Maybe that's why Ralph forgot to show.

My phone rings, and I scramble to pull it out of my bag. But it's Brett calling. "Where are you?" he asks as soon as I pick up. "I'm standing in this bar like an asshole, and you're not here."

So prickly, this one. We're more alike than I care to admit. "Is Ralph there?"

"Why? It's a woman tending bar today, Delilah. I asked if you'd been in here and she looked at me like I'm crazy for asking. Where are you?"

"On the beach," I admit.

"Want to go have drinks with a producer I met?"

"I…" My mind is spinning. Ralph isn't even at work? "I have a headache. I'm in a lousy mood." I'm not in the mood to try to impress a producer. And drinks would mean putting my phobia on display.

"Let me come and find you," Brett says, his voice becoming gentle. "Screw the drinks."

"Screw 'em," I echo.

"We'll walk back to my place and just chill," Brett suggests.

I hesitate. But what difference does it make now? The man I thought was a good one is the guy who stood me up. "Okay," I say. "Let's go to your place."

"Excellent," he says softly. "I'll be right there."

As I get up from my towel and shake out the sand, I take one more look down the beach in both directions.

There's no guy with kind eyes and a surfboard.

When I leave town three days later with Brett at my side, I'll wonder if I imagined him.

JULY

SILAS

"Are you nervous?" Georgia asks, giving me the once-over. "You look great."

"Thanks, I think?" I look down at the Bruisers T-shirt I'm wearing with a pair of khaki shorts. What else am I supposed to wear to a baseball game? "You're making me self-conscious now." It's been two weeks since Delilah Spark made Twitter swoon by accepting a date with me.

Coincidentally, I've been on a two-week high. But now it's showtime.

"Sorry," she says with a giggle. "The girls and I always tell each other how nice we look before a big night out. It's a habit. You're lucky Rebecca didn't show up to do your makeup."

"Yikes. I knew there was a reason I don't really date."

She smiles like I'm adorable. "I hope you have a great time. Are you going to get all tongue-tied in the presence of your idol?"

"Let's hope not." Although it's totally possible. I can still see the scar on my thumb from where I sliced myself the first time I ever saw her. Keeping cool in front of Delilah has never been easy for me.

"Take this. There's a Bruisers jersey in here for her." Georgia hands me a shopping bag. "And there's a teddy bear in here, too. After tonight she won't have any trouble remembering which team to root for."

Or root against, if this goes badly. I'm still a little stunned that she hasn't canceled. That could mean one of two things — either she still hasn't realized that I'm Ralph from Roadie Joe's. Or she figured it out and still wants to see me.

I hope it's the second one. But I'm worried, even if I'm not willing to explain the whole thing to my friends. "Thank you, Georgia." I say, giving her a quick hug. "Thanks for setting up the baseball game." That's the plan for tonight — a seven o'clock Brooklyn Cyclones game, with box seats.

Georgia arranged for us to have a nice but casual meal there. And it's semi-private — the cameras will catch us if they want to, but nobody will be able to harass Delilah for autographs.

"It's my pleasure. Oh! And I got you these." She reaches into her pocket and pulls out a small package of… I'm afraid to look.

I take it from her. "Brooklyn Breath Mints? You're so subtle."

She cackles. "At least I didn't buy you a box of condoms. Knock her dead, cowboy. I expect a *full* report in the morning." Her smile is wide and teasing. "But no pressure."

"Jesus."

She heads for my apartment door, laughing. "Your car will be here in ten minutes. Don't forget to call me tomorrow. In the morning. No hour too early."

Finally, she leaves. My apartment grows quiet again, and I exhale. I'll admit to being a little nervous. Delilah will probably be mad at me for surprising her like this. I'd debated coming clean, but I decided against it, because I'd rather apologize in person.

And maybe she already knows. If you Google my name, you can find team photos where I'm not wearing all my gear.

My phone rings in my pocket, and I pull it out, expecting the caller to be the car company. I'd arranged to pick up Delilah in Manhattan and then drive all the way back to the Brooklyn ball park. It won't be a short trip, but it gives us a chance to talk alone.

It's not a number I recognize, though. "Hello?"

"Hi, Silas? This is Becky, the publicist for Delilah Spark."

"I remember. Hi, Becky."

"Look, there's been a change of plans."

My gut shifts uneasily. "What kind of change?"

"Dee's record label needs her at a meeting at seven tonight. So she can't make the baseball game."

"A meeting. At seven o'clock," I echo stupidly. I can't *believe* she's blowing me off at the last minute. "What about tomorrow?"

There's a pause, because I don't think Becky was expecting me to suggest an alternative time. She didn't think I'd make her turn me down twice. "I'm so sorry—we leave on a midmorning flight. I'm afraid it just won't work."

Again, I'm speechless. But I can't come this close to seeing Delilah again and then have the moment snatched away.

"Silas, look," she says. "You seem like a really nice guy. I just want you to know that this it isn't just a story Dee cooked up so she could stay in and watch Netflix. The meeting with her label is real. She's not happy about it."

A mental image of Delilah arrives in my mind. She's wearing her *Kind of a Big Deal* T-shirt and scowling at Brett Ferris. Back then, she was a nobody and getting jerked around by the Brett Ferrises of the world seemed normal. But now I have to wonder why such a successful woman is still taking orders.

That gives me a bad feeling. "Listen, Becky. Are you needed at that same meeting?"

"Me? No. Why?"

"Hear me out. You name a spot—any coffee shop in Manhattan. Let me meet up with you, so I can give you a note for Delilah."

"A note?" I can hear the hesitation in her voice.

"Yeah. This date isn't a publicity stunt for me. I need to tell her something important."

There's a wary silence on the other end of the line. Becky is trying to figure out if I'm some kind of nutter.

"I won't even seal the letter. You can read it first and decide for yourself. But I promise you'll understand. What I have to say is important."

"This had better be good, Mr. Kelly."

"Oh, it is. I promise."

She sighs again, like she can't believe she's falling for my tricks. And I can't believe it, either. "There's a Starbucks on the corner of Eighth Avenue and Forty-third Street. Be there at seven."

"Leaving now!" I say. "I'm wearing a purple Bruisers shirt. You can't miss me."

"See you there," she says. There's a click. And then I'm running into my bedroom looking for a sheet of paper to write on.

I can't let Delilah go back to California without explaining that I never meant to stand her up. It won't change anything, but at least I'll feel better about it.

DELILAH

I'm stalling.

It's a hot summer day in New York. I'm supposed to be on my way to a ball game with a cute hockey player. But instead I'm staring at the bottled sodas on offer at Starbucks, trying to decide which one will shore me up enough to face Brett Ferris at this meeting.

"Omigod," Becky says. "Choose something while I'm still young."

I wave Becky toward the counter to order her own drink. I don't follow, because I'm busy eavesdropping on the women behind me. They're at a table, each of them with babies in strollers. I don't like to make assumptions based only on skin tone, but after listening to their conversation for three minutes, I've already established that they're nannies of the children in their care.

"It all comes down to four weeks of day camp," one of them is saying to her friend. "If I could pay for August, I could cobble the rest of the summer together with relatives' help."

"How much is Mia's camp?" asks the other one.

"Three hundred dollars a week. So that's twelve hundred

bucks. It's more than a third of my income. But if I don't pay for the camp, then I'm going to have to quit this job or leave her home alone all day." She groans. "Nine is too young to stay home in the Bronx, even if I pay for a second phone instead of camp, and then call her every hour."

I'm still staring at the bottled juices, but my mind is somewhere else now. The Bronx? I'm not familiar enough with New York to guess where this nine-year-old lives. She's sitting on a window seat, staring outside while other children pass by on the street. She's lonely, because her mother is holding someone else's baby for money.

This is how all my songs start out—with a picture in my mind.

"I don't know what to do," the woman says.

"Would you ever ask your boss if you could have a nine-year-old helper for a couple of weeks?" her friend asks.

"A month, though." I hear her sigh. "That would be a last resort, I guess. But the family won't like it. It pierces the bubble, you know? I always try to make them think I put *their* baby first."

"As if," the friend says.

"*Dee,*" Becky says under her breath. Becky never says "Delilah" in public, because sometimes the big sunglasses and the hat I'm wearing aren't enough to keep curious eyes off me.

I pick up a juice bottle and hand it to her, and with a sigh of relief, she goes up to the register to pay for both of us.

By the time she's back, I've already written the check. It's for $1200—enough for four weeks of day camp. I leave the "To" line blank.

"Here," Becky says, handing me my drink. "What are you... Oh, Dee. Really? Which one is it for?"

I tip my head toward the young woman with the blue stroller. "Summer camp for her own child. Trust me."

"You are such an easy target," she whispers.

"No I'm not," I argue. My checks say *D Spark* and the address is a post office box in Culver City. When I make these little donations, nobody even knows.

"Now go, okay?" Becky checks the time on her phone. "You're going to be late if you don't leave now."

"So?" I argue. "Why are you so twitchy today?" Even as I ask, I see Becky checking the door.

"I'm not. But go anyway. I can't give that woman this check until you get out of here."

"Fine." I'm not trying to create some kind of PR moment. When I do my little random acts of kindness, it's supposed to be anonymous. "I'm going. But I don't want to."

Becky gives my bodyguard—Mr. Muscles—a wave across the room. "I just want to say one more thing before you go into that meeting. Every woman has a man she regrets."

"Tell me about it," I mumble.

"I'm trying. Because you tend to beat yourself up over Brett Ferris. But not today, okay? Today he's just an oops. We all have them."

"You are full of wisdom." I uncap my juice and take a sip.

"Now go. Unless you need me to come along as your emotional support animal."

This makes me smile. "I'm going. What are you doing, anyway?" She's glancing around the room again, as if she lost something.

"Maybe I'll sit here a little while and return some emails."

"Whatever floats your boat. Later!"

"Stay strong!" she says, waving me off.

After I step outside, I stop and peek through the plate-glass window.

"Miss?" Mr. Muscles says in his deep, deep voice. "The car is coming around the corner."

"Just a sec," I say, resisting his big hand on my elbow. Becky is bending down, placing the check on the table.

First, the young woman leans down to inspect it. Then she sits up again quickly, astonishment on her face. She claps a hand over her mouth and stares at Becky.

And that's all I need to see. It's done. The rest is just an awkward thank you and Becky's insistence that she fill in the name on the check and go right to the bank to deposit the money.

I let Mr. Muscles steer me into the back of the waiting car. He climbs into the front, and the driver accelerates towards a meeting that I almost certainly won't enjoy.

DELILAH

Brett and I are seated across a conference room table from one another. And it's awkward. Actually, he looks perfectly comfortable. But this is his turf. One year into our three-year relationship, he merged his fledgling record label with part of a bigger company — MetroPlex. He's a partner here.

I'm what they call *talent* in this industry.

If only I had a talent for choosing men. While Brett arranges a folder on the table in front of him, I keep sneaking looks at him. He's familiar in so many ways. He has a tan line in front of his ear, where a recent haircut has exposed a pale spot. And I was shopping with him on the day he bought that shirt on Rodeo Drive.

But after a mere couple months' absence, he also seems strange to me now. I can't imagine kissing him, although I used to do that pretty often. We didn't have a cuddly sex life, though. We fought often and had lots of make-up sex.

That didn't bother me. I've always been a prickly girl, so holding hands at the dinner table wasn't something I'd expected.

And I'd needed someone steady in my life. I was willing to put up with a lot just to belong to someone.

But he wasn't worth the tears. He didn't love me. I think I knew it from the start. I was a trophy for him, a success of his own making. Brett loves success more than he loves people.

He cheated. A lot. And I turned a blind eye because I wanted to believe that we were a team.

There's no Brett in team.

Should have gotten out before he torpedoed my self-esteem...

It rhymes, but I don't hear a single.

"You look good, Delilah," Brett says, leaning back in his chair.

"Thank you," I say woodenly. But inside I'm simmering with irritation. I glance toward the open conference room door. "Who are we waiting on?"

"Nobody, unfortunately," he says with a little shake of his head. "It turns out that Parker can't make it tonight after all. Last-minute emergency at home."

"He can't *make* it?" I repeat, as my internal simmer becomes a boil. "After we rescheduled for this weird hour for him?"

"I know, right?" Brett gives a well-acted shrug. "Vice presidents can do as they please."

Don't react, I remind myself. But this was a setup from start to finish. Originally, the meeting had been scheduled for the perfectly normal hour of three p.m. But at the last minute, Brett had moved it to seven o'clock, ruining my Friday-evening plans.

Becky's reaction had confirmed what I already suspected. "What a shit!" she'd fumed, stomping around my hotel suite. "He did this to ruin your Twitter date. Brett doesn't want to see any photos of you with another man!"

This struck me as a little nutty, even for a manipulative bastard like Brett. Up until tonight, I was never sure how closely he'd been following the finer points of my publicity schedule.

Brett doesn't love me. I know that in my gut. But he *really* hates to lose at anything.

Honestly, the date doesn't really matter. But the incident gives me a very bad feeling. If Brett would wreck an unimportant Twitter date, what else will he do to get back at me?

So here I sit, trying not to fidget in an ergonomic leather chair, wondering how I'll ever be free of him.

Across from me, Brett looks as smug as ever. "So let's just get started. Have you given any thought to my three-album suggestion? If that's the arrangement we decide on, the third one could be a gimme—a concert album, or a holiday thing. Maybe even a 'best of' record. I'd be willing to stipulate that in the contract."

I take another slow breath and will myself not to climb over the shiny table and choke him. "A three-album contract isn't really in my travel plans," I say with practiced coolness.

Neither is a one-album contract or a two-album contract. But my instinct for self-preservation forbids me to admit it. There's no way I'd sign anything for Brett Ferris again. Not even an autograph.

"Fair enough," he says easily. "Then my natural inclination on a two-album deal would be a deadline in eighteen to twenty-four months."

And here's my opening. Finally. "It's a little hard to talk dates for album number three when you haven't released number two yet."

He nods slowly, as if I've said something deeply interesting. But we both know this is the sticking point. I'm here today to make sure he releases my finished songs, and he's here to convince me to sign over more of them.

My new album was done months ago. And he is *sitting* on it. For no reason.

No *good* reason, anyway. It's just a ploy to strong-arm me into signing with him again. We're at a stalemate that neither of us will acknowledge. And since he has all the power, I'm out of ideas.

"What would be the terms of a two-album deal?" I ask. I'm never signing, but I can feign interest if it helps my cause.

"The new terms would be sweeter than your last contract," he says.

"They could hardly be worse." *Whoops*. That just slipped out, though I can't afford to antagonize him.

"Delilah." His tanned forehead wrinkles. "Your first contract was a reflection of your untested marketability. Of course things will be different now."

"Of course," I say tightly. "How different? You haven't said."

He slides the folder across the table toward me. "Read this."

"Thank you, I will." I reach for it eagerly, but it's just an act. The folder will go right into the garbage later. "Now let's find a release date for the album. Get your calendar out, and let's find a good day." *Preferably tomorrow*.

"Hmm. We are still not sure about the cover art," he hedges. "We'd like to find a designer that better understands your demographic."

The cover art? I take another steadying breath. "You know you could put a donkey wearing lipstick on this baby, and we would still do well."

"Is that a suggestion?" He clicks the end of his ridiculous gold pen. "Should I get the art department on the horn?"

"You arrogant fucking asshole," I whisper.

"There she is," he says with a sly grin. "The real Delilah. I've missed you, baby."

Shit. I bite my lip, because it's either that, or say something I can't take back.

"Look," he says, making his hands into a little tent. "We both want the same things. We're both invested in your success."

"You're invested at eighty-five percent, and me at fifteen," I point out. "That's not going to fly anymore."

"Read the contract," he says, clicking the end of his shiny gold pen.

I want to take his fancy gold pen and stab him in the throat with it. "Release my album, Brett," I say, because it's time to stop skirting the issue. "Why would I sign with you again if you're going to sit on my work?" And, damn it, my voice breaks at the end of the sentence. Because I can't play it cool about this.

The new songs are *good*. I'm not just drinking my own Kool-Aid, either. I made great music, straight from the gut.

And he's burying it.

"Sign the contract, and I'll release it," he says. "How can I invest in this new album, if I don't know what the future holds?"

It's a ridiculous point, from an infuriating man. "You're already invested. This is not how it's supposed to work."

"Says who?" He shrugs. "We both want to get paid. Sign the contract, and we will be. *Somebody's* gonna bring out your third and fourth albums, honeybunch. Might as well be me. Better the devil you know, and all that." He winks at me. An actual wink.

I hate him so much. The fact that I used to tell myself I loved this man is just astonishing to me. I was young and naive. Fine—I'll call it what it is. I was really, really stupid.

But no more. "Gotta go," I say, pushing my chair back from the table. "There's somewhere I need to be."

"Let me guess—a baseball game?"

My heart drops, even though I don't truly care about the baseball game or the goalie from Twitter. But I hate that Becky was right. Brett is too invested in me. And I don't know how to shake him off.

"I'm not going to a baseball game," I say because it's true. "I'm meeting Becky for dinner, and she has a reservation."

"Then don't let me keep you." He glowers at me, though.

I can't be civil anymore, so leaving is the only option. "Right. Later." I pluck the contract folder off the desk and hold it up, indicating that I'll read it.

"Safe travels," he says grumpily.

"Yeah, thanks." He wouldn't want anything to happen to his little paycheck.

And then I'm trotting toward the lobby of the empty office suite. Mr. Muscles is waiting by the elevator for me. He presses the elevator button the moment I appear.

"Thanks," I say.

He's silent.

Mr. Muscles isn't a talker. It's not his job to entertain me, but sometimes his silence just seems to magnify all the weird things about my life. I wait impatiently for the elevator, feeling wired and unhappy.

Meeting Brett alone was a mistake. I need to hire a manager to deal with him. I haven't done it yet, because I know Brett won't like it, and I thought maybe I could finesse him.

Not so much.

The elevator doors open, and I practically leap inside. Mr. Muscles follows me, pressing the button for the lobby. Only when the car has begun its descent do I feel the first hints of relief. I take out my phone and tap Becky's number.

"How'd it go?" she asks as soon as she picks up.

Of course I can't tell her much, because Mr. Muscles is probably Brett's spy. "How drunk can we get?"

"That bad, huh?"

"He's willing to play this game of chicken forever. I'm out of ideas."

"Sign with a new manager and let someone else do the negotiating."

"I know, I know." I should have done that immediately. Now I've wasted a few weeks for nothing. I've always been a natural musician and a disaster at the business details. "I can't wait to go back to L.A. Where am I meeting you?"

"Well…" She giggles. "There's been a slight change of plans. Come back to the hotel."

"Why?"

"All will be revealed."

DELILAH

A half hour later I'm in my suite overlooking Times Square, rifling through the mini-bar offerings and wishing Becky would just show up already. I text her again. *Not only do I need a drink, I'm starving. Wasting away, here. And your eyelashes are already beautiful,* I add, because I know her too well. She needs to apply sixty beauty products just to walk out of her hotel room.

There's a knock on the door.

"Finally!" I shriek. "So good of you to mosey upstairs before I starve to death!"

I jerk open the door.

But it isn't Becky who's standing outside. It's a guy. The first thing I see is a muscular chest clad in a purple T-shirt with a hockey player on it. "Brooklyn Bruisers," it says. Then I lift my chin and find a smooth, muscular jaw. And then...

Holy God. Those *eyes*. They're beautiful, and also kind.

They're also very familiar. "What the ever-loving fuck?" I breathe. "Ralph. How did you..." I don't finish the sentence, because I can't decide which question to ask first.

Why is Ralph from California here in New York?

And why now?

And what's with the T-shirt that matches the team from my canceled Twitter date?

And how did he get onto the secure floor of this hotel?

Apparently, Mr. Muscles is curious about that last thing, too. His form looms behind my visitor's. "If you're visiting Delilah, I need to see some ID. Or will he be leaving, miss?"

"No," I snap. I'm confused and more than a little bit hurt, because it's also occurring to me that Becky is responsible for these latest hijinks.

Ralph pulls his wallet out of his back pocket and flips it open to the ID window, showing it to Mr. Muscles. My body-guard/jailer takes out his phone and snaps a photo of it. Then he hands it back.

Or he tries to. I grab it first. *Silas Kelly*, the license reads. *220 Water Street, Brooklyn.*

Ralph from California is my Twitter date? That makes no sense. I hand it back to him. "Get in here," I snap, holding the door open a little wider.

He steps past me, putting his body close to mine for a half second. I get a whiff of his aftershave, and I swear he smells like the ocean and fresh air. I used to love sitting in the bar across from this man as he worked—those muscular hands in action as he made drinks and cut up limes. I liked his quiet company and hearing his thoughts during those rare moments when we were alone.

He was the only person in California who I found completely trustworthy. And then he abandoned me.

Whoa. Easy, girl. I don't know what I did to bring about this weird little blast from my past. But it's obviously unsettling, and emotional overload is not a good look on me.

Still, I slam the door on Mr. Muscles, trapping myself in the room with Ralph or Silas or whatever his name is. I march to the center of the plush oriental rug. "Now talk," I order. "Did Becky send you up here?"

"Yeah." He holds up a hotel keycard. "She gave me this so I could reach your floor." As if he owns the place, he walks over to the bar and sets down the keycard along with a grocery bag he's carrying. And a shopping bag hits the floor.

"You stood me up," I blurt. This is what happens when you greet old crushes on an empty stomach. I'd rather not let him know how disappointed I was three years ago. How I'd arrived on that beach, wearing a bathing suit, feeling freer and happier than I'd felt in weeks. And how awful I'd felt as the minutes ticked by. I waited almost two hours, alone, knowing he wasn't going to show.

The next day I walked past Roadie Joe's and looked into the window, hoping to chew him a new one, but there was a different man behind the bar. And it was the same the next day, too.

That's when I gave up. And anyway, the summer was over. I went back to L.A. and tried not to think about it.

And failed.

"About our surfing date," he says with a rueful smile. "I didn't stand you up on purpose. I wouldn't ever do that." He puts both elbows on the bar and rests his chin on the backs of his hands. "Can I tell you what happened?"

You'd better.

No way.

I am at war with myself.

"It was a Friday, and I was calling around, looking for a training board for you. They're coated with a soft material that's easier to stand on for your first time surfing."

My poor little heart says, *and then what?* Because I want him to convince me. But I just cross my arms and wait.

"I was waiting for a phone call back from a couple of people. And it was already after noon. My phone rang, and I ran out the back door to answer it. It was my agent. She said, 'I need you on a plane to Ontario.' The team that had released me, suddenly needed me back. In the minors, anyway. And you may recall that I was never given your phone number."

"Minor league hockey," I say slowly.

"Yeah." He pats the logo on his T-shirt. "This was always my Plan A. And it came through right after I officially gave up."

It came through. I don't mean to get goosebumps for him. It just happens. "You never mentioned hockey that summer. Not once."

"I know." He regards me with quiet eyes. "It was a sore point. My real name is Silas Kelly, as you saw."

"The guy from Twitter."

"That's right."

"Why didn't you just tell me that—or Becky? Hey, by the way, I'm Ralph from Roadie Joe's. In fact—why call yourself Ralph, anyway? That's just weird."

"I know." He reaches into the shopping bag and removes several limes. And some kind of green herb? Oh my God, it's mint. Lastly, he removes a bottle of liquor. "But I wanted to apologize in person."

"You brought mojitos?" Fuck me, but I'm already salivating. Minty, limey yumminess. The last one I drank was three years ago.

With him.

"Of course," he says calmly. "Now why don't you tell me what I can order you for dinner?"

"*Ralph,*" I say tartly. Because refusing to call him Silas seems like a good reminder that I'm mad at him. "Who says we're having dinner?"

He puts his muscular hands on the surface of the bar and regards me with those solemn eyes. "When you came to the door, you were yelling about how hungry you are. And I'd like to help the lady make her favorite cocktail, but not on an empty stomach. So let me fix that by finding you something to eat."

Well, hell. I'd forgotten how decent he is. And the way he's looking at me right now is doing things to my insides. Nobody ever looks at me like that—like they understand what I need. Except for Becky, and she's on the payroll.

It's going to be hard to keep myself in bitch mode if he's this nice. "I could order some room service. But I'm so sick of room service. The burger, the pasta, or the chicken Caesar salad."

He tilts his handsome face toward mine, and I'm still getting used to the lack of a beard on him. It makes him look younger. "I hope you're not knocking the chicken Caesar salad. Some of my best friends are chicken Caesar salads." He gives me a slow smile. "So how about some takeout food? We could order some Carribean food to go with our mojitos." He rubs his stomach absently. That tight stomach, just over that strong chest, where the T-shirt clings for dear life.

Dear lord. He's only gotten hotter in three years.

What were we discussing? Oh, right. "The takeout guys aren't allowed to come up here to the secure floor. It's a ploy by the hotel to get more business from me."

"I'll run out and get it," he offers. "Or send your giant bouncer friend." He tilts his head toward the door.

"He won't leave me alone," I grumble. "It's policy. And my entourage is in flux right now. I fired my manager and..." This is getting way off topic. "Never mind. We'll have the chicken Caesar."

He holds up his phone, showing me a picture of a plate of churrasco. "This place is on Forty-sixth Street. Not so far away. I'll use a delivery app and run downstairs for it. What do you want?"

I come closer, taking the phone and scrolling, meanwhile trying not to give him sideways glances. I inhale, and there's that scent again. That wonderful, infuriating scent. My thumb pauses on one of the photos. "I'll have the chicken Caesar salad, Ralph."

"Delilah," he whispers from way too close. "I get that you're a little weirded out by me showing up at your hotel. But let me get you some good food and make you a drink. You'll like it. I promise."

There's no doubt he's right. And that's exactly what I'm afraid of.

SILAS

"You again," says the thick-necked guy outside Delilah's hotel suite as I return from the lobby with our dinner.

"I just went down to get the food."

"The boss doesn't like her taking food from randoms," he says, crossing his meaty arms. I'd bet cash money that this guy competes on the bodybuilding circuit. Nobody has shoulders like that without staring at them in the gym's mirror every day.

"I'm not a random," I insist, trying to keep the growl out of my voice. "You want to inspect our takeout meal?" I offer the bag to him, daring him to poke around in there.

His unruly eyebrows knit together as he squints at me. "Naw. Go on."

I tap on the door, and Delilah opens it quickly. "Omigod that smells amazing. It's almost enough to make me forgive you."

"Forgive him for what?" the security guard butts in to ask.

"Nothing. Jesus. I'm joking." As soon as I'm inside, she slams the door on him.

"You two have a great working relationship."

"I don't trust him."

"Seriously?" I put the delivery bag on the bar, and I notice that Delilah already has mint leaves muddling with sugar and lime juice in two crystal glasses. "Seems like you should hire a guard you trust."

"Gosh, why didn't I think of that?" There's an edge to her voice that's unfamiliar to me. Everything she says seems to push me away.

But her body language tells another story. Even now, she's coming closer, standing right beside me at the bar, where I unpack the food. We bump hips. She's like a puppy that barks to put you on notice that it's ferocious, and then immediately wags its tail, begging to be friends.

I wrap an arm around her. It should have been a simple, friendly gesture, but we both go still. Touching isn't something we used to do. But I've been waiting for such a long time. The moment she opened the door on me an hour ago, the sight of her almost stopped my heart. I still want her so badly.

And even worse—my gut is still convinced she's mine. I turn my head to the side and drop a kiss on her temple. The sweet scent of her shampoo almost moves me to tears. But I force myself to take a sidestep away from her. "I'm going to find some real plates," I tell her, my voice thick. "This suite is crazy."

"No need for china," she says. "I'm not the snob that this hotel room makes me out to be."

"Let's not eat this glorious food with plastic forks, though. And you can finish making those drinks."

She gives me a quick glance and then peels the seal off the rum. She's still a little unnerved by me. Not afraid, but stunned. I guess that makes sense. I've been seeing her face everywhere, but she hasn't seen Ralph the bartender in years.

"I don't know how much rum to add."

"Put the ice in first, and then add about this much rum." I pinch the air to show her about an inch and a half.

"Got it."

"Are you still…" I clear my throat, trying to find the right question.

"Crazy?" she offers.

"No. Come on. Phobic is the word I was looking for."

"Yes." She sighs. "It hasn't gotten worse, but it hasn't really gotten better, either. I still don't drink anything that I haven't opened or poured for myself."

I hand her the unopened bottle of soda water and smile at her.

"Thank you, Ralph," she whispers.

"Anytime," I whisper back.

We're staring at each other. I know this whole night is crazy and not what she expected. But it's already perfect. All I ever wanted was to apologize for standing her up and to make another drink for her.

"We should probably eat this food while it's hot," she whispers.

"Yup."

We give our lingering, hungry gaze one more long beat. Delilah looks away first. She opens a drawer to reveal knives and forks.

We arrange ourselves on the sofa, side by side, our plates on the coffee table. She gives me a shy smile as she cuts her first bite of food. Then I watch Delilah tuck away a healthy portion of fine roast beef and plantain fritters.

It's almost embarrassing how much satisfaction it gives me to feed her. "Better now?" I ask, popping a fritter in my mouth.

"Much better." She puts her fork down and leans back with a sigh. "This day, though."

"Do you want to tell me why you're kind of a wreck?"

Her laugh is bitter. "Is it that obvious?"

"Was your meeting awful?"

"Yes. But that's only one symptom of the problem." She crosses her legs on the sofa. "It's…everything. Brett Ferris was so integral to my life that when I finally left him for good, everything got more stressful."

I didn't really come here to talk about that asshole, but maybe there's no choice. "I'm sorry to hear that."

"Not as sorry as I am." She sighs. "Everyone that makes my week easier is his employee. My former assistant worked for him. My security company was hired by him." She points at the door, indicating the bodyguard outside. "He's probably spying on me. But what do I know about hiring a security company?" She puts her head in her hands. "My accountant is Brett's accountant. You get the picture. Only Becky has defected. She quit her PR firm to work for me full time. I didn't even know how to hire someone or how to run a payroll. The first week I stopped by an ATM and paid her in cash."

"So there's a lot of admin stressing you out?"

"Yes." She looks up at me. "And then there's the stalker."

"The—what?" I set the remains of my dinner down. "You have a stalker?"

She nods, and picks at the cuticles of one hand. "I get a lot of weird mail. That's been going on for a while. But there's this one guy who found my home address somehow. He writes these creepy notes about how we're going to get to know each other better." She shivers. "He writes them on cocktail napkins. So that's fun."

I cannot hide my flinch. "Cocktail napkins. From anywhere specific?"

"It's from a different bar every time. There was an interview in *Spin* once about how I wrote lyrics on a cocktail napkin—" She gives me a shy glance. "Your cocktail napkin. I'd forgotten my notebook."

I do remember that, and I'd read that interview. But I didn't know until now that she'd written "Hype City" sitting across from me at the bar.

And now I have chills. Although this story isn't about me.

"I'm sorry," I say. "No wonder you haven't fired your security guy."

"Yeah. I'm not in a hurry to replace Mr. Muscles, because at least he's careful."

"Mr. Muscles?" I crack a smile. "That's what you call your bodyguard?"

She gets a playful look in her eye. She leans a little closer and whispers. "He has no neck."

"I noticed that," I whisper back.

Her smile fades. "The creepy letters aren't really my biggest problem. Brett is holding my album hostage."

"Your album...*Lucky Hearts*? The new one?"

"You know the title?" She perks up. "That's a good sign. I'm worried that people will forget about me before he releases it. It's been ready for months. He won't release it until I sign on for a third."

"But I heard a new song a few months ago."

"You listen to my stuff?" She tilts her head to the side, like she doesn't really believe me.

"Sometimes," I hear myself say. But it's a bold-faced lie, and my friends would convulse with laughter if they heard that. So I have to come clean. "I only listen to your stuff whenever I'm conscious."

She squints at me, like maybe I'm making fun of her. But I'm not, and it's vital she knows. So I turn and scoop her off the couch. My arms are full of warm, cynical girl, just like I've always wanted. I deposit her in my lap.

She lets out a squeak of surprise, and then we're nose to nose, with her straddling me.

Finally.

My pulse kicks into overdrive now. She feels way too good in my arms. "You should know that I own your first album on vinyl as well as CD. And of course it's on my phone."

"You…really?" She blinks at me at incredibly close range. "*Vinyl?*"

"Yup. But it's never been played because I don't have a turntable. And I don't know why you're so surprised. I *told* you I wanted to hear 'Sparkle On' make it big on the radio."

"Yes, you did." She swallows. "As did I. Didn't know it would turn my life into a freak show, though. You were right about Ferris."

"Ah." I tighten my arms around her. "You know, a man usually likes to hear that he's right. But in this case, I'm sorry."

She looks down at my chest, as if taking in the fact that we've never been as close as we are right now. "Are you?"

"Am I what? Right?"

"No—are you *sorry*. Seems like you turned up about ten minutes after I finally kicked him to the curb. That can't be a coincidence."

"No, it really is. I was watching Dallas versus L.A., and there you were. But do you remember last year after your Madison Square Garden concert—taking a photo with a bunch of women from a shelter in Brooklyn?"

"Yeah. A battered-women's shelter, right?"

"That's the place. Those women had my tickets. Second row. I'm still trying not to hold it against them."

"What?" Her eyes widen. "You were going to come to the show?"

"My friends surprised me with the tickets. Or they tried to. We got snowed in on the West Coast. There was a freak snowstorm in Seattle of all places."

"Oh." She traps her bottom lip between her teeth, and it's *right there*. I want to bite it, too. Her weight feels good on my lap, and it's a struggle not to pull her closer to me. "You gave your tickets to battered women? You really are the nicest guy in the world."

"That wasn't my idea," I admit. "Georgia—our team publicist—thought of it when we got stranded." I lift my hand and push a strand of dark, shiny hair out of her face. "But..." I clear my throat. "The fact that you're single right this second? That doesn't make me sad at all. I hope you're okay with me saying that."

"Well..." She gives her head a nervous shake. "If only I felt free like I'm supposed to. I've needed to walk away from him for a long time. I'm still not free of him."

"But you will be," I whisper, because my self-control is starting to slip.

"Eventually." She puts a palm on my chest, and all my synapses fire at once. My body begs her, *Touch me more.* "Listen, Ralph—" She sighs. "*Silas.* Whatever your name is. I really don't need another man to complicate my life."

"Who said anything about complicated? There is nothing complicated at all about me right now." I flatten one of my hands on her lower back and then rub the muscles sweetly.

Her eyes flutter closed, because she likes it that much. But then they snap open again. "Why didn't I know your real name before now?"

"It wasn't meant to be a giant secret. Ralph was a nickname I picked up in high school. And Danny from Roadie Joe's—the son of the owner? He made me that name tag to wear behind the bar."

"Everyone called you Ralph in high school?"

"Most everyone. And they still do. All because once I quite famously ralphed everywhere."

She laughs, deep and low, and I can't believe I went three years without hearing that sound. It gives me goosebumps. I lift a hand and catch her smiling face in my palm. She quits laughing suddenly, as I stroke a roughened thumb over her soft cheek.

"It's really good to be here with you," I whisper. "It means a lot to me."

A pink spot appears on each of her cheeks. "You aren't such rough company yourself."

DELILAH

I'm sitting in his lap, damn it. I have no self-control.

In my defense, it's a really nice lap. And Silas/Ralph is a really great guy. I knew it from the first day I met him. But it doesn't matter. We were never going to be a couple. Fate had other plans for the both of us.

Neither of us cares right now, though. When I look into his pretty green eyes, it's too easy to get carried away.

"Can I have another mojito?" I ask suddenly. If I don't get off this man's lap, I'm going to make a fool of myself.

"Of course you can," he says easily. "If that's really what you want. How's your tolerance these days?"

"Not great."

He nods, a thoughtful look on his handsome face. "Then you have an important decision to make. I'm not sure that having another drink is your best option."

"Why not?" I'm full of food and drinking in the company of the best guy ever.

"Let me explain," he says.

"I'm ready."

"Okay, listen up." But instead of speaking, Silas leans forward.

I make a sound of surprise as his lips graze my neck. His touch is soft and gentle, and goosebumps break out all over my body. He's dropping gentle, open-mouthed kisses down the side of my neck. And when he reaches the juncture of my shoulder, he pauses there, his tongue exploring my skin thoroughly.

A gasp leaves my lips, but I don't jerk away. Nobody has ever kissed me so reverently. I let out an embarrassing whimper as desire floods me. It's been a long time since I was handled so beautifully. Maybe ever. So I lean in, instead of away. Anyone would. In fact, I raise a hand to his soft hair and hold him closer.

He chuckles and sits up quickly. "You see?"

"W-what?" I blink into those green eyes.

"I'm going to kiss you for real in a minute."

My tummy flips over.

"And you're not going to want me to stop. But if you get drunk—" He sweeps his thumb across my cheek again, and— damn it—I lean into his hand. But he feels so good. He drops his voice. "If you get drunk, then I won't be able to fuck you. It wouldn't be right."

The moment I hear that word, I let out a hot breath. I force myself to inhale slowly. "Who says that's on the table?"

"Well." He smiles, and it's the naughtiest smile I've ever seen on him. "It doesn't have to be on the table. I could get you naked right here on the sofa."

I hear myself gasp, because I really don't know what to do with so bald an invitation. My body does, though. My blood heats up by two or three degrees right then and there. I tip my head back and try to think.

This maneuver backfires, because Silas kisses my throat. "That's right," he whispers, tilting his head to drop more wet, sweet kisses up the length of my neck. "Or there's always the countertop. I bet there's a kickass shower somewhere in this suite. And let's not forget the bed."

Unbidden, my hands land on his chest again. Sweet Jesus, he's rock-hard everywhere. I lean back again to look him in the eye. "I just didn't expect you to go there," I say even as my heart rate accelerates. "You were always the nicest guy."

"I am still the nicest guy." He takes my earlobe against his tongue and then sucks on it. "Nice and hard for you..."

If he's trying to make me imagine other places he might put his mouth, then it's totally working.

"I'm so *nice* that I'm going to make you come in every room in this suite. Twice, maybe."

I let out a groan as my nipples harden. "That is a terrible idea."

"Terrible for who, exactly?" He lifts the fabric at my lower back and runs his roughened fingertips lightly up my spine.

And I shiver, because my body is a traitor.

"The clock is ticking. We have one night. If you want to spend it getting blasted on mojitos, I still have the ingredients. But my idea is even better."

And that's when he finally does it—he lowers his mouth onto mine. I make an eager sound at the first touch of his lips, because I never had any self-control. He catches the back of my head in his palm, trapping me in a bossy kiss.

It's Kryptonite. I've never made smart decisions about men in my life, and, apparently, I won't be starting tonight.

He tries to make that first kiss a slow one, I think. His lips are gentle at first, and he tastes of fresh mint and heat. But it's like trying to hold back the ocean. His touch tugs on all my senses. My fingers tingle on the cotton of his T-shirt. The clean scent of his aftershave makes me crazy.

Closer, my subconscious begs. *More*. I lean forward, pressing my breasts against his chest.

Our mouths fuse and his tongue delves into my mouth. My

groan vibrates between us as we deepen the kiss. It feels marvelous and inevitable.

Silas doesn't miss a beat. Those strong hands worship the skin beneath my top. They stroke upward along my ribcage, his thumbs sweeping under my bra to tease my aching breasts. He's not shy. Not at all.

It works, too. I want those hands everywhere. And he knows it. A moment later my top is lifted over my head and tossed aside. Silas looks down at my white lace bra and sighs happily. Then he deftly unhooks it and flicks it down and away. A beat later, my breasts are in his hands, his callused thumbs stroking my nipples.

"Kiss me," he orders in a voice that's hoarse with desire.

So I do. I rise up on my knees and give the man what he wants. I let his bossy tongue scrape against mine, and I stop wondering whether this is a mistake. Because I like it too much to care that he's unzipping my skirt. One of those wide hands slides down the globe of my ass and inside my panties. He scoops his hand down until one questing hand finds the slick heat between my legs.

That escalated quickly. But, *oh hell, yes*.

A better person would probably be horrified at my behavior. I barely know this man. I haven't seen him for three years. Yet I have his tongue in my mouth while his fingers are stroking me right where I need him.

I think I knew this would happen the minute I first opened that door. Hell, maybe I knew it the first time he ever smiled at me.

Still, I feel vulnerable. And I hate to feel vulnerable. "Why am I the only one who's half-dressed?" I ask, pulling back.

He makes a caveman grunt at the loss of my mouth. "You can have whatever you want, Delilah. All you ever had to do is ask."

That's not strictly true. If he'd shown up to take me surfing in California…

I push that thought out of my head even as I tug on his T-shirt, struggling to free it from his muscular body. He lifts his arms to help me out. And—wow. His chest is like a work of art. My hands slide over skin and muscle. Silky skin over steel. "Do you have any body fat at all?"

"Eight percent," he mumbles, reaching for his fly.

I'm in the way, so I scoot back and unzip him myself. Then I reach into his straining boxer briefs and caress his impressive erection.

Silas groans so loudly that half of New York probably heard it. Or at least the bodyguard in the hallway did.

Hell.

"Come here," I say quickly, scrambling off his lap.

"Now?" He catches my hand to keep me close. His eyes are darkened with lust, and his hair is messy from where I clawed at it while he kissed me.

"Please?" I whisper. I don't want to explain myself. I don't want to tell him all the ways that I feel out of my element right now. I just want him to magically know what I need and make it happen.

It's not hard to guess why I've never had a healthy relationship.

Silas stands. He zips his shorts so they won't fall off. Then he actually scoops me up in his arms, the way you'd carry a child. "Where's the bedroom?" he asks quietly.

SILAS

I lay Delilah out on the white bedding and then close the bedroom door. By the time I return, she's kicked off her panties. She's lying back, naked, her big eyes full of an emotion that's not easy for me to parse. Hope and hesitation. Excitement and also nerves.

From the pocket of my shorts I take the condoms that I stashed there hours ago. Unzipping again, I lose my shorts, and then my underwear.

"Really?" she asks in her husky voice. "You planned this?"

"Would you rather I hadn't?" I ask, lying down on the bed beside her. I run a hand down her impossibly smooth hip, and feel the shiver that she tries to fight off. I'm never going to forget this view. Delilah is slim, bordering on bony. In clothes, she's all sharp edges and flashing eyes and quick wit.

But naked? She's softer. I can't help but lean down and lick one tan nipple.

She shivers. "What if I said no?"

"Then I go home and hit the whiskey." I lean over and kiss the other nipple, so it doesn't feel left out. "I learned a few things since the last time I saw you."

"How to get a woman naked, even without her phone number?"

I shake my head. "How not to fear failure. How to have zero ego. You can't get the things you want if you don't lay it all on the line."

A pair of soft hands find their way into my hair. "You always were smarter than me."

"Not always." I have plenty of regrets. But now is not the moment to think about them.

"Do that again," she says, guiding my head back down to her body.

You don't have to ask me twice. I trace her nipple with my lips. Then she gasps as I roll it on my tongue and suck. She whimpers as I kiss my way over to the other breast and do the same all over again.

I want my mouth on her everywhere at once. Finally getting what you need is a heady experience, and I don't even know where to start. So I roam every curve with my hands, and I kiss my way down to the apex of her sex. She smells like honey and musk, and my cock leaks on the bed as I part her legs with my hands.

But Delilah closes her thighs. "Not that," she whispers, adding, "Ralph."

I lift my face and find those giant eyes blinking down at me. "Really? Why not?"

"Because...I didn't shave."

"Oh, honey." I drop a single kiss right onto the thicket of hair between her legs. "The way I want you is so much bigger than that. In fact, the messier the better."

Her head flops back onto the pillows, and she lets out a little sigh that only serves to show me her perfect breasts in motion. "Come here. Please?"

I obey. Of course I do. I cover her body with my own and kiss her again. And again.

Smooth arms come around to hold me. As I stroke her tongue with mine, silken knees rise up to pin my body against hers. My cock settles between her legs, the base cradled against her sweet pussy.

Her dark eyes flash with pleasure as she moves her hips to strain against me.

I settle in, kissing her. Loving her body with mine. Trying every combination of skin on skin that I can think of. I roll us to the side, nipping her lip, slipping my hand down between our two bodies. She moans as I drag a fingertip around her opening in a circle. But I don't venture inside.

She's panting and gripping my body with eager fingers. Her eyes dart toward the condoms on the table. But she doesn't say a word.

"You want me to fuck you," I whisper between kisses. "But you won't ask."

"What are you waiting for, if you know me so well?" she returns. Her tone suggests that she's still angry with me. But she won't admit that, either.

I'll just have to win her trust again, then. But first things first.

I reach out to grab a condom off the table. I tear the packet with my teeth, flick it away, and then roll it on, one-handed.

When I pull her into my arms again, her kiss is fierce. It begs me to love her.

I'm only dimly aware of my surroundings—the fine furnishings, the last of the dusky light filtering through the windows. Time has stopped for us at last. I thought it never would. I palm one of her smooth legs in my hand, and thrust my hips.

And...*finally*. With a groan I slide into her tight heat. She moans into my mouth, and we're a fierce tangle of tongues and teeth and limbs. I rock into her, each stroke more intense than the last. I want to slow down and savor everything. But there's no way. I'm like a starving man who's finally been given a meal.

Delilah doesn't make it any easier, either. Her nails scrape my back, and her breathing is fast and wild. "Don't. Stop," she moans, her eyes dark and hungry.

"I would never," I pant, although I'm fast approaching the point of no return. I bite my lip and groan as my need for release mounts.

Our gazes lock again. My prickly girl can't look away this time. It's too right and too good.

Only pride keeps me going until Delilah makes an achy, desperate noise, her forehead creasing with effort. Like she's reaching for something just beyond her grasp.

I lean down and kiss her as softly as I can manage right now. "I've got you." I roll us over, pulling her against my chest. I take a deep breath and thrust lazily. "Let go, sweetheart."

"I..." She blinks down at me. "I'm still angry."

"I know. Not just at me. At the whole world." I thrust my hips off the bed and she closes her eyes with pleasure. "Show me how mad you are."

"You're..."

I reach up and take her breasts in my hands, my thumbs circling her nipples.

"You..." She leans down and kisses me instead of finishing that sentence. And then she sinks down on my cock and moans deeply. As our tongues slide together, her body quakes around mine.

I can't hold back any longer. I sit up fast, catching her in my arms and pumping her hips onto mine one more time. And then I groan into her neck as I empty my soul inside her.

"Good. Lord," she pants a moment later, her body slumped against mine.

"Still remember why you're mad at me?" I tease, my hand rubbing circles on her soft skin.

"No," she grunts. "But I'm still calling you Ralph."

"Okay," I say, smiling into her hair. "I deserve it." She

moves her hips an inch and I groan at the beautiful contact. "Going somewhere?"

Yes, apparently. She disengages suddenly and studies me.

"What?"

She shakes her head. "You still get to me. I don't know what it is that makes you so appealing."

"Clean living." I fall back onto the pillows with a happy sigh. "I swear I have plenty of stamina. I just need a little rest before I can prove it." I open my arms. "Come here."

She only hesitates for a second before joining me on the pillows.

My arms close around her, and now I have everything I need.

DELILAH

In the morning, I wake up to the sound of texts hitting my phone, one after the other. *Becky*, I realize as my eyes fly open. She and I were supposed to have breakfast. Whoops!

She'll forgive me when she learns why I'm not available.

Beside me, Silas rolls over. He opens one eye, shuts it again, and then smiles at me with his eyes closed. And my poor stupid heart melts a little further. He looks so boyish right now. So *cute*.

He catches my feet with his under the covers, and then drapes a sleepy hand onto my hip. "Morning," he mumbles, as if this were a perfectly normal way to wake up together.

I don't even have words for some of the ways we touched last night.

"Morning," I repeat, as my phone dances a jig on the bedside table. "Sorry. Let me tell Becky that I'm not coming to breakfast."

"Mmm, breakfast," he says with a happy sigh. "Want to go out and get some greasy diner food? We need sustenance."

He's not wrong. There was a round two in the shower. And a round three on the side of the bed.

But I don't answer him for a second, because I'm texting Becky. *Go without me. Still busy here.*

OMG! she manages to text back before I shut the phone all the way down.

"Sorry, you were saying?" I turn my attention back to the sleepy hunk in my bed. And—wow—in the daylight he's even more impressive, crazy bedhead and all.

"Pancakes and bacon?" He yawns. "No—bagels and salmon. And coffee." His stomach actually rumbles audibly.

"Well, going out to eat with me isn't that much fun," I hedge.

His eyes open all the way. "Do fans pester you?"

Yes. "Sometimes. And I'm not in the mood for that right now." Not to mention that Mr. Muscles would be sitting at the next table, eavesdropping.

Usually there's not much happening in my life to overhear. But the things that Silas and I say to each other are private. They're not for anyone else's ears. "How about I order room service?" I offer. "They have good bagels here. From H&H." I sit up.

"Okay," he says easily, catching my hand. "Don't be gone too long."

My poor heart can't take this much niceness, I swear.

I slip my hand out of his, grab a plush bathrobe out of the master bath, and order breakfast. When I get back, Silas is squinting at his phone with a scowl on his face.

"Something wrong?" I ask, sitting on the bed, smiling at him.

He looks up at me and his expression softens. "You look so relaxed this morning."

"Are you looking for compliments?" I ask, giving him a poke in the hip.

"No!" He snorts. "Just saying." His phone buzzes on his chest. "Let me just tell my roommate I'm not dead."

"You have a roommate?" I flop back on the pillows, where his screen is visible to me.

"Yeah. I actually have two at the moment, because his girlfriend moved in. Now there's a long story..." He unlocks his phone and checks the messages.

And—good lord—there are bunches. I swear, a dozen people are all pinging him. "Your phone is like LAX on a Friday night."

He sighs. "Teammates. They're nosy."

"I'm sorry," I say, realizing that I'm being rude. "I won't look over your shoulder."

"Hey, I don't care." He reaches up and tugs me back down again, arranging me under one arm. I never met anyone as tactile as him. He makes cuddling seem inevitable. "I don't need to answer all of these, anyway. Let me just check this one." He taps a face, which belongs to a woman named Georgia.

I'm standing in your apartment and you're not here, she writes.

"Uh-oh," Silas says.

My stomach drops. "Who's Georgia?" I ask. Could he have a *girlfriend?* It's not like I asked.

"My publicist—the one who set up the ball game."

"Does she always make house calls?"

He must hear it in my voice, because he turns his head and studies me with those clear, guileless eyes. "We all live in the same building. It's like a college dorm sometimes. It just didn't occur to me that Georgia would show up looking for details at..." He checks the time on his phone. "Eight thirty in the morning."

"Oh," I say as my face heats.

"Yeah." He reaches out to touch my cheek. "Sorry. She's going to assume..." He starts to laugh.

"Well, she'll be right," I point out.

But he doesn't answer Georgia's message. He goes back to

the main menu. "Georgia is married to Leo." He points at another face, also with a pending message. *Buddy have a great time at the ball game!*

"And my roommate Jason lives with *this* chick…" He points to a cute blonde woman who has also texted him this morning. "We're like one giant, gossipy clan. But the only message I need to answer right now is my roommate's." He taps on Jason's face.

Okay, it's midnight, Jason writes. *Must be extra innings? Bad traffic? Heidi and I are wondering where you are.*

We both snicker.

And then, an hour later: *Dude, wow. I'm impressed. Way to make the date a success.*

"Oh man," Silas says, while I laugh. "I'm so sorry."

"Why? Because you have friends who pay attention? That's kind of their job." He has no idea how envious I am. Besides—if you want to know whether someone is a good guy, just look at his phone. If he has a dozen friends hazing him at once, then he is obviously loved.

It's a shame I didn't figure that out a long time ago. All of Brett's messages are from people who fear him or loathe him.

Jason's final text has a timestamp from a half hour ago. *Wow, man. I didn't know you were such a stud. A sleepover with your idol? Georgia is here looking for you. She and Heidi are laughing their butts off right now.*

Silas taps out a reply. *Shut it down, will you? Can't you just tell Georgia that I went out for an early run?*

The roommate replies immediately. *Too late!* He adds a laughing emoji. *Georgia and Heidi are reading this over my shoulder.*

"Oh, Jesus." Silas tosses the phone onto the nightstand again. "I'm never living this down. Totally worth it, though." He encircles me with both arms.

I tuck my face into his neck and sigh. It's odd how comfortable he feels to me right now. I don't feel as if I'm snuggling an acquaintance I haven't seen for three years.

"When am I seeing you again?" he asks me.

And even I'm not cynical enough to pretend I'm not wondering, too. Not that seeing him again will be easy. "No idea. My life is such a mess right now."

"I know." He strokes my hair. "But here's the thing. I have six more weeks before training camp starts again. I can travel any time before mid-August. After that, I'm unavailable, except in New York, roughly on alternate weeks."

"How do you spend the summers?" I ask, realizing I know so little about his life.

"Well, I always fly out to Cali and visit my mom. But I did that the week after we got knocked out of the playoffs. Then usually the single guys rent a cottage somewhere, for golf or hiking or whatever. But this year we're all going to a destination wedding instead."

"You visit your mom...in Darlington Beach?" I ask. The idea gives me a chill, because I've made frequent visits to Darlington Beach, too. Has he been right there under my nose before?

"She lives inland, now," he says, his big hand flattening on my back. "I haven't been back to Darlington Beach for more than a couple hours."

"Oh." Still. Even a single glimpse of him will always affect me. I know that now. "Want to hear something funny? I'm headlining the Darlington Beach music festival this year."

He laughs, and the sound echoes under my ear. "Of course you are. How long will you be in town? Maybe I could arrange to be there at the same time."

"It's not until August," I point out.

"Ah. You're right. If you give me the dates I could try, though."

I kiss his neck. He makes a happy sound, so I do it again.

Lying here with him makes me feel like a different Delilah — a sweeter, less crabby one.

A hopeful one.

He rolls to his side so he can see me, and his eyes are already smiling. "Does this mean I can finally have your phone number?"

For about a half a second I contemplate teasing him. But I can't do it. "Sure. Grab your phone," I say, turning to reach for mine.

"*Sure*, she says. Finally."

I smile, although I can't help wondering what life would be like if I'd given it to him years ago. When I refused him before, I was so sure I was protecting myself from confusion and heartache.

Joke's on me!

"What's your number?" I ask, and he rattles off a 646 number.

Hi, I text him.

He texts me back a heart emoji.

Is there an emoji for a heart exploding? Because I think I need it. "You're going into my phone as Ralph," I warn him.

"I'm fine with that," he says, putting his phone back on the bedside table. "So long as you call me Silas the next time I'm inside you." He punctuates this thought by reaching between the halves of my hotel bathrobe and cupping my breast.

And my body is instantly like one big heart emoji. He smiles, as if he can read my thoughts.

There's a knock on the door. "Room service!"

"Aw." Silas laughs. "That was fast. But it's probably for the best. You must be a little sore."

It's true. But I wouldn't even care. I straddle him and kiss his forehead. "Would you pull on your shorts and get the food?"

"Of course, girly. But you have to move your hiney off me first."

I move away, hiding my smile. I just love the way Silas speaks to me—as if we're back at Roadie Joe's. As if I'm still wearing an ironic T-shirt, and he's cutting up limes. Those were golden hours, and I didn't understand how special they were.

Silas departs for the living room, whistling, wearing shorts and nothing else. I admire the muscles in his back as he crosses the thick carpet and answers the door. And I step out of sight, because I don't want to show off my sex hair to the hotel staff.

"Just leave it here on the table," Silas says.

"Can I take this away for you?" a voice inquires, probably in reference to our discarded takeout containers from last night.

"Oh, would you? Thanks a lot. You have a nice day." He speaks to the porter the way everyone should—like he's done that job himself before, and he remembers how it is. But then I hear him say, in a different voice, "What are you looking at?"

It's Mr. Muscles's murmur that follows.

"Do me a favor? Delete my ID from your phone after I leave in an hour."

I can't hear my bodyguard's reply.

The door closes again. "Breakfast is served," Silas calls out.

I show myself. "What was that about?" I whisper.

"Nothing," he mouths. "Coffee?"

"That's for you. This is for me." I pluck a sealed bottle of orange juice off the tray. "And this is for you." There's another glass, this one with a paper hat as its only cover. "Fresh squeezed."

He looks from his juice to mine. "Still opening all your own bottles?"

"Habit," I say, popping the lid off of mine. Although we both know that *phobia* is more accurate.

He watches me take a sip, but he doesn't say anything more about it. He sits down on the sofa with his glass, and pats the cushion beside him.

"Can't believe I have to fly out this morning. I'll have to

leave here in forty-five minutes." I put a hand on his knee and squeeze. Not like it's easy. His leg muscles are like iron.

He covers my hand with his. "What's your least favorite airport?" he asks. "Let's compare notes.

"Boston!" I say immediately. "And Fort Lauderdale."

"I dislike Chicago, myself," he says. "Bagel?" He hands me a plate with an easy smile.

And I fall for him a little harder.

DELILAH

On the flight home, I'm all keyed up inside.

"I say this with love," Becky starts from the generously sized seat beside mine. "Stop tapping your heel or I'll throw those shoes into the first-class toilet."

My feet go silent for a minute or two, but then start up again when I return to thinking about Brett and his stupid meeting.

I have to get my songs back from that man. I just don't know how.

"For the love of God," Becky hisses, pressing down on my wiggling knee. "You're not behaving the way someone who had sex three times last night should behave."

"Wait." I rotate in my seat to face her. "Who told you that?"

She bursts out laughing. "You did—just now. And I do appreciate it." She tips her head back onto the headrest. "Wow. Three, huh? Does he have any friends? That is some serious stamina."

"Shh." I rise up and peek into the row behind us. But the octogenarians in 2a and 2b are both asleep. And Mr. Muscles is back in the main cabin, because I didn't upgrade him like I did for Becky.

"Tell me *everything*," Becky whispers. "Is he good with his hands? Do goalies do it better?"

Her question makes me picture Silas's hands, which have always fascinated me. And my face heats just thinking of all the places he put them...

Becky laughs again. "Your face says it all. And nobody deserves a fun night like you."

"Thank you, I think."

"You're welcome!" She beams. "Look, there are a few things we need to talk about before we get back to California. Some are more fun than others. I have a few business items for you, and then today's Sparkle. It's the best one ever."

We have this silly tradition. Becky deals with a lot of bad news—gossip pieces and other bullshit in my life—so every night she gives me something good. It might be a fan letter, or it might be a video of a kitten being rescued off the median of a highway. It's always something worth cheering over. We call it the daily Sparkle.

I fucking love Becky.

"We still have this meeting with Charla Harris, right?" I ask first. The whole point of a morning flight was getting back in time to see a manager in the late afternoon. Of all the names we reached out to, Harris was the only one who said it would be tricky to "squeeze me in" this week. Though she has a great reputation.

"Yep," Becky says. "I emailed her your existing contract with Ferris. But last night she asked for a royalty statement, and I balked. I didn't want to send her any dollar figures without talking to you first."

"Wow. She needs to make sure I'm worth the money, so she knows whether to cancel the meeting?" I'm only twenty-six years old, and already I have a jaundiced view of the music industry. Music is beautiful, but its business people are all sharks. Most days I think I should just go live on a mountaintop somewhere with my guitar.

"You can give her the royalty statement this afternoon, if it still seems like a good idea," Becky says.

"Okay. What else?"

She makes a grim face. "Two items. Neither is very nice."

"Spit it out already."

"A news thing." She sighs. "Just a stupid gossip column about you and Brett. I just want those stories to die."

"Where? What does it say?"

"The *Post* has a shot of you walking into his office building yesterday. And there's a snarky line about how you were done with Brett Ferris because he already gave you your big break." She rolls her eyes. "It's the typical misogynistic bullshit. Men deserve all their successes, but women probably sleep their way to the top."

"The joke's on them," I grumble. "I only wanted him to love me." Or anyone to love me, really. I was such a needy little thing. And Brett knew that. He spend three years doling out affection with an eyedropper, and I was always waiting there, needing another hit.

"Someday the record will be set straight," Becky says. "Brett Ferris is a weasel, and the world will know."

I feel another rush of love for Becky, who—in spite of trading in gossip for a living—still believes in justice and happy endings. She's twenty-three, exactly the same age as I was when I met Silas but then started sleeping with Brett. It's an age where you still believe that anything is possible.

"Nobody cares, though," I point out. "The people who read those stories aren't looking for justice. They just want something lurid to enjoy with their morning coffee."

"I *know*, Delilah. Jeez." She opens the folder on her lap. "But I can't do this work every day without imagining that the good people can come out on top."

"There's a sex joke in there somewhere."

"Yes! At least you're making sex jokes. That's progress."

"What's the other bad thing?"

"You got another cocktail napkin in the mail."

My gut twists. "From where?"

"The Polo Lounge."

I stare at her. "Who did we tell that we had a drink there? It wasn't even planned."

She shrugs. "Could have been that somebody Instagrammed it, and we didn't notice."

"Ugh. Was the note creepy?"

"They're all creepy, Dee."

I suppose that's true.

"The guys are going to send the envelope and the napkin out for fingerprinting. He'll screw up eventually. Are you ready for today's Sparkle?"

"At this hour? What if we're back to gloom and doom by evening?"

"Then I'll find another one. But I can't wait to show you this. It's a letter from Silas Kelly."

"What? Why?"

She clutches a folded piece of paper to her chest and sighs. "When I called to break your date with him, he said he needed to give me a letter to you. Said it was really important. And since he could tell that I thought it sounded creepy, he told me I should read it and decide for myself if I should give it to you."

"Oh," I say slowly.

"So while you were at that meeting with buttface, I met Silas at Starbucks. And he gave me this." She tosses the page into my lap.

Delilah —

I don't know if you'll remember me. But three years ago I was the bartender at Roadie Joe's in Darlington Beach, and you were the highlight of my day. I was going through a really rough time, thinking I had to start from scratch on my Plan B.

It would have been a terrible summer, except you came in every day for a beer — a cold one in a bottle, unopened — and just talking to you made the whole day right.

You might remember that we were supposed to go surfing. I deeply regret that I did not show up that day. I was in a mad dash to the airport with all my belongings. Now there's a story I'd like to tell you in person. I sent a friend to the beach to find you and tell you why I didn't show.

He was two hours late, though. Because obviously an employee of the restaurant I'd just walked out on wasn't the right person to ask this favor. That's on me. I'm sorry for that screwup and for leaving you standing there.

(Although, I feel obligated to point out that if only you'd given me your phone number the 73 times I asked, this could have been avoided.)

Lucky for me, I haven't needed your number to see that your Plan A is kicking serious ass. Even though I don't see you between the lunch rush and happy hour anymore, I am still paying attention. My wish came true — I heard Sparkle On playing on many different radios. You don't know how happy that makes me. (Spoiler: really happy.)

Every time I hear your songs, I smile. And while I'm still wishing I had your phone number, I just want you to know how proud I am of you. You deserve every good thing that comes your way.

And I hope you're still wearing that T-shirt — the one that says Kind of a Big Deal. Now it's not ironic anymore.

Love always,

That Guy Behind The Bar With the Ralph Name Tag

AKA Silas Kelly

Becky is dabbing at her eyes when I look up. And — fuck — I'm dabbing at mine, too. "That boy is seriously good at letter-writing," I sniff.

"See?" Becky squeaks. "There are good men in the world, Dee. The rescuers of kittens are out there."

I laugh and wipe my eyes again.

"When are we seeing him again? I think we need to get that on the schedule."

"It's hard," I hedge. "We live on opposite coasts. He has a job with hours that are even crazier than mine." I peeked at the Bruisers schedule on the way to the airport. Silas wasn't exaggerating when he said his schedule was inflexible during the season.

"But you want to see him again," Becky presses.

"Of course I do."

"I can't believe he spent the night in your room!" she whispers. "His letter is just about the most romantic thing I ever read. But it didn't sound like you guys were, um, super close."

"Oh, I had it bad for him," I admit. "But I was in town for just a few weeks, so it would have been only a fling." Even as I say it, I wonder if that's really true. "And I was trying to juggle Brett and trying to get heard. It was not an easy time."

"There are no easy times," Becky says. "And this guy really likes you."

"Yeah." I sigh. "And he likes me for *me*. I don't have to wonder if he's just interested in my strange job."

"He has his own strange job!" Becky reminds me. She sounds gleeful. "Again, if he has any friends..."

"I know just where to send them," I promise.

———

There isn't time after our flight lands to make a stop at home before my meeting with the manager. And I don't even mind, because the hollow little furnished studio I'm renting doesn't hold much appeal for me.

Mr. Muscles drives me to an Art Deco building on Wilshire

Boulevard, where the offices of Charla Harris Talent Management reside. It's a pretty little building with a stern security checkpoint and thick carpets.

But Charla is not what I'm expecting. She's not L.A. glamorous. She's...

Okay she's terrifying. She's wearing a black power suit. Her salt-and-pepper hair is cut short in a way that makes her head surprisingly cube-like. She has pale skin, accentuated only with bright red lipstick.

And the first thing she says—even before hello and introducing herself—is: "Never show your contract to anyone who's not representing you." She waves a sheaf of papers in the air. "This right here is enough ammunition to make your life hell. Christ, your social security number is on here."

I'm speechless, hesitating beside the chair facing her desk. Did she just threaten me?

"Girl, I'm not actually going to use it against you! But stop being so trusting. Let's break that habit right now."

"Oh," I say, sounding quite stupid. "It's a lifelong habit, I guess. And I have the scars to show for it."

"I'll bet." She throws the papers onto the desk. "Sit already. You should know that this is the weirdest contract I've ever read. And I've been in the business twenty-five years. Way to pick 'em."

"Should I just go, then?" I ask, trying to keep the exhaustion out of my voice as I collapse into the chair. Only jet lag and a night of great sex prevent me from crawling over this woman's giant desk to choke her. "Is there a point, here? Or did you only need someone to patronize for a few minutes?"

For a second she just stares at me. And then her square face splits into her version of a smile, and she promptly cracks up. Her laugh is a lot like her personality—big and unpredictable. "We're not done yet, girl! I can help you, but first you need to acknowledge that you need help."

"Like it's not obvious? After I brought you the worst contract in twenty-five years."

"Indeed. This document is both arrogant and strange. It reads as if he spent, oh, fifteen minutes researching recording industry contracts before deciding he could do better than a lawyer and a hundred years of entertainment law."

"That sounds very much like Brett Ferris," I admit. "Mine also might be the first contact he ever wrote."

"He was a producer first, right? With Daddy's help?"

"Right. But I was the first artist on his brand-new label." It had seemed like a victory at the time. And maybe it was. I lacked confidence. I still do. "And then he sold out to Metro-Plex two years ago, because he needed more capital."

Charla's smile becomes more motherly and less terrifying. "Brett Ferris told you not to bother hiring a manager, right?"

"Yes," I say glumly. "I was twenty-three, and nobody else wanted to sign me, and I was afraid that if I got a manager, Brett would be scared off."

"And now all you wish for is to scare him off," Charla Harris guesses.

I nod.

"Oh, honey," she says. "You're in pretty deep here. And he's sitting on your second album?"

"Yeah."

"Whether it's Brett's decision or someone higher up at MetroPlex, that's a vindictive, shitty maneuver," she says.

"Tell me about it."

"I notice you didn't send me the royalty statement I asked for."

"That's because I knew better than to share information with a stranger who might use it to hurt me."

She gives me a big, evil grin. "Good girl. But I have a theory, and if we work together, your royalty statement might prove it." She pats my contract. "You have an escalator in here."

"A… what?"

"Your contract stipulates that he has to pay you a big bonus once you sell a million records. He probably never expected that to happen. If I had to guess, you're nearing the threshold. So he doesn't want to bounce you into the top one hundred right now with new music."

"Why?"

"Your first album will get a big boost when your second comes out. That always happens."

"Oh," I say slowly. When industry professionals talk business, I always feel incredibly stupid. "I should know all of this already."

"Nah," she says with a wave of her hand. "You should have a manager to keep track of it for you — to be your bulldog."

"I just want to write the songs and have my label release them on time," I whine.

"Yeah? Well I want a month in Fiji and pony riding lessons. If you sign with me, I will try to bully these assholes into releasing your record. But it will not be easy. I can't promise success. In the meantime, you're going to have to hold your head up high and get to work on album number three."

"Because…?"

"Once they see you're lining up a third album, they'll have to release the second one. There are some things we could do to make it look like you're making an end-run around them." She rubs her hands together, as if there's nothing more fun than manipulating Brett Ferris.

Against all odds, I'm starting to like her. "So, if the contract is weird, does that give me any way to break it?"

"Delilah, I will never ever lie to you. Breaking any contract is very hard. If we work together, I'll lean on him to release your album. And if he doesn't, I'll try to break this contract. But in my twenty-five years I have never gotten an artist out of a contract, no matter how bad. And even if we found legal grounds to sue him, it would take years."

I slump down in my chair. "My career will be dead by then."

"That's the risk. That's why suing him isn't your best option. You're going to have to force him to come around to doing things your way. Now, you know you can't release a single on another label, because your contract prevents that."

"I know," I grumble.

"*But.*" She grins. "My attorney agrees with me that you can *independently* release an entire album without violating this contract. He hasn't rejected your work, right? He's just sitting on it."

"Right." Although the word "rejected" makes my stomach hurt. "There is *nothing* wrong with that album."

"Good. So my best advice to you is—after signing with me, of course—go home and ask yourself, 'What does my third album sound like?' We'll find you some collaborators. You'll record a couple things with a new producer. You play the role of someone who's getting on with her life."

I try to picture this, and it sounds fun but also terrifying. "So I'm just supposed to pretend that my second album doesn't exist?"

"For now," Charla agrees. "Brett Ferris needs that second album, too. He doesn't work alone anymore. He has overlords, and they'll want the cash."

She's probably right, I realize. MetroPlex is one of the biggest record companies in the world. Brett still retains creative control over his artists, but he answers to Metroplex on financial matters.

"Maybe it isn't going well for him at MetroPlex," I say slowly. "That's why he'll do anything to get me to sign. He could fight even dirtier. He could reject my album."

"He won't," Charla says. "And that's where your weird-ass contract is going to help you for once. Because it says that if he rejects it, we can buy the album back for production costs. And even if those costs are as inflated as Brett Ferris's ego, the price tag is still peanuts compared to that album's worth."

My head is spinning. "I can buy it back?"

"Only if he rejects it. And you'd still owe him ten more songs. You're locked in this dance until he releases something. So go home and write your angriest music yet. And force his hand."

"Okay," I say, taking a slow breath. This madwoman has finally shown me a path forward. It's not easy, but I never thought it would be.

"Look, I know this isn't exactly what you wanted to hear. But Brett Ferris isn't stupid. He's arrogant, but he's not dumb. If you hire me and meet some new producers, that looks serious. That means action. He's going to notice. His little plan to bully you into a new contract isn't going to look so good anymore."

Every cell in my body hopes she's right.

"I can't make this easy for you. But I promise you this—if we work together, I will not *ever* back down. And you don't have to do this alone. It will become my job to get in that weasel's face. And I will do it with pleasure. In fact, I'll have to insist that you don't take his calls and you don't meet with him face to face."

"That's worth fifteen percent right there," I mumble. "Send me your contract."

"I will. But what are you going to do with it?" she asks.

"Read it. Is this a quiz?"

"Get an entertainment lawyer to read it, too," she says. "I need you to become less trusting. Don't trust anyone who isn't on your payroll. Don't trust strangers who offer you candy. Don't trust men who want to get in your pants. Or women, if you swing that way." She lets out another peal of that deep, weird laughter. I wonder if I'll ever get used to it.

"Got it," I say.

"Now, shoo!" She waves me off. "We'll talk soon. Chin up, Delilah. You're going to be okay."

I like hearing it. I only wish I believed her.

When I get back into the car with Mr. Muscles, I check my texts. There's one from Silas. A long one.

Hi girly. I was trying to play it cool so you won't regret giving me your phone number. Note that I waited at least one hour after your plane landed to send you a message.

I can't play it cool when it comes to you. Last night was special to me, and not just the naked parts. Although the naked parts do stand out in my memory. My whole day is like:

He includes a GIF that's an actual photo of him with flames flickering in front of his crotch, and I laugh out loud.

Kidding aside? You will always fascinate me. And I can't wait to spend more time with you. So please tell me how that can be accomplished.

Signed, your love slave, Silas Kelly/Ralph.

I lean back against the seat and mentally compose my response.

Dear Ralph, your message is pretty hard to top. And that's basically how I feel about you in general. You are smart and funny and kind, as well as...

I can't actually type that. He makes me feel unworthy. If we actually tried to have a long-distance relationship, I suspect that I'd ruin everything. And how would that even work?

The car moves slowly through traffic, and I feel overwhelmed. Last night was incredible. It was so great that I'm having trouble putting my mask back on. And I need that mask right now—it's going to protect me from the assholes in my life.

When I reread Silas's message, it's pretty hard to believe it's really about me. So I don't compose a gushing reply, even though he deserves one. I'm going to respond another way—a rock-star way. With a gift.

I send a message to Becky. *Could you get Silas's home address on the sly? I'll bet that nosy female publicist would give it to you. I want to send him a gift.*

On it! she replies immediately

"Change of destination!" I say to Mr. Muscles. "I have some shopping to do."

SILAS

"She didn't reply to your texts?" my roommate asks.

"She did. But barely," I puff as we jog past the carousel. It's a humid July afternoon, and even the seagulls on the promenade look hot. But we decided to punish ourselves with this outdoor run, anyway.

"And you think she's blowing you off?"

"Maybe."

"That sucks, man."

That's putting it lightly. I feel...tortured. Delilah warned me that her life was complicated. She was very clear about that. But I thought our night together should change everything.

It did for me.

"Here's what really bothers me," I tell Jason. "I met her three years ago. We spent some hours together. They were casual hours but we had a connection and I felt it deep."

"I know you did. Maybe she did, too."

"But here's where it gets confusing. She has this big career, right? And I got to listen to every note and follow along for three years." I can't explain out loud what that was like. Delilah poured raw emotion into my ears every night. "So, I'm still right there with her every step, but she's not with me."

Castro doesn't say anything, either out of respect for my stupidity, or because he's just winded.

"Back in California, I know she felt it, too. But now I wonder... Am I just another idiot superfan who thinks he knows what's happening in her mind? Am I like my grandma who used to talk back to Pat Sajak while she watched *Wheel of Fortune*?"

My roommate laughs and then slows down to a walk.

I stop running, too. "Maybe I'm holding on to an illusion."

"But maybe not," he says. "All you can do is remind her of the parts that are real. You two obviously need to be in the same room together again. Evidence suggests that works well for you." He snickers.

He isn't wrong. But I'm well aware that I can pull off that kind of big gesture maybe one more time before I give up. "Eventually, she's got to come to me."

"Give the girl a chance. What's it been, a week? You said her life is blowing up. She might not be ready for you. Timing is everything."

"That's not comforting. Timing has never been on our side."

"Ice cream shakes?" Castro asks, changing the subject.

"Hell yes."

"Here, or at home?"

"Home," I grunt, because I can't wait to get into the AC. It's funny how I yearn for the fresh air during the hockey season. And now that summer is here, the heat is killing me.

I'm grumpy, and I have been ever since I kissed Delilah goodbye at the hotel elevator last weekend. I need her in my life, and I don't even know if that's possible. Meanwhile, my summer break is flying by at a rapid rate.

"Then giddy-up," Castro says.

Like horses who can't wait to get back to the barn, we run a final fast mile back to Water Street, arriving sweat-covered and panting in front of our building.

"Lookin' good," teases Miguel, the doorman.

"We're not supposed to look good right now," Castro pants. "We're just supposed to hear the Rocky theme music inside our heads."

"Are we?" I grumble. "All I hear is my fat cells crying out in pain."

"You don't have any fat cells," Miguel says. "But you do have a package to take upstairs."

"A package? I don't remember ordering anything." He waves me inside, where there is indeed a large box addressed to me.

It's from "D. Spark," with a return address in L.A.

"Oooh! Somebody got a present. I can't wait to see what it is." Castro actually jumps up and down.

"Help me carry it upstairs, would you? I don't want to sweat all over it."

Together we carry the box into the elevator and then into our apartment. "Ice cream time!" Jason says as we set it down.

"You start, I'll be right there." First I have to locate some scissors and cut the tape sealing the box. When I finally get inside, I find... A turntable? And several records. Also a note.

Silas —

I know that I'm supposed to be a writer. But I don't think it's possible for me to write a letter as lovely as the one you gave Becky for me. That was basically the nicest note I've ever read.

But I just wanted you to know how wonderful it was to see you again. And now you can listen to music on vinyl if you want to. I didn't want to give you a gift that was all about me, though, so here are some of my favorite albums, too.

Still thinking of you,

D.

Oh. Well. I feel a little better now.

I've been trying not to be the kind of pest who won't stop texting when he's being ghosted. But now I find my phone and tap her number, hoping she'll answer.

She does. "Ralph," she whispers into my ear. "Did you get my present?"

"I did."

"That Clapton album is collectible. I hope I didn't screw it up by shipping it."

"I'm sure it's fine," I say hastily. "What a great gift. But you know I'm going to play your album first."

"You ass-kisser, Ralph."

"If you were here right now, I'd happily kiss your ass and every other part of your body."

"GET A ROOM!" yells Castro from the kitchen. "Also, your shake is ready."

Delilah laughs. "Better get your shake. Is it chocolate?"

"Probably. But Jason probably put some kind of healthy crap in there, too. His girlfriend is turning him into a nutritionist. None of the rest of us can stand it." I walk into the kitchen and take the pint glass that's waiting for me.

"You can clean the blender, you freeloader," Jason says.

Ignoring him, I take the shake back to my room and close the door. "How are you? Still stressed out about what's-his-name and the album?"

"I'll be stressed out until he releases it," she says. "But a few things are looking up. I have a new manager, and she's a tigress."

"That's good." I take a sip of my shake and wonder what to say. It's really none of my business. But I want Delilah to know that I'd do anything to help her. "Look…" I say slowly. I need to stay in my own lane. But my lane can be fun, too. "Do you ever take beach vacations?"

"Not often. Shit, I can't even remember the last time I took a real vacation. When I travel, it's always for a show."

"Well, I have to go to a wedding next week. It's on an island in the Caribbean."

"Fancy."

"I know. I promised not to give the date or location to anyone who wasn't accompanying me to the wedding."

Delilah laughs. "Who's the paranoid bride?"

"It's the groom. Do you know who Nate Kattenberger is?"

"The billionaire? Sure. He owns your hockey team."

"That's the guy. So you're a hockey fan now?"

"Shut up. So I did a little harmless Googling on my way home to L.A."

It's embarrassing how much pleasure it gives me to picture Delilah stalking me on the internet. "It's his wedding. Why don't you come with me? I get a plus-one."

"But..." She hesitates. "I'd feel weird crashing a wedding. And I'm not the easiest guest. My security guy goes everywhere I go."

"What if you could leave him behind?" I think it over for a second. "Let me make a couple of calls. If I can promise you four days on a private island with me, and if security was provided, will you do it?"

"Well..."

I hold my breath.

"A few days won't kill off my career, right? I would really like to try."

My relief is all-consuming. "Awesome. Stay tuned. I need to make some plans."

———

I spend the next several days on an expectant high, working out with my friends and looking forward to the trip. "Maybe I need a new bathing suit," I tell Jason as we trade off sets on the squat rack in the training facility.

"Fashion crisis?" he teases.

"We're going to a beach. I only have one suit in New York and it's all bleached out from hotel hot tubs. Where do I buy a bathing suit?"

Jason grunts as he sets the barbell back onto the rack. "Heidi. Duh." His girlfriend has a business where she does errands for hockey players for extra cash. He hasn't set foot in a store since last summer. "One more set?" he asks me. "Bonus round?"

"I'm done," I decide. I have some shopping to do.

After I get out of the shower, there are two texts on my phone. One is from Delilah, and it's a photo of palm trees. *This is my last view of the sky for the day*, she writes. *Recording studios have no windows.*

Neither do hockey rinks, I reply. *Every year I feel like a vampire by April.*

Vampires can be sexy, she replies. *Hello, Edward Cullen?*

And now I have a dilemma. Do I cop to knowing exactly who she means? *Can a real man admit that he once watched the Twilight movies on a plane? Asking for a friend.*

She replies with a Twilight gif where Edward is looking pretty sexy, if everyone is honest.

My other text message is from Heidi, whose full-time job these days is assisting the team's general manager. *Are you in the building? Carl Bayer is looking for you. He's set up in the security office.*

I'll be right up, I reply.

Whistling to myself, I jog through the sunlit tunnel connecting the practice facility to the Bruisers' office complex, then take the stairs two at a time.

Carl Bayer is the head of the security company who watches over Nate Kattenberger's empire, including the hockey team. He's also the father of my retired teammate, Eric Bayer.

Carl rarely shows his face in Brooklyn. He runs a big company, and his minions usually do all the legwork. But today I find Carl seated at a conference table, papers spread out in front of him.

"Hey, kid," he says as I enter. "How's life?"

"Not bad. You're working here today?" His office is somewhere in Manhattan, I think. This office is usually occupied by the security staff member who works full time for the team.

"Yeah. I have a meeting with Nate and Rebecca in an hour. And I'm just working on the guest list. Next week is showtime. So let's chat about your date."

My stomach flips over. "Is she coming?"

The older man tips his head from side to side, as if to acknowledge his uncertainty. "I hope so. But yesterday, her security company tried to convince me that she can't go anywhere without them. And we can't accommodate a security team on the island where you are staying."

"She won't need security on this island, right? It's tiny."

"Tiny, isolated, and guarded by my team as well as two dozen professional athletes." Carl grins. "But her security guys are pissed off that I won't provide the name of the hosts, the coordinates of the island, or the guest list. It's frankly obnoxious that they'd ask. Bayer Security isn't just a couple of rent-a-cops. We have a global reputation for protecting high-net-worth clients. The whole thing kinda rubs me the wrong way."

"I'll bet. But Delilah is an adult. She can go wherever she wants. She doesn't need their approval."

"Agreed. I can't imagine they'd convince her that this trip is dangerous. Honestly, her coming along is an inconvenience to me, not the other way around."

"Why?"

"Crazy fans." He shrugs. "There are people who would rent a boat and follow a popstar around the Caribbean. You do my job for forty years, you see some things."

"I, uh…" I hadn't thought this through. "Sorry to make things complicated."

"Don't be!" Carl chuckles. "Aside from being a little extra-vigilant when we bring her to the island, it's not a deal killer. I assumed her security guys would just get over themselves. But then I got a Skype call from her bodyguard. He called me from home, from his roommate's computer. And I didn't get the feeling that it was an official call."

"Wait, what? Was he a giant dude? No neck?"

"That's the one. No idea where he shops for shirts. Anyway, it was a strange conversation. He says, 'I'll bring her to the meetup, no problem. But they keep tabs on who she's with. They'll know afterwards. Maybe she should stay out of pictures.'" Carl shrugs. "I'm thinking—fine whatever. After the wedding is over, the whole thing will be public anyway. Photos will be draped across the internet."

"That guy didn't strike me as the sharpest tool in the shed," I point out.

"That was my first impression, too." Carl clicks the button on his pen a few times, thinking. "But reading people is my job, and it sounded as if he was trying to warn you. He mentioned that her security detail is provided by her record company."

"Right. She wants to change that, but she hasn't done it yet."

"Because she broke up with the producer guy? I Googled."

"Yeah."

Carl puts his meaty forearms on the desk. "I think the bodyguard is saying that if she vacations with you, the ex is going to blow his musket."

"So?" My blood pressure spikes. "Again—adults can do what they want. He's her ex for a reason."

"Agreed. But I'm a cynical old man who's met a lot of assholes. Wouldn't want this to blow back on her."

"He's a sore loser." I know this all too well. "But she's never going back to him. He needs to understand. And I don't see how denying her a trip to the beach is even a little bit fair."

"All right," Carl says simply. "I'll tell those assholes that I'll bring her across on the launch myself. They can just deal with it."

"Thank you," I say, getting up. "I appreciate it."

He chuckles. "Oh, to be young again. See you on the island, kid."

DELILAH

I'm seated with a dozen or so people on a boat that's cutting across turquoise waters, clutching my floppy hat against the breeze. It's so beautiful here.

I almost didn't come. And not because this trip is inconvenient. Charla Harris is working hard to line up songwriting dates for me, and I had to delay them for this trip. And getting here wasn't easy—a flight to San Juan, followed by another to Tortola. I put Mr. Muscles up at a hotel there for five days, because it was cheaper than flying him home.

Besides, who wouldn't want a free trip to Tortola? But my bodyguard seemed more anxious than happy. His security company didn't like this trip. At all. Not that I care.

But the biggest problem with this trip is me. I'm a nervous wreck. What if it's weird? What if Silas and I don't have as much to talk about as we thought? What if he'd rather party with his friends than spend time with me?

What if it's just not the same? I'm worried that I've built up our one night together in my head.

The woman next to me reaches over and covers my hand

with her own. And I realize that I've been drumming anxiously on the gunwale. "Sorry," I say quickly.

She laughs, and I turn to see that we're wearing almost identical big dark sunglasses and floppy hats. She also has thick, dark hair. We could be cousins. The biggest difference between us is the squirmy toddler on her lap, who is currently trying to pull her own sunhat off.

"I'm Zara," the woman says. "And I can't believe I just did that. It's a mom thing. If your drink was too close to the edge of the table, I'd also move that away from your hand. Hopefully I won't actually wipe your face with my napkin. It's a sickness."

"I'm a nervous tapper," I admit. "My assistant does the same thing, but she isn't as nice about it."

"Not a fan of the water?" she asks.

"No it's…" There's no explaining it to a stranger. "I'm Delilah, by the way."

"Oh!" Her eyes light up. "I thought you looked familiar, and now I remember why. You're Silas's date. He's the cutest. They're taking bets over whether you'll show up."

"Yes. Right." I am stammering. "Wait, why?"

"Just to tease him. He never brings a date anywhere." She smiles again. "They're always betting about something. You get used to it. There's also a betting pool over whether Dave and I will have a second child by the end of next season. Dave just retired, so I guess that's where their minds go." She rolls her eyes.

"Daddy coming now?" the little girl asks.

Zara replaces the hat on her bright red hair. "You'll see Daddy in five minutes, I swear. Now leave that hat on before I glue it to your head."

The little girl gives her an evil grin.

"We've lived apart," Zara says. "Long story. Nicole is fascinated with the idea that Daddy is going to live at our house."

She laughs. "But when you're two, normal is whatever you know."

"I think normal is generally pretty elusive. Right now, for instance." Flying to a private island to see Silas feels so crazy. And yet here I am.

"Too late now," Zara says cheerfully.

I look up to see an island on the horizon. On one end, the land rises to showcase a mansion with a multifaceted roofline and a sweeping terrace. Trees hide any other buildings on the property. There's a little harbor with a dock. "Wow."

"I know!" Zara says.

"Daddy!" the little girl screams, scrambling to climb up her mother for a better look.

"Easy, killer." Zara sighs, freeing a small, sandaled foot from her crotch. "The flight was basically just like this. Hey—I think the whole team is waiting for this boat."

Indeed, there's a crowd of handsome men standing around in swim trunks and sunglasses. I scan their faces, spotting Silas on the end. He's wearing a tight gray T-shirt and has his hands thrust into his pockets.

And, wow. *Hi, hormone rush*. If there's a more appealing man on the planet, I haven't ever seen one.

The moment the boat nudges the dock, the dark-skinned pilot hops out to secure it. That's when Zara's daughter gets free of her mother and scrambles, dodging other passengers as she breaks for the dock.

"Nicole!" Zara calls, her voice sharp. She stands up, but there are others in her way now.

The pilot steps back into the boat and catches Nicole neatly by the T-shirt before she can climb overboard. And a redheaded man, laughing, runs down the dock toward the boat. "I'll take that off your hands."

"DADDY!"

There's a wave of laughter from the people onshore.

"Mom fail," Zara says with a sigh. "I may not sit down the whole time we're here."

"That sight, though." The redheaded man has his little girl wrapped in a tight hug, and it's so sweet that watching them makes me feel like I'm intruding.

When it's my turn to step off the boat, Silas is waiting. "Hi," he says quietly, lifting the brim of my hat a few degrees so he can see me. Then he gives me a quick kiss on the jaw.

"Hi, yourself."

He smiles, and the corners of his eyes crinkle. I could stand here admiring him all day, but a gauntlet of his friends are waiting, and I am suddenly intimidated.

For someone who is required to meet and charm strangers all the time, I'm not very good at it. And Silas has a *lot* of friends. They're all tall and healthy-looking and staring at us.

"Guys," Silas says, taking my hand. "This is Delilah. Say hi."

I swear they shout it in unison, goofy smiles on their faces. "Hi, Delilah!"

"I'm Georgia," says a blonde woman about my age. She pushes her way past the players to shake my hand. "We spoke on the phone."

"Nice to finally meet you," I say, my voice squeaking.

"If you need anything while you're here, just holler," Georgia adds. "But I have a feeling Silas will take very good care of you." She turns around. "Guys, no photos of Delilah unless you ask her first. And no social media at all. Not until Monday. Then you can post family-friendly photos of the wedding."

"But I was going to sell wedding pictures to *People!*" a handsome guy argues.

"That one is my husband," Georgia explains with a shake of her head. "He's smarter than he looks. They all are, actually."

"Good to know," I say.

Silas clears his throat. I just want to stare at him, honestly. I can't because there are all these people here, but I feel his calming presence beside me. I swear, it isn't even the chance at more sex that brought me to crash a wedding on an island full of strangers. It was the chance to stand close to him again and experience the weird magnetic energy between us.

"You don't have to remember all these names," Silas says. "But this is Leo and Jason and Heidi and Ari and O'Doul."

I go down the line, shaking hands. He's right—there's no way I'm going to remember all these names.

"Ping-pong time!" O'Doul says, clapping his hands. "Let's do this."

"Awesome," Silas says. "We're just going to put Delilah's bag in the cabin. Go on and start."

"You guys want a doubles bracket?" O'Doul calls over his shoulder.

"Nah," Silas says. "We'll take over for someone else, maybe."

Jason—the handsome, olive-skinned roommate I just met—looks back at us and smirks. "Later," he says, and then his cute girlfriend swats him on the arm.

Silas ignores all of it. He scoops up my suitcase in one hand, putting his other hand on the small of my back.

"That has wheels," I say.

But superheroes don't use wheels, apparently. He leads me away from the group and into a grove of well-pruned fruit trees —oranges, maybe?—with occasional palm trees mixed in. I don't know anything about the tropics.

"Wow. This place is so beautiful."

"Isn't it? I'll give you the tour before dinner," he says. "Wait until you see the pool." Silas stops suddenly, putting the suitcase down and turning to me.

When I look up into his eyes, the intensity I see there steals my breath. "What?" I whisper.

"I wasn't sure you'd come."

"I almost didn't," I blurt. "I thought that..." He waits for me to finish, but my hesitation isn't easy to describe. "I thought I'd ruin it. That maybe we wouldn't be the same again." Like maybe I'd imagined how alive he makes me feel when we're in the same space.

"And?" he asks quietly.

And you're just as amazing as I remember. That sounds crazy, though. It's hard to put into words how strongly I feel the pull every time he shows up in my life. "I'm really glad I got on that boat."

He pulls me in until I'm folded against his solid chest. "Goddamn, I missed you," he says, removing my hat and kissing me on the forehead. "That was a really long two and a half weeks."

My heart swells. "You amaze me," I tell his T-shirt.

"Why? Because I'm smitten?"

"No." I laugh. "That you can say so. Like it's no big deal to say how you feel."

His big hand has a pleasant grip on my back. "But you do the same thing all the time, no? You put a lot of heart into every song."

"It's not the same at all." I take a step back so I can look up into those warm eyes of his. "The song isn't personal. It's for everyone. And if I do manage to say something personal, I disguise it very carefully. So nobody could ever guess why I ever really felt the things I'm singing about. I never have to look someone in the eye and lay myself bare."

"Ah." He gathers my hair in his hand. "I'm willing to make a very large fool of myself if it means I have a real chance with you."

Even though it's eighty-five degrees on this island, I feel goosebumps. "I want to be more like you, Ralph. But I don't know how."

"Sorry, can't tell you," he whispers, his lips grazing my hairline. "I've been me all my life. It comes easy."

That's when his eyes lock on mine, and I know he's finally going to kiss me. Suddenly, I feel incredibly self-conscious. I'm standing here in beach clothes that I obsessed over and lipstick that I touched up on the boat, for a guy I barely know but desperately want.

"Shh," he whispers, as if he can hear the clanking of the gears in my head and the thumping of my heart. Then he takes my face in his hand and draws me in.

His lips are warm as he takes my mouth. His kiss is slow, like he knows I still need a minute to accept that this is real.

The first kiss calms me down. I feel my mind go quiet as he tilts my head and deepens our contact. His eyes close as my lips part for him. He tastes me slowly and then not so slowly. My arms grip him, pulling him closer. His hand tugs on my hair, and I lift my chin, exposing my neck.

Silas crushes me to his chest and kisses me ten different places in quick succession. "Jesus," he whispers against my skin, and I shiver.

He steps back with a grunt and lifts my suitcase again. "Right. Where were we?" He takes my hand in his. "The cottage is just through here. They all look alike, so if you get confused, remember that ours is Number 11."

Ours. I like the sound of that. I'm a silly girl who can't wait to play house on an island for a few days.

There's a tidy paved path between the little structures, and Silas opens the door to Number 11 with just a twist of the knob. "We haven't been locking up. Everyone on the island is either a hockey player or a rich tech executive, so..." He shrugs. "There's a safe in each bedroom. For valuables. You could put your wallet in there."

"Got it," I say as he leads me into a comfortable living room with rattan furniture and throw pillows. There's a kitchen area along one wall and a basket of muffins on the countertop.

We pass through into a short hallway with three bedroom

doors. "They gave me the smallest bedroom," Silas says, walking in and placing my bag down in a corner. "I never show up with a date, so it's a habit."

It is a small room. Small enough that I can reach out and place a hand on his chest. "Never?"

"Nope," he whispers. "Didn't have the right girl. So what's the point?" He covers my hand with his.

And—like gears in a clock—we each turn a few degrees, fitting ourselves together. His chin tilts down, mine tilts up, and our kiss is inevitable. There's nothing tentative about it. One kiss turns into a quick dozen. Then he lifts my top off and sheds his T-shirt.

No words are exchanged at all as he nudges me onto the bed. When I turn to crawl farther onto the mattress, he catches me by the hips and relieves me of my skirt and my bikini bottom in one smooth pull.

I spread my body out on the bed, face down, inhaling the scent of clean linen as his kisses make a path up my back. I hear a zipper as he frees himself from his other clothes. His skin slides against mine a moment later, his erection a hot brand against my ass as he draws my body against his. He's all hands and hot kisses and fervor. We are twisting, aching bodies on a bed, reigniting the flame that sparks so effortlessly between us.

Chemistry is something I'd forgotten about entirely until Silas showed up in my hotel room to reacquaint me with the concept. I roll over and cling to him shamelessly as he kisses me and teases me into a desperate fever.

He moves down my body, his mouth burning me up inside. This time I'm prepared. I've buffed and shaved and smoothed every naked inch.

Or at least I thought I was ready. I grow self-conscious as he parts my knees with those magic hands. I look up at the white ceiling and wonder if I can do this—spread myself so bare for a man.

But then Silas rests his cheek on one of my thighs and kisses the other one. His hand strokes my leg, and he lets out a happy sigh, as if arriving home at the end of a long day. The sensitive skin of my inner leg gets another kiss. And another. Now I can feel his warm breath on my pussy, and my nipples get impossibly hard.

I catch myself arching toward him. Because even if this scares me, I still crave him. I couldn't fall asleep last night, I was so full of expectation, so desperate to have him inside me again. My usual solution—getting out of bed to fetch my guitar—wasn't an option. Any song I wrote would have been filthy dirty.

As he slowly turns his head to kiss my achy body, all my hesitation flees. And, as his tongue makes the first, slow lick, I sink further into the mattress, bearing down, letting go. *Just take me*, I want to say. *Don't ever stop.*

He makes a hungry sound, which only makes me crazier. And I lose myself in kisses and licks, until I'm panting and begging him to fuck me. By the time he flips me onto my stomach again, kicks the bedroom door shut, and tugs my hips up to meet his, I'm desperate. He fills me with one primitive thrust that makes both of us groan.

"Silas," I gasp, realizing something. "Condom."

He goes absolutely still, his big hands easing their grip on my hips. "I didn't forget. You want to see?"

"Oh," I say as my pulse pounds in my ears. "No, it's okay."

But he's already gone. Cool air hits my back. "Sweetheart." He lies down beside me. "That's not something I would mess up. I won't hurt you like that."

"Okay. Sorry." I move closer to him. But I've broken the mood now.

He pulls me onto his body and studies me. "You'll trust me eventually. I'll make sure of it."

"It's not you," I whisper.

"Oh, I know it." He runs a finger down my nose. "It's okay to slow down, anyway. I walked you into this cottage and went right into Beast Mode. How was your trip?"

"Fine." I run a hand down his sculpted chest and take a good look at his beautiful body. And, yup, there's a condom looking back at me. "I kind of liked Beast Mode," I admit. "And we're home all alone."

He smiles. "So you wouldn't rather go outside and play ping pong?"

"I suck at ping pong. You?"

"Champion of the team league. I fucking love ping pong." He rolls on top of me and kisses my neck. "But not today."

"No?" I gasp as he takes my nipple against his tongue.

"Nope." He hooks a hand under my knee. Then he lifts his chin and gazes right into my eyes as he slides his way home again. "I'm right where I need to be."

———

We spend the whole afternoon in bed. Eventually we're so spent that lying under the sheet watching the ceiling fan turn is all we have left.

"How's the new manager?" he asks, his fingers combing through my hair.

"Nice. No—that's the wrong word for her. She's fierce. She has ideas for how I can move forward without Brett's cooperation."

"Yeah? Tell me all the news."

My head rolls lazily to the side, resting on his magnificent chest. "My contract isn't easy to break, but there are some odd loopholes. Get this—I can't make another solo album until he publishes the one he's sitting on. But I could, for example, make a new album that's credited to a *band*."

"You mean the new album could come from—" His deep

voice vibrates beneath my ear. "—Delilah and the Sparkle Puppies?"

I lift my head. "Did you say *sparkle puppies*? What the fuck is that?"

"Puppies are a crowd-pleaser, Delilah. Everyone likes puppies."

"You're mocking my demographic," I tease.

"Puppies are universally appealing," he insists. "Wait. Are you a puppy hater? Have I bedded a monster?"

We both crack up. I feel so loose right now. I love the way he teases me. We're discussing all the most stressful things in my life, and he's got me *laughing* about it.

"I know." He snaps his fingers. "You should call the new band Free Beer. Everyone loves free beer."

I let out an unladylike snort. "You're off the marketing team."

"What? I'm a marketing genius. Obvs."

"Obvs," I repeat happily. My troubles seem smaller when I'm lying next to him. "I'll run them both past my terrifying manager."

"Does she really want you to start a band?"

"Only if she can't find another way to force Brett to do the right thing. That's our nuclear option. The thought of walking away from my finished album makes me sick. I honestly spend several hours of each day trying to think up an alternative solution. Those songs represent more than two years of my work, and I can't imagine a future where they're not out in the world."

I need Brett to release that album. I need him to blink first. Some days it's all I think about.

"Is there no way to release *those* songs as a band?" he asks. "Like, rerecord them?"

I shake my head. "He already accepted them as fulfillment of the second and last album on my current contract. I can't retract them without handing over another ten songs."

"But doesn't he need this release, too? Isn't he sitting on millions of dollars right now?"

"Yes. That's what's so maddening. But apparently I care more than he does, and he's willing to take some pain to cause me even more pain. Which shouldn't surprise me." I roll over and look him in the eye. "I should have listened to you when you warned me about him. I should have asked you to tell me the whole story."

Silas closes his eyes. "Shit," he says. "I think you did ask. And I refused."

"Why?"

"Because it doesn't reflect well on me, either." He turns to prop his head on one hand. "Brett wasn't the only cheater. And I didn't want you to know."

SILAS

Delilah blinks back at me. "What happened?"

"Well..." I haven't told this story in a long time. Or even thought about it, really. It brings me too much pain. "Back in high school, hockey wasn't my only sport. I also played—"

"Tennis," Delilah says. "You told me that Brett didn't like to lose."

"Does he still play?" I hear myself ask. Because I never touched a racquet again. Not after what happened.

"Sometimes. But there are trophies in his parents' beach house. I mean—that house is impeccably tasteful. It's all wood and beiges and blues. But right there on the sideboard are like a dozen gold, gaudy tennis trophies. I always thought of it as the Shrine to Brett."

"All trophies are ugly, but it doesn't matter. You still want them. Never get between a man and his trophies."

"Now, Ralph." She squeezes my arm. "Do you have an apartment full of hockey trophies?"

"Nope. They're in a box somewhere in my mother's garage. But if my team ever gets a Stanley Cup, you can bet your cute little butt that I will have my photo taken in every possible combination with that thing. I will treasure it as non-ironically as I'll treasure my vinyl edition of Delilah and the Sparkle Puppies' first album."

She snorts. "Fine. I've been warned."

My smile dies, though, as I realize she's still waiting for me to tell her about my life's greatest disaster. "Brett won trophies because he was good. It didn't hurt that he had the best coaches and the most expensive equipment I'd ever seen. But before I showed up at the school, nobody could beat him."

"And then you did?"

"Sometimes. Freshman year I was still learning fast. But sophomore year I began to dominate. Especially once I learned about the Darlington Beach scholarship. It was sponsored by the country club—there was one winner each year. It went to whichever Darlington student was the highest ranked tennis player. Male or female."

"Fancy."

"Yeah. Usually that prize went to a senior. But as juniors, Brett and I were already setting records in our division. Our school was cleaning up all the meets. My mom and I moved to Darlington Beach to make me eligible for the scholarship. You had to be a resident. If I won, it would be like getting a blank check. I could use the money at any private college that would have me."

Delilah's hand skims my arm. "And Brett wanted it, too?"

"Yup." I shake my head. "Richest kid in town, but he hated the idea of losing to me. And tennis is weird. There are no team-mates in tennis. It's a pretty brutal setup, where every man is ultimately out for himself."

"Sounds perfect for Brett. That man is not a team player."

She's right. I prefer hockey for exactly this reason. Tennis is the loneliest sport in the world. You're not even allowed to speak to your coach during a game.

"So he started to cheat," I tell her. "Do you know anything about tennis?"

"No." She shakes her head. "Not a lot of tennis happens in foster care."

"I took up tennis just so I could see how the other half lived," I admit. "And because Darlington Beach was crazier about tennis than about hockey."

"How does a California boy take up hockey, anyway?"

"That's a different story. Hockey is all about the refereeing, right? If they don't call it, it didn't happen."

"Okay."

"In tennis—unless you're on the pro circuit—there's like one official for every eight games in progress. When a ball lands on the line, the player has to call it in or out."

Her eyebrows draw up into arches. "And nobody argues the calls?"

"Not usually. So Brett started cheating during his games."

"Against you?"

"Me and anyone else who'd threatened his standing. Eventually he was sort of famous for calling his opponent's balls out when they were on the line and should have been good."

"And nobody noticed?"

I shrug. "People noticed. But he was careful not to do it in front of the officials or his opponent's coach. Once I watched a parent get up in his face, and he just lied his ass off."

I remember these days like they were yesterday—the heat of the clay courts and the sound of the balls thwacking off racquets all around me. I'm competitive, too. I lived for that shit.

"So that's how he got an edge on you?"

"Yes and no. We had to play each other in a tournament at the end of the season. I felt *intense* pressure to win. The recruiters were circling. My SAT scores had come back better than my counselor had expected. 'You could do this,' he said.

'You could win the Darlington Beach Club scholarship. Or maybe even a tennis scholarship to Stanford.'"

At that point I probably didn't even need the damned town scholarship. But that doesn't mean I'd give up.

And there's a reason I never talk about this. A tightness grips my chest as I remember how this felt. Teenage me would have done anything to avoid failure. It took me years to get past this stupid incident. And there are days when I still feel the lingering damage to my psyche.

"So…" I can almost smell my own nervous sweat as Brett and I waited on the sidelines for the officials to tell us we could start that last game. It was the stupidest week of my life. And I really don't want to tell Delilah all the ways I failed myself. "We both cheated. I sank right to his level."

"And?"

I can't do it. I'm not going to tell her the whole story. "He cheated better," is all I say.

"He won the scholarship?"

"He did." *And so much more.* Only one of us walked away with our pride intact, and it wasn't me. "At least I had senior year to switch gears. I ended up taking a gap year and playing juniors hockey while applying to colleges. And that went well, so a hockey scholarship paid for everything." I didn't get to go to a private school like I'd planned, though. I had to settle.

Some days I blame Brett. Most days I blame myself.

"He took a bite out of both of us," she whispers. "But no more."

"No more," I agree. I want to be done with this conversation and with him. "Should we get up and shower?"

"Soon." She puts her head on my shoulder.

I smile at the ceiling. "Okay. Soon."

The ceiling fan makes another lazy rotation, and I try to relax. But now I'm all keyed up inside. The specter of Brett Ferris has me thinking about my failures.

I cheated on the tennis court. My teenage brain had been sure I was only reclaiming what Brett had stolen from me. You need luck to win by cheating, though. Not every game offers up a ripe moment for an ethical lapse.

That match had done the trick for me, and I'd won the day. The season had been drawing to a close, with me in the lead. The following weekend would have sealed to deal — I would have been the first Darlington student to ever take home the scholarship in his junior year.

But before the weekend, Brett had left a note on my beat-up car. *Meet me behind the Quickie Mart at six. There's something I need to ask you. I think we can both get what we want.*

Teenage me hadn't been very cunning. I'd hated cheating, and I wasn't eager to do it again, but I was intrigued. So I met him like a goddamn fool. He'd been standing there beside his BMW, waiting for me.

"What's up?" I'd asked, wondering if he'd suggest that we take turns. One of us wins this year, one of us wins next year. I wouldn't have been able to trust him to stick to a plan, though.

"Here's the thing," he'd said, picking his fingernail. "The scholarship has more than one factor."

"You need a B grade-point average," I'd said. I'd read the scholarship rules many times.

"And a good standing in the community." He'd looked up at me. "Which you don't have."

"What do you mean?"

He'd folded his arms. "I wonder what the board chairman will think when he finds out your dad is in prison for a violent felony?"

My head had snapped back as if I'd been punched. My mother had gone to great lengths to make sure that nobody knew that. "Who's going to tell them?"

"I am," he'd said. "Unless you get injured tomorrow at practice and don't play on Saturday."

He made air quotes when he'd said the word "injured."

There are so many things I might have done in that moment. I might have laughed. I might have lifted my chin and told him where he could shove his obnoxious threat. I might have turned around and walked away without another word.

Any of those solutions would have been better than balling my hand into a fist, wrapping my thumb, and punching him right in the face. He went down in a soul-chilling tumble of limbs onto the dusty asphalt.

"You're so fucked now," he'd said as the blood began to run out of his nose.

That's when I'd finally turned and walked away. And the security camera he'd scoped out ahead of time showed my departure—centered, in crisp detail. The video is the first thing they showed me when I was arrested a day later.

Sometimes I can still picture the grainy image of me coolly walking away from my bleeding competitor. He just lays there on the ground for a while after I go.

The only blessing was that my mother hired a good lawyer immediately. We didn't have the money, but she did it anyway, putting down her tax refund and borrowing the rest.

Since I wasn't eighteen yet, my lawyer got the charge knocked down and made sure that the conviction would be expunged a few months after my birthday.

My stupidity had no lasting effects on my prospects. But it got me kicked off the tennis team. With a broken nose, Brett Ferris won the championship the following weekend. He went on to receive the Darlington Beach Club tennis scholarship and a spot at Stanford.

I lost my scholarship to the prep school and had to attend a public high school instead for senior year. So my tennis career was over. Without the prep school to back me, I couldn't train.

We moved out of Darlington Beach, too, because we couldn't afford it. Rents were higher. And my mother got tired of hearing women whisper about us in the grocery store. *Did you know the kid's father is in prison? Aggravated assault. Just like his dad.*

Hockey became my outlet, and I didn't look back. Never played tennis again. I liked being part of a team. And let's face it —if my hockey team had found out about my violent offense, it wouldn't have made headlines. I'm a nonviolent guy who was convicted of violence. Who now plays a violent sport.

Not in a fighting role, though. The goalie is a puck eater, but he rarely throws a punch. If you ask my teammates, they'll say I don't even have a temper.

I hit Brett, though. I (briefly) had a criminal record, which was hideously embarrassing to me and heartbreaking for my mom.

"You're *lucky* he won that final tennis championship!" my mom had sobbed the night before my court date.

She was right. It meant Brett couldn't tell the judge I'd given him a head injury or a permanent disability. Nine years later I'm still upset, though. I let Brett Ferris outplay me.

Never again.

DELILAH

It's dusk by the time Silas and I finally venture outside. We're both starving.

"Dinner is at seven," he says. "But there will be snacks and drinks on the beach. I feel like an ass for starving you all day."

"Oh, I think it was worth it."

He gives me a hot smile.

Hand in hand, we walk along a path that winds past a cove where kayaks are waiting on the shore. The water is an impossible shade of turquoise blue. "This place is mind-blowing. I think I need to get out more."

"It is. And I'm all for you taking more beach vacations with me."

I squeeze his hand and feel as though I'm walking through a dream. A really good one.

The path leads us toward a beach where a couple dozen people gather. I'd rather have Silas all to myself, but that's not what I signed up for. So I put on my People Face and let him lead me into the fray.

"Look who it is!" his roommate calls from the water's edge.

He's holding a soccer ball. "Decided to show your face? You missed ping pong entirely. Afraid of the competition?"

"I thought someone else should be allowed to win sometimes," Silas says easily.

"Get over here," Jason says. "You need a beatdown for saying that."

"Patience. You'll get your beatdown." He grins at his roommate.

"Go head and play," I urge. I don't want to be the kind of date who needs babysitting.

"We need a drink and some of those appetizers, first." He scans the beach, taking in a little tiki hut where a bartender waits. But someone else is flagging us down.

"Over here!" A short, smiling woman waves at us. "I have munchies. Introduce me to your date!"

With a grin, Silas leads me toward her. "Rebecca, this is Delilah. Delilah, this is the bride."

"Oh, hello!" I sit down on the empty beach chair beside her and shake her hand. I don't know why I'm surprised at her appearance. She's completely adorable. But I thought billionaires married supermodels. I was picturing someone six feet tall with a European accent and hair that rarely leaves the salon. "Thank you so much for letting me crash your big day. This place is exquisite."

"It's my pleasure. The groom is—" She points at another man in swim trunks. He's in a circle of men kicking the soccer ball around. "That guy. I'll introduce you after their tournament ends. It's an elimination game, and Nate usually doesn't make it to the final four."

"Who usually wins?" I ask.

"I do," Silas says. "Duh."

"Look at the ego on this guy," Rebecca teases.

"It's not bragging if it's true," Silas argues, sitting down right beside me on the chair. He lifts a tray from the little table beside

Rebecca's chair. It's piled with skewers of shrimp and crab cakes. "Delilah, I ate about twenty of these last night, and they are worth it."

"Have some!" Rebecca encourages me. "I put the snacks next to me so that everyone would have to stop by. We also have this." She hefts a pitcher of what looks like frozen margaritas and grabs an empty glass off an inverted stack. She pours the drink, and it looks delicious.

And now we arrive at the awkward part. "Oh, Silas can have that," I say as she offers me the glass. "I'm not ready."

Honestly, I wish I could just take the drink like a normal person. Nobody on this beach is trying to drug me. But some habits are so deeply ingrained you can't even imagine breaking them.

Silas takes the glass and then stands up. A warm hand lands on my head. "Back in one sec."

"So," I say to Rebecca. "How did you end up working in professional sports? Did you always love hockey?" I help myself to a shrimp skewer, because I really am starving.

"Hockey is the best," she says. "But I didn't see my first pro game until Nate bought the team a few years ago. Now it's my life. The same could happen to you if you're not careful." Her eyes sparkle. "But I heard you went to your first game only a couple of months ago."

"True story." My eyes cut to Silas, who's speaking to the bartender. I'm realizing now that Silas underplayed his relationship with the bride and groom. Rebecca isn't just an acquaintance. She's his friend. "The first time I met Silas, I didn't know he was a hockey player. He was just the guy behind the bar who brought me my beers."

"Really?" she squeaks, wide-eyed. "That is adorable!"

"Yes, ma'am. And I had a thing for him right away. Even though I thought his name was Ralph."

"Ralph," she repeats at a whisper.

"Yeah, it's a nickname they gave him in high school." I shrug, but it occurs to me that I've made a tactical error.

"Ralph...as in vomit?" she gasps.

"Um..."

Rebecca puts two fingers between her lips and whistles toward the soccer circle. "Georgia! Come here."

"What did I miss?" The publicist comes bounding over.

"Did you know that Silas's high school nickname was *Ralph?*"

"As in..." Georgia makes a face. Then she bursts out laughing.

Uh-oh.

Silas returns a moment later holding an unopened can of Coke in his hand. Rebecca and Georgia are still laughing. "What did I miss?"

"Not a lot, *Ralph*," Georgia says.

"Really?" He frowns down at me, then checks his watch. "I step away for ninety seconds, and you manage to give that up? Three years of discretion, gone in an instant."

"I'm sorry! It was an accident."

He gives me a wry smile. "You're lucky I like you."

"You are a perfect man." I pop open the can of Coke. "And I will endeavor to keep all your other dirty secrets private."

"Which dirty secrets?" Rebecca asks, laughing.

"Yo! Silas! Get your booty over here!" Castro yells from the sand.

I put a hand on his hip and nudge him toward the game. "Go on. I swear I'll behave. I won't tell them about the time you cut your thumb—"

This bit of silliness is cut off by Silas's mouth, which is suddenly on mine. I receive a *blazing* kiss. It's a very effective form of censorship. With his hot mouth on mine, I can't actually remember what I was saying.

"Dude, leave the poor girl alone for ten minutes!" Leo yells from somewhere nearby.

Silas breaks our kiss, and for a split second we're staring into each other's eyes again, wondering where the nearest bedroom is. But then I blink. "Go on. Show me how you're a legend at sportsball."

"Try not to do too much damage to my rep, okay?" He grins, pivots like a ninja, and jogs off toward the guys.

"You can play too, you know," Georgia says. "I made it through five eliminations today."

"My personal best is three." Rebecca sighs. "My coordination is legendary. And not in a good way."

"Unless we're doing manicures," Georgia argues. "I'm the one who's not allowed to apply polish anymore."

"That's just because you don't care enough to do a good job." Rebecca turns to me. "I have to put Netflix on in front of her so she won't get up and walk away in the middle of a manicure."

"Well, I'm *very* busy!" Georgia argues.

"How's that manicure holding up?" Rebecca asks, grabbing her friend's hand for an inspection.

"Fine." Georgia tugs her hand away like a naughty child.

I eat another skewer and wonder if I can just stay here on this beach permanently.

"The chef is flagging me down," Rebecca says.

"Want me to handle it?" her friend offers.

"Nope. You stay here and nibble. I'll make sure that dinner is almost ready." She gets up.

"The hardship!" Georgia says, taking her spot. "More margarita?" Georgia says to me. "Oh—you're drinking soda. Never mind."

"Thanks, though."

"Hey, I didn't make them. So Silas was a bartender? I feel

like we should be exploiting that more often. What's his specialty?"

"Mojitos," I say, even though it's the only drink we've made together.

"Yum."

"But let's talk about *your* job and the obvious fringe benefits," I say, as another hockey player dives for the ball. He sort of flops onto the sand, somehow casting the ball into a neat arc with his foot. All the other players cheer.

"I do have a *gorgeous* workplace," Georgia says with a happy sigh. "The office itself is okay too."

"I can see how it might keep your spirits up."

"Oh, they're up." She gives me a smile. "Do you work with a lot of hipsters in music?"

"Well, sometimes. My job definitely has its star-studded moments. But mostly I write music at home in yoga pants and bunny slippers. If I had coworkers, maybe I'd be more skilled at human interaction."

She laughs. "You have Becky, though. Your publicist."

"I couldn't manage without her. Lately she's doing the work of three people. But poor Becky doesn't know how she's missing out." I watch the athletes clowning against a tropical sunset. "All Becky sees is my grumpy ass, day in and day out."

"Well, you've had some chaos lately. A recent breakup. That must be heartbreaking."

"Uh… Heartbreaking isn't the right word."

"I guess that's good, right?"

"Sure. Although if I were truly heartbroken, I'd be less embarrassed. I should have walked away a long time ago." Brett never loved me. He probably isn't even capable of love.

"I'm sorry."

"Don't be. For a long time I confused his attention with love. He made my life easier, so I let him. I wanted a minder, and he wanted the job."

"I can see how that could happen."

I steal a glance at her. "Can you? It's okay if you're just saying so to be polite. Because I didn't follow any of my own hunches. But in my defense, I always thought you had to be a meek person to end up in a controlling relationship. I didn't know it could happen to cynical people like me."

It happened, though. I grew up with nobody. Before Brett, nobody in my life had ever tried to take care of me. When he did, it seemed like a miracle. Even if I knew in my gut it wasn't love, it still scratched an itch that I'd had all my life.

"I've never been with a controlling man," Georgia admits. "But I have been young and stupid."

"Yeah. I guess it just stuck to me a little longer. This isn't even the first time I broke up with Brett. But it sure will be the last. Every time I walked out on him, it was because I suspected him of cheating. But it was always just a feeling I had. I never could prove it. There would be a weird lipstick stain, or a night out of town that wasn't easily explained." Or a voice in the background of a phone call. I'd ignored a lot.

"Oh, ouch."

"Finally he was busted in the tabloids, and I didn't have to give him the benefit of the doubt anymore." I didn't have to try to make Brett Ferris love me anymore. It was like quitting a bad job. I was more relieved than sad.

"Oh, geez," Georgia says. "I'm sorry."

Someone plays a flourish on a set of steel drums.

"The dinner bell! Let's eat." Georgia leaps off her chair. "Sorry for my excitement, I have a really fast metabolism."

She's not the only one. Silas is already jogging toward me with a smile on his face. "Ready to eat?"

"Of course."

On our way toward the dinner tent, we join hands, and somehow it feels completely natural to me. Silas doesn't let go until we reach the buffet, where he hands me a plate. "Would you look at this? I'm going to weigh five extra pounds an hour from now."

"Me too." I've never seen so much food in one place. I take a portion of Caesar salad and a dinner roll. But let's face it—I'm really here for the grilled fish tacos, the jerk chicken, savory rice, and crispy plantains. There's a tropical-fruit salad, too.

We sit down at a table with Jason, Heidi, Leo, Georgia, and the head coach for the Brooklyn Bruisers—who I quickly learn is Georgia's father.

"Every day is take-your-daughter-to-work day," he says when I figure out their connection.

"Bullshit!" Georgia makes a face. "I had the job first. You're the interloper."

"Becca actually put a plaque on the wall of her office," Leo volunteers. "It says, *I was here first.*"

"Damn straight."

Silas pats my knee under the table and laughs at his friend's joke. His friends all radiate health and self-confidence. It would be disgusting if they weren't so nice.

I pick up my fork and dig in.

SILAS

The satisfaction I feel sitting beside Delilah at dinner cannot be underestimated. Not only am I happy to finally feed the poor girl, but I've been craving this for three years—a few easy moments in her company.

I have nice friends, so that part is easy, too. For me, anyway. I get the feeling that Delilah is less confident than she lets on. Back in California, she always seemed unshakable to me. Cocky, even.

But none of us really are, right? Delilah's confidence has its limits, just like mine.

"What does the rest of your summer look like?" Heidi asks her. "Isn't this the season of big, outdoor venues?"

"Usually," Delilah says slowly. "But my new album hasn't come out, so there's no tour yet." She shakes her head. "I have one big concert in California, at the music festival where I met Ralph the first time."

"Ralph!" Georgia giggles.

"I thought we talked about this," I say, poking Delilah's arm.

"That one was an accident. I swear." She picks up a cornbread mini-muffin and pops it in her mouth.

"Ralph ought to fly out for that concert for old time's sake," Heidi says. "And he should probably take his roommates, just to be nice."

"I could probably scrape up a few tickets in the first couple of rows," Delilah says.

Heidi squeals.

"Maybe Silas can finally give you that surfing lesson," Jason says. "And me too, right? I want to surf." He tugs on his girlfriend's ponytail. "Let me guess. You already surf."

"Just a little," Heidi says.

"What does *just a little* mean to you?" I ask Heidi. She is one of those people who is mysteriously good at everything.

"I only won one competition." She waves a hand like it's nothing.

Jason just shakes his head.

"Oh!" Georgia stands up suddenly. "I have to say my thing before people get up and wander off." She picks up a water glass and a spoon, pulls back her chair, and climbs onto it. Leo braces the chair with one hand and eats another chicken wing with the other.

Georgia clinks the spoon on the glass, loudly, and heads swivel in our direction. "Good evening, friends!" she begins. "I want you all to know that last year Rebecca planned *my* wedding. She did everything from choosing the dresses I tried on, down to the bunches of..." She makes a motion with her hands. "What are those tight little bouquets called...?"

"Nosegays!" Rebecca calls from two tables away.

"Right! Because that's something every girl should know." Everyone laughs. "We all have our skill sets. Anyway—I want you all to know that I offered to plan Rebecca's wedding. Fair is fair, right? But she would only give me one job, and that's tonight. I planned the after-dinner entertainment! When you've finished your meal, please make your way to the great lawn for carnival games."

A cheer goes up.

"No way!" I holler, because that sounds awesome.

"Yeah, if you'd left your bedroom at all today," my room-mate says, "you might have seen them setting up."

Georgia holds up a hand, asking for continued silence. "You might notice that no dessert or coffee have been served. They're at the carnival, too. But you have to win a ticket — or a ticket for your sweetheart — to claim something at the dessert stand. Since I'm surrounded by two hundred of the most competitive people on Earth, I'm thinking that's going to be fun to watch. Good luck, everyone. I'll see you over at my favorite game of all. It's called Dunk the Hockey Player."

"Uh-oh," Leo says as she climbs down. "Please tell me you didn't really get a dunking tank."

"Oh, I absolutely did. You're wearing swim trunks, anyway."

Leo sighs. "Did you take any practice shots during setup?"

"What do you think?" Georgia asks.

He gets up without her.

"Where are you going?" Georgia calls as Leo turns away.

"To get towels. Duh. See you over there."

———

"Georgia is clearly a genius," I tell Delilah as we stroll down the impromptu midway. There's a ring toss, Skee-Ball, and a booth with pop guns capable of firing corks at a stack of soda cans. It's all set up on the vast lawn in front of the mansion house.

The air smells like warm wind and sea salt. And nearly everyone I care about in the world is standing around me, their faces lit by candle torches and tiny string lights.

Delilah's hand is in mine, and it feels like it belongs there.

We stop in front of a basketball shooting game, where O'Doul and my retired teammate Bayer are already talking smack. Apparently ice cream isn't high enough stakes for these two.

"Ten bucks a ball," Bayer says.

"Twenty," O'Doul counters.

His girlfriend Ariana just crosses her arms. "Would somebody just sink one so I can have ice cream?"

"You're sporty," I remind her. She's our yoga instructor. "Not a basketball fan?"

She shakes her head. "I bend things and balance things. I don't throw things."

"We gotcha covered." Bayer, without turning around, throws the basketball backwards over his shoulder, sinking it on the first try.

Ding! the machine chimes, spitting out a ticket with an ice cream cone printed on it.

"Works for me," Ari says, tearing the ticket out of the machine.

"I am so fucked, aren't I?" O'Doul asks.

"This is going to be fun," Bayer says with a chuckle.

Ari shrugs. "Sink one for Delilah before you start the Great Basketball Battle of the Century."

"I want to win my own," Delilah says. "But not at basketball." She glances around. "Actually, this might take a while."

Ariana laughs. "I'll be eating ice cream and staying out of trouble."

We stroll on, hand in hand. "What should we play first?" I ask her. "The ring toss looks hard. Those rifles might be fun. Or pick something where I don't have to let go of your hand." I lift her palm to my mouth and kiss it.

Her eyes go a little soft. "I'm not great at throwing things, either. But that looks like fun." She leads me toward the bouncy obstacle course. "We could have a bet, too. Loser pays the winner ten bucks for every second he comes in behind."

"That could add up," I say with a shake of my head. "I don't want to take your money. Do you want a head start?

"Head starts are for sissies." She toes off her sandals.

"You talk a good game." I step out of my flip-flops. "But no crying afterwards. Deal?"

"Please remove your shoes," says a bored-looking young man who's stationed in front of the inflated red archway that marks the beginning of the course.

"Got it," I say, resisting the urge to point out that we're standing in the grass in bare feet. "Thanks."

"Thirty seconds until your race starts."

"Thanks," Delilah says, giving me a fierce glance. "Is there anything I should know? You're not the league champion at bouncy courses or anything, right?"

"Never done this before in my life," I admit. "But there is the whole professional athlete thing."

"And the eight percent body fat," she adds.

"It'll be nine after I win the first ice cream."

"And, go!" says the worker.

All I see is the back of Delilah's head as she shoots through the arch ahead of me.

I should have seen that coming. But I take off after her, and since my legs are longer, we reach the inflatable climbing wall at the same time.

Like some kind of sexy spider monkey, Delilah has found her first handholds and footholds before I've even assessed the challenge.

But my arms and legs are longer than hers, and I'm a goalie, so I'm super limber for a dude. Three seconds later, I'm halfway up the wall in just two lunges. "How's it going down there?" I ask the top of Delilah's head.

"Not bad," she puffs, reaching for her next handhold. "Wouldn't get complacent if I were you."

I laugh. But laughter is dangerous. It shakes my body just

enough to dislodge my foot from the weird rubber ledge where I've stashed it.

Before I even know what's happened, I'm bouncing on my ass at the bottom of the wall.

"Guys, look! Silas is getting dusted by a girl."

I hear my teammates laughing somewhere behind me. But I'm already grabbing at the wall again.

Above me, Delilah clings like a cat as the wall ripples under my bulk. The second it calms again, she climbs one more step and then disappears over the top.

Huh.

Concentrating now, I scale the wall. There's a slide at the top, which I career down just as Delilah is righting herself at the bottom. As I slide, she disappears into a forest of man-sized tubes poking up from the bouncy floor. As if she were ducking between a giant's whiskers.

I plop to the bottom of the slide with a jaw-jarring bounce, giving myself a world-class wedgie. But this is no time to worry about personal comfort. I spring forward, plowing between the inflatable obstacles, pushing blindly onward.

I can't see Delilah, but I can hear her laughing up ahead of me. When I emerge from the forest, her arms are just disappearing through a low tube on the left. So I dive headfirst through the one on the right. It pitches downward at an angle I wasn't expecting, and I hear myself yell as I accelerate toward the unknown.

We both land with a bounce and a gasp on the other side.

"Omigod!" she squeals from her back.

"That was kind of like being flushed down a bouncy toilet," I gasp.

She rolls over. "We're not done." And off she goes.

By the time I'm on my feet, Delilah is making her way up another wall. This one has two thick ropes, one for each of us to grab as we haul ourselves upward. Instead of leaping for my rope, I reach up and catch Delilah by the hips, holding her in place, preventing her progress.

"Silas!" she shrieks.

"Oh, I'm sorry. Were you going somewhere?"

She lets go of the rope, destabilizing me.

Falling is sort of a secondary specialty that all hockey players cultivate. So I brace her in my arms and lie neatly back on the inflated surface until we both bounce to a stop.

Delilah rolls out of my arms. When she looks down at me, she's flushed. Hair wild. Eyes bright. "If you weren't so good in bed, I might actually be irritated right now."

I laugh, and she kisses me once, quickly. Then she leaps up and scrambles over the wall.

And I chase after her.

We swing over a gap like Tarzan and Jane. I hold back a couple of seconds just so I can watch Delilah's hair fly past the darkening sky and hear her whoop of joy. All that's left after that is a quick scramble through a corkscrew thing that looks like it belongs in a Dr. Seuss book.

Panting, we roll up at nearly the same moment to another archway, where an employee waits with ice cream tickets. Delilah slides her toe over the line first. "Better luck next time, Mr. Professional Athlete."

She gives me a glee-filled smile and takes her ice cream ticket.

"Do I get one for almost tying?" I ask the attendant.

"Sure." He hands me one. "You know you don't even need the ticket, right?"

I do know that. This place is a fantasy land constructed to give rich people pleasure. "Thank you," I say. "Have a nice night."

Nothing here is real. I'm all too aware of that as I slip my hand into Delilah's, and we reclaim our shoes. In three days we'll be headed back to our regular lives.

I dread it.

"What flavor are you getting?" Delilah squeezes my hand as we head for the ice cream stand, where a cute young woman with ebony skin is serving sundaes and cones.

"Do I have to pick just one kind?" I ask.

"They have German chocolate," Delilah says, letting out a low moan. "I need that in my life."

Forget ice cream. I need that sound she just made in my life. We've had our clothes on for maybe two hours. And it already feels like too long.

When it's our turn, the young woman staffing the dessert stand turns to us. She lets out the kind of high-pitched shriek that shatters glass in cartoons. "Oh my God!" She clutches her face. "Delilah Spark! OH MY GOD." She darts around the stand and grabs Delilah's hand, like they're long-lost friends. "This is amazing! Can we take a photo?"

"No!" barks a voice. Carl Bayer—security extraordinaire—is jogging toward us. "No photos of Delilah or anyone else."

The woman's hand flies to her mouth. "I'm sorry. I knew that. I'm sorry," she stammers.

"Don't worry," Delilah says quickly. "If you have a pen I can sign something for you."

"Oh!" The young woman's face lights up. "That would be amazing!" She grabs a napkin off the stand.

"Wait, does anyone have a pen?" Delilah asks. "I don't have pockets…"

Carl reaches into his pocket and produces one. He stands like a tank beside us, arms crossed, keeping order. That's just Carl's way.

Delilah is unbothered. She asks the girl's name, and writes a message on the napkin, signing it in looping script with a heart over the "i" in Delilah.

The woman is overjoyed, babbling her thanks and then

scooping generous portions of German chocolate ice cream into waffle cones for us.

"Thank you," Delilah says. "It was lovely meeting you."

Eventually we're free of the smiling young woman, and Carl follows us toward the lawn furniture where people are gathered with their desserts. "Sorry about that, Miss Spark," he says.

"Oh, please." She waves her spoon, dismissing it. "Nobody has asked me for a photo all day. I'm going to forget I'm a diva."

He smiles, because we're all smitten with Delilah, who doesn't come across as a diva at all.

"By the way," she says to him, "thanks again for helping to settle down my bodyguard."

"My pleasure," Carl says. "I don't think he settled down much, though. He looked like he was ready to dive into the harbor and swim after us. Either he's extremely dedicated to you, or he works for assholes who will string 'im up for letting you out of his sight. I hope it's the former."

"Actually..." She frowns, taking a dainty bite of ice cream. "There's a third possibility. I think that guy's job is half protection, half spying."

The older man's eyes brighten. I can't tell if it's because he has the same theory, or because he just likes a good story. "Spying for whom?"

"My record label, and more specifically, my ex who runs it. I am trying to detangle my life from his, but it's not like I can fire my bodyguards before I find someone new." She makes a face. "Actually, it's tempting. But they come in handy about once a week. And I've been getting some creepy mail, so..."

"What kind of creepy mail?" Carl barks.

She shakes her head. "Just some guy who likes to send cocktail napkins from every place I've gone. Telling me how good we'd be together. It's eerie, but they don't come to my actual home. They go to my PO box."

I hate this. But I bite my lip, just like I did the last time she told me about this. Delilah's security choices are none of my business. Even if I wish they were.

"If there's any chance that you know people at security firms in California," Delilah says to Carl. "I would love to hear about them."

He clicks his pen absently. "Let me think about who I could send you to. I assume you have security 24/7? One man or two?"

"One. There are three guys in rotation, unless I'm going to a big event and then they beef it up. It's…" She sighs. "To be honest, I haven't paid enough attention to the details, because it was done for me."

"Don't worry." He puts a hand on her shoulder. "California is full of companies that can help you. We'll find you someone who knows what they're doing and won't pad the bill." He pulls a charming little notebook out and offers the pen again. "Put your number right here, missy, and I'll call you next week."

"Thank you," she says, scribbling on the page. "I use exactly the same notebooks. Great paper, right?"

He snorts, takes his book from her, and closes it. "The paper is fine. But I liked the cover." It reads: *I'm surrounded by complete fucking assholes.*

"Are you?" she teases.

"Well…" He tucks the book away. "I have two sons who haven't listened to a thing I say since 1999. That's when Eric became a mouthy teen. And Max was born mouthy. So it depends on the day."

"What do your sons do?" she asks.

"That one over there—" He gestures toward my teammate. "—is a hockey player. Thirty-four years old and still playing games for a living. My other son does something with technology."

I burst out laughing at this description, because *something with technology* is a bit of an understatement. His other son is a tech genius who made a fortune in cyber security. Nobody has any idea how much Max Bayer is worth because his company — and his entire life — are private.

"You kids enjoy your night," Carl says. "I'm around if you need me. And I'll help you find someone new after the wedding."

"Thank you!" Delilah calls after him. "God, could it be that easy? I just want people to tell me what to do."

"I have a few ideas," I mutter.

She gives me a smile over the edge of her ice cream cone. "Do you, now?"

"More than a few," I whisper.

She licks her lips. "Well, I have a few ideas of my own."

"I can't wait to hear them."

———

Maybe I could have waited to hear her ideas. Because now I'm sitting on a plank suspended over a tank of water, while Georgia warms up her throwing arm.

I watch her wind up and throw. Then I hear — but can't see — the smack of the ball near the target. And just as I'm wondering whether that "oooooh" from the audience means a hit or a miss, I shoot downwards at a surprising rate, splashing into the water.

I come up snorting, water in my nose. And this isn't even for charity. *Fuck.* I'm a good sport, so amid the laughter, I climb back onto the bench.

It's Delilah's turn. "I don't know if I can throw," she says.

"That's okay, baby," I call. "I like you better if you can't."

Everyone laughs.

She tries an underhand throw. I hear a swish and a soft plop. The bench beneath me doesn't move.

"Bummer, honey!" I call. "Can I get out of here now?"

"Everybody gets three tries," Georgia says cheerfully, passing Delilah another ball.

I grit my teeth as she throws again—harder this time. But the audience's "OH!" clearly sounds like a miss.

"Last one, honey. More ice cream?"

"What you need is a spotter," Jason says, stepping forward. "Let me help."

"Nope! No spotter necessary!" I argue.

Jason stands behind my girl and captures her hand in his. "On account of three. One, two, thr—"

THUNK!

I hit the water again.

Only for Delilah.

DELILAH

Can you live a lifetime in three days? I feel as though I have.

When I first stepped off that boat, Silas and I weren't strangers, but we weren't really a couple, either. We were some third category. Let's call it, *hungry for more*.

But then came a rapid succession of hours on neutral ground, where the only work to be done was fitting into one another's lives.

We're quite good at it already. Each night we sleep like puzzle pieces fitted together—his arm flung over my waist, his knees bent into the crooks of mine.

And when the mornings arrive, we make slow love on the tousled bed, and then fit our morning routines together, too. We swap places beneath the showerhead, we pass the milk, we exchange tooth-brushed kisses and breakfast pastries.

There is no end to our ease and pleasure. We splash in the turquoise ocean. We share beach towels and spread sunscreen on each other's backs.

It's been way too easy to find our rhythm. And I don't ever want the song to end.

But the time flies past at the speed of a movie montage. The ocean. The sparkling pool. Drinks at sunset and a nap in a hammock somewhere. At night, while frogs sing in the trees outside our window, Silas lays breathing beside me. It would be way too easy to get used to this.

No, too late. I'm already used to this.

It's not just Silas, either. I grow accustomed to Heidi's sunshine and Jason's good-natured complaints. I don't have to wonder why my life is such a mess, because I'm surrounded by happy people.

For three days, I'm not a pop star with a late record and relationship baggage. I'm just a girl on vacation who doesn't need a bodyguard if I want to run to the snack bar for more bottled water and a plate full of cookies for the guys on the beach.

Now I understand why there's an entire genre of music devoted to beaches and summer love. I'm a believer.

But then suddenly, it's late on Saturday afternoon. We've all had enough sun, so we're lounging around the cottage. I'm curled up on my favorite sofa cushion, flipping through a magazine of Heidi's, while Silas, Leo, and Jason do pushups and sit-ups on the rug.

When Silas starts stretching out his limber body, I give up the pretense of reading and flip the magazine closed so I can watch. "Do you have to work out all summer to prepare for the season?"

"Yeah," Jason grunts through yet another set of sit-ups. "But this extra set right here is just for vanity. Gotta keep the abs looking fine. Heidi? Come and hold down my feet. This is for you, babe."

"Okay." She comes over and plops herself on to his sneakers, while biting into a donut. "Feel the burn, honey," she says, licking icing off her finger.

"That. Is. Just. *Mean*," he says through gritted teeth as he curls his abs.

"What? You asked for my help." She takes another bite and moans.

Silas claps his hands. "Five more, man. Then you get your own donut."

"Use your anger," Heidi coaches through a bite.

"Three...two...one..." Jason rises for the last time, reaches out and grabs the rest of the donut. It disappears into his craw a split second later.

Heidi only shrugs. "Good work. I have to fit into my dress right about now, anyway."

"Is it already that time?" I glance at the clock. The wedding starts in ninety minutes.

"Yes! Primp time!" she says, rising. "What are you wearing?"

"Maybe you can help me decide before I jump in the shower." I put the magazine aside and stand up. But all I really want to do is climb into Silas's lap and pretend my trip isn't almost over.

Heidi follows me into the bedroom, where I've hung three dresses. "Hmm," she says, eyeing them one by one.

"Which one says, 'tasteful, appreciative wedding-crasher'?" I ask.

"They all do. They're very conservative. None of them says, 'I'm a fabulous pop star on a private island living it up with my buff boyfriend.'"

"Dresses aren't my thing. Most of the time I wear snarky T-shirts and jeans. I'm terrible at makeup. And I'm not really a pop star."

Heidi cackles. "Millions of young women say otherwise."

"I mean, I'm not like Taylor Swift. I don't dance, or "Shake it Off," or influence fashion. I'd rather sit on my stool and make a squinty face while I play my guitar and sing."

Heidi ignores all of these objections. "We'll go with this one." She holds up the simplest dress, but it's also the barest.

Dove-grey, sleeveless, with a soft drape of fabric at the bosom. "I'll handle the makeup. Silver, I think? With rosy highlights for that suntan, maybe. Do you have heels?"

"Two-inch sling-backs." I wasn't quite sure what shoes to wear to a beach wedding.

"Phew. So you're not totally hopeless."

"'Not totally hopeless' is exactly what I aim for." That would make a good song title, actually...

"Focus, Delilah," she says just as my mind wanders off in that direction. "Show me your accessories."

"Hmm. I don't remember if I brought any." It's Becky who usually thinks of these things. And I've been wearing only bathing suits, sundresses, and sunscreen for three days.

It's been heavenly.

I cross to my carryon bag and zip it open. "Oh, here we go." There's a small quilted bag, and it contains two necklaces and three pairs of earrings.

Heidi picks up a necklace and makes a happy noise. "You must have a great stylist. This is from a designer I could never get near, let alone afford."

"People send me things to wear," I admit. "And when I go on tour, a stylist steps in to put all those clothes together. But that's more like costume design than clothing. They match the sheen of the fabric to the lights and the video effects. It's literally the job of three people to make me seem bigger and more like a star than I really am."

"Huh." Heidi looks more thoughtful than impressed. "And I thought my job was weird."

"You're the team manager's assistant, right?" It seems like everyone I've met works for the team.

"Yeah, I run his office and his life."

"Is that a lot of travel?"

"Sure is. But it lets me see more of my honey, so I'm not complaining. Their schedule during the season is *brutal*."

A fresh, new worry pokes its way out of my subconscious and scurries to the forefront of my brain. Even if my magical vacation with Silas was the start of something big, how would I ever see him? We both have strange jobs.

"Now let me see..." Heidi squints at the dress. "Which eye palette goes best with this?"

"I wouldn't know a palette if it bit me in the backside. I just radiate incompetence, don't I?"

"Not at all," Heidi argues. "You radiate indifference. That's not the same thing. Hold this up to your face so I can see how it plays with your olive skin tone."

I do it, and Heidi smiles. "Perfect! I'll hitch the fairy dust to the genius pony and be right with you after you shower."

"Don't spend too much time on me," I caution her. "It's not like I'm the bride."

"Not this time, anyway," she says cheerfully.

As if me getting married didn't sound as unlikely as taking a trip to the moon.

———

"Hold still. Last time, I promise."

I close my eyes and wait while she strokes something onto my brow line.

"Ladies." There's a tap on the door. We're in Heidi's room, which is twice the size of mine. "Let's roll." Jason prods through the door.

"One sec!" Heidi calls.

"You said that ten minutes ago! Walking in late to the big boss's wedding is not a good look on you."

"We're totally ready!" Heidi calls, sitting back and admiring her work. "Let's go! This is going to be great."

I stand up and slip my feet into my shoes. In the living room, Silas is looking out the window. He turns my way, and then those green eyes widen. He gives me a onceover and a slow, sexy smile. Then he presses his lips together, like there's something he needs to hold in, because it's not for everyone's ears.

Nobody has ever looked at me like that before. Like I'm half of an important secret.

It takes me a long moment and a slow blink to notice what he's wearing. "Is that a seersucker suit?" In *pink?*

"Of course." Still smiling, he smooths a hand over a jacket that looks like something you'd see at the Kentucky Derby. "Perfect for warm weather."

"And for looking like a geezer," his roommate snarks.

"You look adorable," I argue, walking toward him. "Like a Southern gentleman."

"And you two match!" Heidi squeals. "I'm all amazement."

"Whereas I feel a little nauseated," Jason mutters.

"Let's go!" Heidi chirps. "Weren't you in a big fat hurry?" She slaps his butt and scoots out the door ahead of him.

Silas gives me one more longing gaze, lingering particularly on my cleavage and then down to my bare legs. "How did I get so lucky to have you on my arm tonight? Love your dress."

"Do you?" I'm not sure it's my dress he's admiring.

"Mm-hmm. It will look great on the floor later." He leans in, and his lips sweep down my cheekbone.

"This wedding starts in four minutes," Jason says from outside.

"All right." With a sigh, Silas takes my hand. "Let's go sit through the stuffy parts so we can get to the carousing that comes later."

We walk out the door, hand in hand. And until this moment I don't think I ever knew what being part of a couple was meant to feel like.

———

Apparently, a billionaire's private island home comes equipped with a ballroom seating two hundred people on prim white chairs. The room is also *filled* with tropical flowers in pinks and oranges. It's gorgeous. Flower petals line the sides of the aisle, too.

Piano music plays while the mother of the bride proceeds down the aisle on the arm of her son-in-law. After she sits, our gazes swing to the front of the room, where a rotund officiant appears. His white collar sets off his ebony skin as he walks, chin high, to step behind the flower-covered altar. He smiles happily and beckons to Nate and the best man, who enter in light-grey suits.

As the music changes, two hundred heads turn to look up the aisle.

The bridesmaids come into view, escorted by groomsmen. Their dresses are all the same shade of deep pink, but in different styles cut to suit them.

So this is how weddings are done. I admit I never paid much attention before. But this is classy.

And I don't *feel* like a wedding crasher, even if I am one. I spoke to everyone in the wedding party at some point this weekend. I feel weirdly invested.

Rebecca's sister is the maid of honor. Smiling sweetly, she walks slowly down the aisle alone. But when she's made it about halfway down, she stops and turns around.

And a tiny little boy in a miniature tuxedo toddles into view. He's carrying a small sign that reads: *Here Comes the Bride*.

"Awwwww," says the crowd.

Rebecca's sister waves to him. He looks up, locking onto the sight of his mom, and then starts to toddle, hustling down the aisle until he is scooped up into her arms. She carries him to the front of the room, then hands him off to his grandma before taking her place at the front of the bridesmaids' line.

"Well, that's about the cutest thing I've ever seen," Silas whispers.

I give him a quick glance, taking in the curve of his freshly shaved cheek. The wedding must be making me a little crazy, because suddenly I have a crystalline image of Silas holding a baby boy in his arms, speaking to his child in a calm, even voice...

Okay, *danger*. Weddings are clearly like strong drugs, sending my emotions into overdrive. *I don't even know these people*, I remind myself.

Then the crowd makes a happy noise, and I turn reflexively to see Rebecca in the doorway. And, wow. She's resplendent in a white dress that reminds me of 1950s styles—with a wide V neckline falling in soft folds to a tea-length, asymmetrical hem. It's fancy and simple at the same time.

And even though it's a lovely image, what I notice most about Rebecca is the look on her face. She's absolutely beaming. Her clear, happy smile tells me everything I need to know about her, and about how much this all means to her.

It's not just pageantry that I'm witnessing. It's more like hearing a great song for the first time. The melody is both new and familiar. And you're tapping your foot along to the beat without even realizing you started.

When I glance in the other direction—at the groom—his face is flushed. He smiles, too. But then his lip trembles, and he raises a hand to flick away a tear that's threatening to fall.

I bite my lip. Here we have this famous man—one of the wealthiest in the world—reduced to tears over the sight of Rebecca walking toward him in a white dress.

Suddenly I have the sniffles. Dear lord. I don't know if I can survive this.

Rebecca makes her way toward her fiancé. She's escorted down the aisle by Hugh somebody-or-other—the middle-aged manager of the team, and her coworker. Because the Bruisers give new meaning to the phrase "one big happy family," apparently. After she takes her place across from her dazed groom, the officiant begins.

"Greetings to friends, old and new! It's an honor to stand here today to celebrate the marriage vows of Nathan and Rebecca. This is my favorite part of the job. Christening babies is nice, too, but sometimes they cry."

The crowd gives him a laugh.

"Now, in olden days—or maybe this only happens on television—" The crowd chuckles again. "—the minister would begin by asking whether anyone has an objection to this union. But I won't be asking that question today. The two people standing before me are ready to make this commitment before God and their families."

I swear the room lets out a happy sigh.

"I only mention this old tradition because in their case, I've learned that Nathan and Rebecca were their own worst obstacles to finding their place together. Some of us have to search the Earth for our soul mates. Sometimes we find that person right in front of us. And a few of us are too busy writing code and taking over the world to see her clearly."

The crowd roars.

"Or…" The pastor waits a moment for the audience to quiet again. "Or maybe this is you. Maybe you do see that special woman, or that special man. Perhaps you know with whom you'd like to share your life. But you're wasting precious time wondering whether you deserve this person. Maybe you've put aside your own heart, thinking that if you could just get that next promotion, or quit smoking, or lose another ten pounds…" He pats his belly. "Maybe *then* you'll deserve the love your heart is ready to give."

Why am I holding my breath? I let it out as quietly as I can.

Beside me, Silas squeezes my hand. But I don't turn my head. I can't. Because I don't trust my expression right now. I don't know what to think about this time on the island or Silas's excellent company.

I don't know if fate is trying to tell me something like: *Hey girl. There's more in store for you than that asshole you dated.* Or if this trip is just a diversion so lovely that only a fool would try to make it last.

The pastor has asked Georgia to read a bible passage, and her lilting voice is the backdrop to my wandering thoughts. Tomorrow I'll be on a plane back to L.A., where my manager is busy lining up collaborators for me to write and record with. "Business as usual," she'd told me. "We will not be cowed."

In a few weeks, Silas will be back to work, too. Ours is not like the story the pastor tells—where your true love is waiting right outside your office door. Even if my favorite bartender and I have that special something that makes sparks fly, we don't have it on the same ends of the continent.

"Let us pray," says the pastor up front.

SILAS

The night is almost over, and I can't stand it.

Under a tent on the lawn, we were fed another perfect meal —locally caught fish with a mango slaw. There was a seven-tiered wedding cake and passionfruit sorbet. There were champagne toasts and music and now dancing.

But it isn't enough. It will never be enough, because I'm supposed to put Delilah on a plane back to California tomorrow.

"Hey," she whispers as I turn her slowly on the dance floor. "What are you thinking about in that big brain of yours?"

I hold back a sigh. "Nothing useful. Want to go look at the stars?"

"You know I do."

That's just it, though. I don't know what she's thinking at all. I know she had fun this weekend. A lot of it. But I don't know what it all means.

I lead her off the dance floor, trying to choose my direction. My coach is to my left, so I head right instead, weaving carefully between clusters of teammates and acquaintances, so nobody will talk to us. I'm in no mood.

"Beach?" I ask, because that's the way we're headed.

"Always." She pauses to remove her shoes. So I do the same.

Then we're tiptoeing through the cool sand, the half-moon our only guide. It's a clear night, so it's enough. Another couple ahead of us has had the same idea. Nobody is ready for this trip to end. Me, least of all.

"When am I going to see you again?" I ask, because beating around the bush isn't my style.

"Good question." Delilah hesitates. "It's been nice to be out of touch with reality for so long. But I expect Charla Harris will have put a bunch of meetings with songwriters on my calendar. She said she would."

"Okay." I stop and push a strand of hair off her face. "Talk to me about the music festival. August is almost here already." Shit. Training camp starts in...four weeks? Could that even be right?

"I'm playing the first Friday night. Main stage."

"Well, duh." She gives me a smile. "I meant—do you want me to come?"

"Of course," she says quickly. But then she looks away, and the breeze pushes her hair everywhere again. "Anytime, Ralph."

"I'm back to Ralph now?" She hasn't called me that in days.

"No, not really." She sighs. "This is just going to get trickier. We both know that we can't be like all those other couples." She points back toward the tent. "We live on different coasts. We travel a lot. I honestly just want to stay on this island for the rest of my life. But that isn't an option, so..." She shrugs.

She's right, of course.

I take her hand again and walk farther down the beach. We only have a few hours left. We should be getting drunk and making out like happy fools. But I'm all torn up inside. "Look, I don't mean to go heavy on you. But this isn't over for me. I won't just walk away after this. Unless you need me to."

She shakes her head. "I would never ask you to lose my

number. But I warned you that I had things that needed sorting out. This is the first week in forever that I didn't spend a lot of time worrying about how to get my second album back. But the minute I step off this island, that problem comes right back."

"I know." The wind rises up again, and I can see Delilah rubbing her arms. "Are you cold?" I wrap an arm around her. "You know I want you to get what you need. I'm not asking you to prioritize me. But I want you to leave the door open."

"Okay." She leans against me. "Take me surfing, Ralph. In California. Maybe everything will work out."

"All right," I agree. It's the least I can do.

———

In the morning, Delilah has to take the earliest launch back to the mainland, but I have to wait for my teammates. So our goodbye happens on the dock in the morning.

I put a brave face on it, but I'm not a happy guy.

As the boat comes into view, Delilah turns to me. "Thank you. Seriously. I had a great time. I can't remember ever having as nice a time as I did this weekend."

I'm certain she means it. I can hear it in her voice. I'm about to give her a kiss that will last her all the way to L.A., when a girl makes a high squeal.

"You guys are so cute *it's insane!*"

"Elsa," growls Beacon, the other goalie on our team. "Leave them alone. Put away your phone."

Holding back a curse, I turn to greet the Beacons. Elsa is fourteen. Her baby brother—in a baby carrier perched on my teammate's chest—is not quite six months old. "Hey, guys," I say.

Beacon smirks. "Sorry."

"The photo ban is over," Elsa says with a big, cheeky smile.

She's a handful, and some days I don't know how Beacon hangs onto his sanity. "Could I please have a picture with Delilah?"

"Sure, sweetie," Delilah says.

We step apart. The launch is coming. The weekend is over. And I'm just not ready.

Elsa shoves her phone into my hand. "Silas—you take it." The teen steps between me and my girl.

"*Please*," Beacon growls.

"Please!" Elsa adds with zero remorse. She poses beside Delilah, who's smiling patiently. I hold up the phone and snap the photo.

The boat docks a minute later. All I can do is pull Delilah aside for one last kiss. I take her beautiful face in my two hands and touch my lips to hers. "Take care of yourself. I need to hear from you that you got home okay."

"Okay." She gives me a shy smile. "Thanks for everything. This was amazing."

It's true. And I'm still so sad. "Call me anytime at all."

"I will." She stands up on her toes and kisses me one more time.

After that, she's gone.

SILAS

"No." Heidi shakes her blond curls. "It looked better under the windows. Let's move it back."

"For fuck's sake," I grumble. "Give me a second, here."

"Don't let me interrupt your texting session," Heidi says. "That phone is like permanently attached to your hand now."

Ignoring her, I sit down in the middle of the mostly empty apartment where my teammate Dave lived until just last week. And I continue my conversation with Delilah.

Silas: Do you get to see your manager today?

Delilah: Yup. But she's making me drive to Malibu to meet with her. I can't tell if her schedule is really that booked up, or if she's punishing me for missing my appointment Tuesday.

Silas: The word Malibu makes me think of rum drinks behind the high school gym. **Shudder**

Delilah: Let me guess. You drank Malibu and Coke and then ralphed.

Silas: Well I wasn't always this cool.

Delilah: <3

Silas: Are you getting a nice lunch out of your manager at least?

Delilah: I wish. She's so booked up she could only fit me in if I met her at the spa.

Silas: Get a massage. I need a massage.

Delilah: I thought you told me there was an on staff massage therapist?

Silas: Not in the summer, sadly. If I wanted an appointment with her I'd have to leave the building. And I'd have to actually pay for it, too.

Delilah: Oh the horrors.

Silas: I know right? So enjoy yourself.

Delilah: Don't bet on it. She said I was meeting her between treatments.

Silas: I heard that LA has some weird spa treatments. Isn't that where they invented colonic cleansing?

Delilah: Well now I'm terrified. Thanks for that.

I laugh.

"Listen, lover boy," Heidi says, clapping her hands. "If we don't get this done, then I can't order you a pizza from Grimaldi's."

My stomach rumbles, because she's right. And I'm hungry. "Okay, when can we eat?"

"We should be done here in about three hours."

"*What?*" I let out a howl of anguish. We've been moving furniture around my retired teammate's empty condo all morning. I don't know how I got suckered into this.

"Kidding!" Heidi giggles. "Jeez. Just move the couch one more time. Then I'll fluff the pillows and we can go."

Still grumpy, I sign off with Delilah. Then I pick up my end of the sofa and relocate it to the spot where Heidi indicates. "Happy? How much are you making on this gig, anyway?"

"My standard rate per hour."

"And why are you furnishing an apartment for a guy who's already moved out?" Dave lived here in this amazing two bedroom with a den and a view of the Manhattan Bridge. But now he's moved to Vermont with Zara and their toddler.

"The place was under contract to be sold. But Dave lost his buyer at the last minute." She fluffs the pillows, as promised. "The realtor said it's harder to sell an empty house. So I rented this furniture for three hundred bucks a month."

"And you rented me for the price of a pizza."

"I'll throw in a six-pack of beer because I love you."

"I'm a cheap date."

"The cheapest," she agrees. "But you're also a good friend, so that's understandable."

"Thanks?"

"What I don't understand is why you aren't buying this place."

"Wait, what?" I turn to Heidi, who's studying me. "Now you're trying to evict me?" I mean, living with a couple is a little weird. But Castro and I just had a conversation about how much money we're all saving.

"No, buddy. I'm trying to get you to think big."

"If you want me to think big, then let's order the large pizza."

Heidi gives me half a head shake, like I'm the dumbest man in the world. "If you want to convince Delilah Spark to move to New York, you're going to have to figure out where she can do her thing. And you know there are recording studios in the Navy Yard complex, right?"

"There are?" I look out the window, befuddled. "Wait. How do you know that? And why do you think Delilah would move to New York?"

Heidi blinks. "Well you can't move to L.A., dummy. So she's going to have to move here. It's not that complicated."

"You say that like it's so obvious. We barely—"

"—know each other. So you've said. But I think your relationship is happening in dog years. The time you've spent on texts alone this week is more togetherness than some married people have in a year."

It's true that Delilah and I are talking. A lot. And I can't wait to go to California to see her concert. Unfortunately, I'll have to leave the day after the concert. Even so, I'm missing the first two practices of the season. Nobody does that. Ever.

And Delilah seems to have even more on her plate than I do.

There are a few things that Heidi's chirpy, upbeat attitude just can't fix. I'm afraid this is one of them.

"You could give Delilah one of the bedrooms as a studio," Heidi says. "The master bedroom would be that one—" She points. "That leaves you a nice living room, and the den could have a foldout couch for when your mother visits."

"That is a lot of life planning," I say tightly. "Didn't you say it was time for lunch?" But now I'm glancing around the space again. It's gorgeous. Beringer's pad was the sweetest one. "How much is Dave trying to get, anyway?"

"The buyers he lost were paying two point nine."

"Million?" I gasp.

"It's the biggest unit in the building."

"Why didn't the sale go through?" I hate that she's making me think about this. But I want this little picture she's painting. I want to walk through that door after practice and see Delilah on the sofa with her guitar.

I want that so bad.

"The buyer was getting transferred here from San Francisco," Heidi says, backing up to take a photo of the couch and its well-fluffed pillows. "Then his company went belly-up and he no longer has a job. Dave let him out of the contract." She spins around. "I think he'd take less now. He just wants to sell and be in Vermont with his cute family and have another baby."

"Are you getting a commission or something?"

"No." She walks over and pats my arm. "You should take a few photos, too, in case you want to discuss it with your girl."

"She's not my girl," I say reflexively.

"But she could be. I'm going to go order that pizza. Meatball and roma tomatoes. With olives?"

"Yeah, thanks," I say, trying not to buy into Heidi's fantasy.

It's already too late. I'm busy wondering if I could afford this apartment. It's not an easy question. I make nine hundred thousand a year, and when my contract is renegotiated this year, I'll make more.

But I'm so superstitious. If I make an offer on this apartment, Delilah will probably freak out that I'm moving too fast. Which I probably am.

Or I'll get traded to another team nowhere near Brooklyn, and I'll still be on the hook for nearly three million bucks. This shit happens. Since luck isn't always on my side, it would probably happen to me.

Buying this place would be a terrible idea. What's the down payment on three mill? Almost a half million dollars? I don't have that much money in the bank. Maybe I will in two years. But not yet.

Still. So tempting. I pull out my phone and take a couple of photos, damn it. I already asked Delilah if she wanted to visit me in Brooklyn next week. August is too long to wait. She said she'd check with her scary new manager.

I wonder how casually I could mention the unit for sale in my building...

It's crazy to think this way. Even so, I pull out my phone and search: *how much house can I afford?* And I don't like their answer.

So I go back to our rental unit to stuff my face with pizza.

DELILAH

"I'm here to see Charla Harris," I tell the woman behind the frosted glass desk. She's dressed head to toe in what's supposed to be a soothing shade of seafoam green. Instead of a regular desk chair, she's sitting on something that resembles a giant pebble.

"Namaste," the woman whispers, giving me a chin dip that's meant to be a bow. "One moment please."

I can't wait to tell Silas about this. The thought pops into my head, as it seems to do all the time now. We talk all the time, too.

It doesn't feel like enough.

"Right this way."

I follow the seafoam woman through a doorway marked, *Dressing Pod.*

Dressing Pod?

"Clothes off, please. All of them. Here is your robe," she says once we're inside.

I don't take the robe. "I'm sorry, but I'm not here for a treatment. Only a chat."

She points one perfectly manicured finger at the opposite

door, where a sign reads, *Robes Only Beyond This Point*.

"Um…"

She thrusts the robe in my hands and opens a locker door. "You may put your things in here. When you're properly attired, follow the yellow healing dots to the oxygen room."

"The what to the what?" But she's already disappearing through the door.

Silas is definitely hearing about this later.

I remove all my clothes and put on the robe. Feeling like an idiot, I walk barefooted out the far door. At my feet there are large, bubble-shaped dots in various colors painted on the floor. They lead off in various directions. I follow the yellow ones down a corridor.

I pass a door marked *Serenity Pool*, and another marked *Revitalizing Waters*. Finally, I locate a door marked *Oxygen Room*. I don't know if I'm supposed to knock or not. After a moment's hesitation, I turn the doorknob and gently poke my head into the room.

There sits Charla Harris on a chaise lounge, her short legs crossed at the ankles. Her eyes are closed, and she's breathing very deeply, like someone in a yoga video.

"Hi," I say, and it sounds too loud in all the silence.

"Close the door," she says without opening her eyes. "You're letting all the oxygen out."

I step in and shut it behind me. "There's oxygen everywhere, though. Are you sure this isn't a scam?"

She ignores the comment and takes another deep breath.

"Usually in Hollywood, when you have to take off your clothes to see your manager, you can file a sexual harassment claim later," I add, crossing to one of the lounge chairs.

"You are hilarious, darling. Let's see if we can get you some standup comedy gigs after I earn you another ten million on your fucking album." She still does not even open her eyes.

"Why didn't we just have dinner?"

"Oxygen is more important than dinner. And all my dinners are booked through October, anyway."

"All of them? Don't you ever eat alone?"

"I would, but there's always somebody who slept through her regularly scheduled appointment and therefore needs to have dinner."

Touché.

Charla finally opens her eyes. "My goodness. Where did you say you went on vacation?"

"I went to a wedding."

"Was it your own? Because you look twice as healthy as last time I saw you. And by 'healthy' I really mean sexually satisfied."

"Well. The oxygen is clearly doing its magic."

"Don't sound ungrateful, darling. You're the reason I'm so busy this week. I've been chasing down lawyers to help you get out from under Brett Ferris."

"Don't say his name. It depletes the oxygen."

My tough manager actually cracks a smile, and I feel like I've won an Oscar. Pulling out my phone, I Google *how much oxygen is in the air.* "Twenty-one percent," I tell her. "That's how much oxygen is in the air already."

"Doesn't it say, 'except in L.A.?' Have you heard of smog? You are in a very goofy mood. You did meet a man on the beach, right? You had a fling."

"There *was* a guy. Sure." But how does she know? "You're a little creepy, Charla. I say this with love."

"It's just years of experience. So you spent the weekend with a guy on a beach. Then you returned to L.A. where you remembered that your life is in flux. And you're not sure why you came back."

Get out of my brain. "Yeah, something like that. It was a pretty amazing time. I don't know what to think about it, honestly. But this isn't your issue."

"Isn't it?" Her expression softens. "You hire me to help you reach your goals, no matter what those are. So if you sit here and say—Charla, find me a couple million dollars so I can go off and have three kids with the guy from the beach—" She shrugs. "Then that would become my task."

"That doesn't sound like me. I've spent my whole life trying to make it in music. I can't even imagine just walking away."

"Maybe not. I just need you to understand that getting what you want out of life is all about making tough choices. You have to ask yourself, 'What can't I live without?' Will it kill me to lose that second album? Do I need to make Brett pay? Or will it hurt worse if the guy from the beach gets away. Who is he, anyway? Wait, let me guess." She squints at me. "I see...a hockey player."

"Charla!" I realize I'm being punked. "Who told you?"

"Instagram. There's a photo of you kissing him. The post was from a teenage girl. You took a photo with her, too."

"Oh. You're stalking me on social media?"

"Of course I am. Or rather my assistant is. So tell me about this hockey player."

"I'm not sure what you need to know. He lives in Brooklyn."

Charla rolls her eyes. "I don't need to know anything. I just like gossip. Does he have a really muscular butt? What position does he play?"

"Goalie."

"A puck eater. Interesting. They're very bendy." Charla Harris is full of surprises.

"I didn't take you for the kind of woman who's impressed by professional athletes." I reach for my phone to show her the lock screen, which is now a selfie I took with Silas.

She whistles under her breath. "So this is a rather large problem, then."

"You can't tell just by looking at him."

"The hell I can't. He has kind eyes. That's the kind of man that could make you stop and realign your priorities."

I hear myself take a deep breath of air that might or might not have extra oxygen in it. I'd just spent forty minutes driving here to talk about writing new music. So why were we talking about Silas? "My priorities haven't shifted. I want my second album released."

"Okay," Charla says. "So then it's a good thing I set you up with three different producer teams and a buttload of studio time all over L.A."

"Why three? Why all over?"

"That weasel needs to hear about it, that's why. And I'm not even done. I still want you featured on an Ed Sheeran track, or something. Or we could go the opposite way—a hip-hop tune. We're going to be as fresh and unexpected as good taste on a Kardashian! We're going to be *everywhere*."

I love that she's full of ideas. "So it's probably not a great time for me to take a few days in Brooklyn, then?"

"Oh, honey. What did we just talk about? *Choices*."

"I know. Because..." My gut already knows how to prioritize. "The thing I can't live without is my second album."

"Then I need you in the recording studio, looking fresh-faced and ready to work. Gossip will be hounding Brett on the right, while my lawyers are hounding him on the left. We're going to give this man no choice but to release your record."

"Sounds good," I say, wondering what I'm going to say to Silas. I would love to visit Brooklyn. And I've heard all about the cool old apartment building where he lives with his teammates.

Looks like I won't be seeing it anytime soon, though.

———

Two days later, I'm sitting in a recording booth with a female songwriter named Sarah. She has giant glasses and pale skin that probably never sees the sun. She also has a voice like Joni Mitchell's, and a fierce, lovely personality that I came to adore about ten seconds after walking into this room.

"I don't know how to collaborate," was the first thing I said after "Hello." But Sarah didn't care at all.

"Oh, nobody knows how to collaborate. We just have to sit here and spit ideas at each other until one of them doesn't suck. Just unpack your guitar. Let's do this."

Four hours later, we're feeling a little slaphappy. We've already written one song that's not bad. It's called "Not Totally Hopeless."

We were going to stop, but we still had an hour of studio time. So we started fooling around again, her at the piano and me on my guitar.

"I think we're coalescing around this line." She sings it. "*Ask the universe.*"

"*Ask the universe,*" I repeat, adding, "*Anything could happen.*"

She plays it back, trying two different melodies.

"I think this song is about hitting Send. Asking for things." I think that over. "Okay, 'hitting send' is not fucking lyrical."

Sarah laughs.

"So I definitely need to think of another way to say that. But I like this idea that hitting Send is scary, but also exciting."

"It is." Her eyes light up behind those giant lenses. "When you hit Send, nobody has said no yet. Nobody has turned you down. Nobody has taken a shit in your cereal bowl."

I snort. "Let's avoid that imagery, maybe." Then we both giggle like idiots. And I needed this laugh almost as much as I needed all the sex and cuddling I got last weekend.

"Who did we hit Send to, anyway?" she asks.

"Anyone. The cute boy. The job opening—"

"—the Grammy-winning producer," she suggests.

"Exactly! Hitting Send is a moment that's pregnant with

expectation. This could be the thing that you've always needed. This could be the thing that changes everything."

"Write that one down." She points at my notebook. "The moment that changes everything. The day that changes everything. The hour... The minute..." We both stare into space, considering the possibilities. "What are you doing when you actually hit Send? What's the visual?

"Pushing a button. Using...electricity. Electrons! Copper wires."

"A little bit of electron magic, sending your dream out into the world."

"Yes! Now I've got chills."

"Good," she says. "Let's play this verse again to see if any of it flies. I'm going to bring up the tempo a little bit."

As I strum my guitar, I can see Becky on the other side of the glass. She's taking photos of us on her phone. There are other onlookers, too. Maybe they wonder what we're doing in here. I close my eyes to shut them out.

This is one of those moments when I recognize just how spectacular my job really is. This never happens when I step onto a red carpet. That's just stressful. It turns out that the glamorous parts of making music are the unglamorous parts. Today I'm making something out of nothing. All I need is my guitar vibrating against my breastbone and my warmed-up voice.

Anything could happen.
Ask the universe.
Send that message flying.
Ask the universe.

———

"I wrote a song with a stranger," I gush into the phone when

Silas answers. I'm in the back of Mr. Muscles's car.

"That sounds fun," he says, breathing hard.

"It was! I thought it would be so much pressure, you know? All my songs suck when I start them. I didn't see why that would be fun in front of someone else. But it's magic. She solved some of the snags that I hit, and then I solved some of hers."

"Teamwork," he pants. "We could get you jerseys. What number do you want to be?"

"I don't know. What's your number?"

"You don't know already? I thought you liked me."

I laugh. "What are you doing? You sound like you just ran a mile."

"I just ran five of them," he says. "Still am. I'm on a treadmill at the practice facility."

"Oh!" I try to picture a room where Silas and his pals are all flexing their muscles at once, but the idea makes my brain short out. "You can run and talk to me at the same time?"

"Sure, unless you don't like the panting."

"Panting can be fun," I point out. "Under the right circumstances."

"I completely agree." He chuckles.

I close my eyes and wish that everything was easier. "I called to give you some bad news. Unfortunately I can't fly out this week or next."

"Oh. Shit," he says. "You aren't coming?"

The disappointment in his voice is so genuine that I already regret my decision. "My manager came through for me on a whole bunch of songwriting dates at once. So my schedule is really tight. I thought about asking you to fly out here instead, but that's a shitty offer. I'd be spending a lot of hours in the studio with composers and producers."

He's quiet for a moment. "So this is good news for you, right? You need this."

"Yeah. It's forward momentum. Charla did exactly what I

asked her to do, which is create opportunities for me. She's trying to put pressure on—" I refuse to bring the jerk into this phone call. "—my record label. To get off their butts and do the right thing. She's making it look like I'm producing all kinds of new music without them."

"Okay," he says. "Let me stop this thing." I hear a beep, and then more deep breathing. "Glad to hear that your first session worked out."

"It really did. I'm not sure yet if the song is a keeper. But I learned a lot."

"What if you don't come up with anything good? Does that ever happen?"

Nobody ever asks me these questions. I mean—Brett asked me questions about music all the time. But he never asked me how I felt about the process. "Sure, it happens all the time. I can finish a song and then later decide it doesn't fit the album, or it doesn't sound right in my voice."

"Huh. I can't imagine having to sit in a windowless room and just *invent* things with music. Hell, I can't imagine even playing music. I can't even whistle in tune. Next time I see you, will you play me some guitar?"

"Sure." And the sooner the better. I want to pick up my guitar and fly to New York to give him a private concert.

Can't I just have everything? Am I a horrible person for wishing I could?

"The next time I see you will probably be in California," I point out. "I'll be playing for you and ten thousand of your closest friends."

"I know," he says. "Where are you staying, by the way? Should I get us a hotel room? Now there's a fun thought."

It is a fun thought, but I've already beat him to it. "Oh, I got a room. Big enough for both of us. Brett offered me the Ferris guesthouse again, but I didn't even respond to the email."

"He did? You're *shitting* me."

See? I shouldn't have mentioned him. "It's just posturing. He wants to appear accommodating in the hopes that I'll sign on for a third album."

Silas makes a noise of displeasure. But he doesn't say any more about it. And I love this about Silas—he lets me know that he cares, and yet I know he's not going to lecture me, either. That's what real support looks like, I guess.

"Anyway." I try to lighten the mood. "You and I are going to make mojitos and go to the beach. And then I'm going to play a concert where you'll be in the first row. And I'm sorry I can't come to Brooklyn."

"I understand. I knew I signed up for this."

"For what?"

"Missing you. Lots of phone calls and tricky travel arrangements."

"How early can you come to Darlington Beach? I got the hotel suite for four nights."

"Well..." He chuckles. "That's still under negotiation. In order to see your concert, I have to miss the first two days of training camp. Nobody ever misses training camp."

"Ouch. Maybe you shouldn't—"

"Oh no, I totally am. I made a deal with my coach that I'll show up to work out with the prospects in Hartford—the young draftees that Coach is looking at. I'm giving him the end of my vacation in trade."

"Wow. I'm sorry."

"Don't be, it's fine. But I'll be racing back to jump on a plane to you, that's all. There are lots of flights to L.A., and we'll just play it by ear to see which day I can get there."

"Okay. Don't stress over it."

"I won't. Pack a cocktail shaker and very little clothing."

I laugh. "Fine. Pack your big hot self and some surfing shorts. I still want my surfing lesson.

"You got it."

The next night I have a date. With Becky, of course. She's my entire social life these days. I find her seated already at the trendy new Melrose Mexican restaurant we've both been wanting to try. "Don't look now," she whispers as I slide in next to her. "Brad Pitt is three tables over."

"No way, really?" I crane my neck.

"Didn't I just say not to look?" she hisses.

I can only see the back of his head. I guess I can tell people that I saw Brad Pitt's neck at dinner. "Did you order the guacamole?"

"A double portion. What do you take me for? And I see that Mr. Muscles got a nice seat at the bar."

"Good for him," I grumble, eyeing the margaritas at the next table. I suppose I could break my streak and just order one like a normal person. But Becky would eventually end up drinking it, because even though I know my phobia is irrational, I don't feel like fighting it right now.

So I order a bottled beer unopened. We eat too many tacos and get a little slap-happy over Becky's crush on our waiter. It's all the more amusing because it's mutual. Over the course of an hour, he checks on our table thirty times.

"Is there anything else I can bring you ladies?" he finally asks, his gazed locked on my assistant.

"Just the check," I say.

"My *pleasure*." He winks and turns away.

"Those dark eyes," Becky hisses. "So hot."

"He's going to slip you his phone number," I predict.

"He'd better." She sighs. "I just hope he doesn't assume I'm someone important."

"What?"

"Sometimes people are nice to me because I'm sitting next to you."

I blink. "But there are, like, hearts in his eyes when he looks at you. I don't think you can fake that kind of attraction."

"Maybe." She shrugs. "But if he has hearts in his eyes and a demo tape in his glove compartment, it will still come up."

"Well, I hope it doesn't." How depressing it is that my success complicates Becky's life. Fame is paying for this dinner. But it has hidden costs.

"Hey, don't worry about me. Your bonkers life doesn't follow me home at night. It's worse for you. You can't ever stop being Delilah Spark."

"Sure I can," I argue as a reflex. But immediately I think of Silas. He liked me when I was just another failing musician. He liked me when I was broke and scared and had nothing to give but good conversation.

"You've got that dreamy look again," Becky says. "The Silas face."

"I do not," I lie, picking up my beer bottle. But it's already empty.

"You so do. Did he send you a goodnight photo? What is it this time?"

"Since you asked..." I dive into my purse and pull out my phone. Silas's nightly photos have become the thing I most look forward to. The three-hour time difference means I'm often busy when he's tucking himself in. So I always get a photo and a nice little note instead of a phone call.

I open my email and there he is. *Goodnight from Brooklyn* reads the subject line. Becky leans in.

"Hey," I tease. "What if it's a dick pic?"

"It won't be. He's more romantic than that."

She's right. These nightly notes are sweet and PG-rated. Usually there's a shot of him reclining in bed—shirtless but not naked. Or of him putting a record onto the turntable I sent him, or drinking milkshakes in the kitchen with his roommates.

Tonight's photo is different, though. When it loads, he's not in the shot at all. Instead, I see an attractive room with wood floors and fancy old windows set into a brick wall. There's a view of a bridge outside and sunlight glinting off the glass.

Hey D.

My teammate Dave is selling his apartment, and it's putting a lot of crazy ideas in my head. For the first time in my life I've got the itch to buy an apartment and figure out my life. I'm not buying it, though. There are a lot of reasons to hold off.

But it sure would be nice. Especially if you were here with me.

And before you remind me that I'm not allowed to make serious plans, I get it. I'm not asking you to make big sacrifices for me, and I don't know what the future holds. But I wanted you to know how appealing it is to me to think about waking up together every morning for the rest of my life. I want us to stand beside each other in this kitchen, making toast while we're still too sleepy to talk.

You and I can't make plans. But I still have goals. I'm okay with filing them under "someday." I'm a patient man.

Sleep tight.

S.

I finish reading the note with a lump in my throat. But I'm not too broken up to take another good look at that photo. I like what I see. Maybe I'm a reckless girl, but I want to stand in front of those windows and plan my weekend with Silas.

"And I'm dead," Becky announces. "No comment from me, because I have died."

Someone clears his throat. "Does that mean I can't ask you out?" asks our ever-present waiter. "Because I totally put my phone number at the bottom of this check."

Becky blinks up at him. "Oh, I think I can stay alive long enough for that."

"Good deal." He gives her another hot smile. "Call me tomorrow and we'll make a date."

She glances down at the check to read what he's written. "I'll do that, Carlos. I'm Becky by the way."

"It was a real pleasure meeting you, Becky." He gives her one last grin that's full of heat and promise. Then he walks away.

Becky lets out a happy squeak the moment he's out of earshot. "I feel lucky tonight."

"Because you're *getting* lucky soon."

"Was that way too easy?" she asks. "I should have made him work for it."

"Embrace the easy," I say. "Trust me, here. Making them work for it sometimes backfires." I have the scars to prove it.

"Right!" Becky claps her hands. "So does that mean we're moving to New York? I've always wanted to see shows on Broadway. And the pizza is really pretty great!"

"No! That's not what I was saying. It's not *that* easy."

"Isn't it? Let's review..." She gives me an appraising glance. "You're living in your cramped little studio right now, which is supposed to be temporary. You work for yourself and could easily wear those ratty slippers of yours in any city. Besides— think of all the miles you could put between you and Brett Ferris."

"He spends half his time in New York at the label."

"Fine." She waves away this thought with her bright red manicure. "He's not a factor. But somebody else is. A cute man —a *nice* man—wants to settle down with you. Why aren't you asking me to find you a plane ticket?"

"Because it's way too soon. We can't just move in together."

"Uh-huh. Aren't you the one who spent yesterday afternoon writing a song about this? *'Ask the universe,'* Dee. *'Anything could happen.'"*

"You are such a pain in my ass," I grumble. "Those are just lyrics. We all know that I'm more cynical than my music."

Becky frowns at me. "This is true. But it's also fixable.

There's really no reason why you can't make a grand gesture for Silas. You two can't do things the ordinary way. You're not ordinary people. You don't lead ordinary lives."

I put a pile of cash inside the bill wallet. I know what Becky is trying to say. And there are some pretty extraordinary things about my life. Like getting a table at Cactus when other people are waiting months for a reservation.

But the fact is this: on the inside I'm super ordinary. And this ordinary girl does not have the courage to up and move thousands of miles across the country to ask a man to love her. Even a man as great as Silas.

What if it didn't work out? I barely have roots in L.A., but I have none at all in Brooklyn.

"Look. Time to roll."

My reverie is ended by Becky's announcement that Mr. Muscles is now outside with the car. She shows me his text as proof. "Great." I gather myself together and follow her outside. She can't resist giving our waiter a cute little wave goodbye.

Outside, Mr. Muscles practically vaults out of the running car in order to escort me across those treacherous fifteen feet of busy Melrose sidewalk. I roll my eyes as he takes my elbow in hand.

"Please, miss. Spare some change?" I hear the rattle of coins in a cup.

Turning, I slow our progress. This causes my bodyguard to roll his eyes. At least we annoy each other evenly.

The panhandler is a youngish man with long hair and a tie-dye shirt.

And call me sexist, but I don't usually hand cash to men who look so healthy. This one, though? He happens to have very small baby sleeping on his forearm, her tiny head cupped in his palm.

There's a cardboard sign propped in front of him. *Just*

became a single parent. Wife OD'd. Need a bus ticket to South Dakota where family can help me.

"Oh man," Becky mutters, but I can't tell if she's moved by the story or just very intuitive about what will happen next.

Mr. Muscles nudges me toward the car, and I let him tuck me inside. But already I'm searching my bag for my checkbook.

"What if he spends it on drugs?" Becky asks, hopping into the other side. "At the very least you should write the check to Greyhound."

"I suppose that's a good point. Google it?"

"Ladies, we need to..." my bodyguard tries.

"In a *moment*," I demand in my best diva voice. Becky and I are both tapping at our phones. I'm pricing bus tickets to South Dakota.

"I'll be damned," Becky says. "You can pay by personal check if you buy your ticket in person at the station."

"Sweet." I'm already scribbling the fare onto the check. It's several hundred dollars.

I count out three twenty dollars bills and hand them to her with the check. "For food and diapers. Bus trips take days."

"But drugs..." she mumbles.

"You're too young to be so cynical."

"You're too cynical to tell me I'm too young." She gets out of the car anyway.

I watch through the tinted glass as she hands the man the check and the cash, and explains what to do. His eyes widen. And then he puts a hand in front of his eyes, and his shoulders shake.

So I look away, making myself very busy putting my checkbook away when she gets back in the car.

"Okay. Well. He was very moved," she says.

"Good."

We sail away from the curb on the perfect suspension of the

Mercedes I'm paying for. Nobody says anything for a few minutes.

"Why do you do that?" Becky asks finally. "You're super cynical. And then you give large sums of money to strangers. It doesn't make any sense."

"Sure it does. I have an unhealthy relationship with money. When I didn't have any, I was always embarrassed about it. And now that I have a bunch, that embarrasses me, too."

"That's kind of pathological."

I won't argue that point.

We pull up at Becky's a few minutes later. "Goodnight, honey," she says. "Sleep well and dream of hockey players."

"You too, sugar. Sleep well and dream of waiters with dark, soulful eyes."

"He *was* a looker," comes a mumble from the front seat.

My gaze locks with Becky's, and both of us nearly burst out laughing. Who knew Mr. Muscles had a thing for waiters? Who knew he had opinions at all?

She gives me a little wave and leaves. The car pulls away again, and I squint at the back of my driver's thick neck, wondering if I imagined that comment. "Mr. M, you don't usually offer your opinion. I'm startled."

"Nobody wants my opinion. I gotta tell you something, though. Bad news."

"Okay?" And I have a bad feeling that I know what he's going to say.

He glances at me briefly in the rearview mirror. "We got another napkin tonight."

"Ugh. From where? Who says?"

"That's the weird thing. I'm sitting there at the bar eating the world's most overpriced tacos. I get this text from Mr. Wilde."

That's the guy who owns the security company. "And?"

"It's a photo of a cocktail napkin he just pulled out of an

envelope. And it's exactly like the one under my soda at the bar."

"From...Cactus?"

"Yeah."

Chills run down the back of my neck. "But we were just there. Whoever sent it to my P.O. box would have to have sent it before tonight."

"Right. Yesterday at the latest. When did you make this dinner plan?"

"Um..." I close my eyes and try to think. "Last week, I guess. Becky and I read about it in *Time Out*, maybe? We decided to try it. I told her to make a reservation."

"Do you remember where you had this conversation?"

"Well, we were in the guitar shop. Or leaving it. But we mentioned it a few times since then. And..." My mind clicks through the possibilities. "Restaurants aren't private. Maybe someone saw the reservation."

"Was it in your name?"

"Maybe? It's new and trendy. Becky might have dropped my name to get that table."

"Then we can't do that anymore," he says immediately.

"So I guess I'm never eating out?"

"Use Becky's name."

"But...!" If I finish this sentence, I'm going to sound like the diva I always claim not to be. The truth, though? Sometimes it's useful to be Delilah Spark. I don't have to plan ahead. No restaurant will ever turn me away. "Right. Okay," I say glumly. Those napkins freak me out. "What did this one say?"

"'*Have a margarita with me.*'"

"I never order mixed drinks," I point out. "See? This guy doesn't know me."

"Well, I hope you're right about that," Mr. M says. "I really do."

SILAS

"I'm not usually so easily excited. But this could be a big deal," Delilah tells me.

"Yeah? That's great, baby. Tell me more." I'm walking through the lobby of the Bruisers headquarters, my phone pressed to my ear, my gym bag on my shoulder. When I push open the door, it's like stepping into the tropics. Brooklyn in August is pretty brutal. Good thing I'm about to get on a plane to California.

"You're probably busy, though. I could tell you tonight."

She's right, because in nine or ten hours, we'll be together. Finally. "Tell me now. I'm walking home. Besides—tonight I'll have other things on my mind. Rawrrrr," I growl.

The effect is awfully silly, and she laughs. "Okay, fine. Remember when I told you that my contract with the jerk was strange? There are loopholes that Charla is trying to exploit."

"Of course I remember. That's why I named your new band."

"Right, smart-ass. But the Sparkle Puppies are now on a permanent hiatus. Because the other loophole is for movie soundtracks. I can write for film without breaking my contract.

So that's what my genius of a manager found me. A savagely cool film gig."

"What kind of film?"

"It's based on a true story about the first woman to fly in combat. There's a female writer, a female director, and a female production team. It's going to be so amazing. Charla is trying to attach me to this project. It would be six new songs. There's no guarantee I'll get it, though."

"Of course you will. They'd be lucky to snag you. Come *on*." Who's better than Delilah?

"You are very loyal. But I have a certain sound, and if it doesn't match their vision, then they'll call someone else. This is going to be really high profile and they can have their pick of female recording artists."

"But you want this, right?" I'm already walking up Water Street, my building in view. Upstairs, I have to put a few more things in my suitcase and then call a car to the airport.

"I do want it. Not only does it get around Brett, but I'm excited for it. And I haven't felt jazzed up about something in so long."

I can hear it in her voice, too. "That is fantastic." *Come write those songs in Brooklyn.* I manage not to say that out loud, of course. But it's on my mind as I walk up three steps to my building.

Miguel—the concierge—holds the door. I give him a salute and march toward the elevators.

"Now tell the truth," Delilah says as I push the button. "Is your coach still pissed at you?"

"Eh," I say, unwilling to make it Delilah's problem. "He'll live." Even though I'd carried through with my promise to skate for all the rookie sessions, and even though he'd already approved it, Coach Worthington still gave me a bunch of guilt over my trip to California.

But it was only a couple of days, and the man would soon

forget all about this. Nobody was more dedicated than me. I always show up and work hard.

"I made a dinner reservation for tonight," she says as I step into the elevator.

"Yeah? Where?"

"Roadie Joe's."

"Really?" I laugh. "Okay. Are we going to eat at the bar for old time's sake? Or can we sit outside?"

"You can pick."

"Okay. Can't wait. I'd better go."

"Bye! Don't miss your flight."

"Never."

We hang up, and I'm smiling to myself as the elevator doors open on my floor.

———

Thirty minutes later, I'm basically ready. All I need is a carryon, because a trip to the beach doesn't require many clothes. All the important things fit into a small space—phone charger, bathing suit. A nice shirt to wear while I'm taking my girl out to dinner. A new box of condoms.

One last thing needs folding. It's a T-shirt I had made for Delilah. Okay—Heidi did the legwork to figure out where to have it printed. But it was my idea. It's black, with a pink design on the front. *Delilah and the Sparkle Puppies*.

Jason looks over my shoulder and laughs. "That came out well. I hope your girl likes it. Because my girl is a genius."

"Hey! I did the design myself. I drew the puppy freehand."

"Yeah, if this hockey thing doesn't work out, you can be her merch guy. Have a good trip, okay? I'm going for a run. I'll see you at practice when you get back."

"Thanks, man." He lifts a hand, and we high-five.

In the kitchen, my phone starts ringing.

"Want me to grab that?" Jason offers. "It's probably your driver."

"Sure. Thanks." I fold the T-shirt carefully and tuck it into my bag, then zip it up.

"Yeah, he's here," I hear Jason grunt. "Don't get your panties in a wad." He appears in front of me with a grumpy look on his face. He points at my phone and mouths, "*Some asshole.*"

I take the phone. "Hello?"

"Silas Kelly. Long time no speak."

My pulse jumps at the sound of Brett Ferris's voice. "How did you get this number?" is the first thing that comes out of my mouth.

"Really? That's your question? If I were you, I would want to know *why*, not how. But that was always your failing. You always focus on the wrong things. And when you figure out what's really important, it's always too late."

I'm standing in my own home, stunned and pissed off at once. "What are you playing at? Make this quick. I have a plane to catch."

"See, that's where you're wrong. You're not going to go to L.A."

The smug sound of his voice fills me with rage. "Of course I am." And how does he know my travel plans? Delilah must be right about her security team spying on her.

"You won't want to go after you hear what I have to say."

"Bullshit. Nothing you could say would make one difference to me." I take a deep breath and remind my body how to feel calm. Oxygen into the lungs. Looseness in the limbs. *We got this.* I'm not the same freaked-out kid that I used to be.

"No? I'm not so sure about that." He pauses, and I know manufactured drama when I hear it. "Delilah is at a crossroads right now," he says. "She's about to write her third album and launch her second."

"Sure, but I'm not stopping her," I argue.

"Yeah, you are," he argues. "You're a distraction. And I won't allow it."

"You won't *allow* it?" My voice sounds almost level. "She's not a child. You don't get to arrange her play dates."

"*You're* the child." His voice is hard. "You have no idea what's at stake for her. She can be a one-album wonder, or she can be great. But you and that pit bull of a manager need to back the fuck off."

"Or what?" I don't know what this temper tantrum is meant to accomplish.

"Simple. It's like this. I will not release her album so long as you are in her life."

"What? That album doesn't have the first thing to do with me."

"Like hell it doesn't. You're the guy whispering in her ear that she doesn't owe me anything."

"She doesn't," I snap, and then instantly regret it. I care too much. And now he knows it.

"Bullshit," he fires back. "I put too much time into this to let you walk away with it. You're just a piece-of-crap jock from a family of criminals, and I will let the world know."

"Uh-huh," I say, feeling suddenly calmer. "You played that hand before. And when I was in high school, I fell for it. But you don't get to play me twice. Tell whoever you want."

"Check your email."

"For what? I can't do that when I'm on the phone with you."

"Check it later, then. I just sent you a parole-release notification."

"A what?" But even as I ask the question, I realize what he means. "Wait, he's out?"

Brett's chuckle makes me want to lean over and throw up. Because he's done it again. He's two steps ahead of me. When I open that email I know what it will say. *Everett Joseph White is released on parole, subject to the following conditions...*

"When?" I ask through gritted teeth.

"Almost two months ago."

Two months. And I had no idea. I don't even bother to play it cool anymore. "Where did you learn this?"

"It's public record."

A few more gears click into place for me. My father's parole was just a lucky find for Brett Ferris. But it means that he went digging for something on me, and this just happened to pop up.

Unless it's not true.

Fuck, it probably is.

"So?" I say, unclenching the fist that I've made with my free hand. "Thanks for that fun little news nugget. But I still have a plane to catch." I have to talk to my mom, for one. Now more than ever.

"No. You don't go near Delilah. If you do, I won't release her album. And furthermore, I'll send someone to find your daddy and tell him your mother's brand-new name and where she lives."

My mouth goes dry.

"Just walk out of Delilah's life," Brett says. "No explanation. No blame. She's the biggest new voice to break out in a decade. She doesn't need you, anyway."

That is probably true. But it doesn't mean she doesn't want me. I find my voice. "You know, high school has been over for seven years. You and I are not in competition anymore."

"Yeah, sure," he says. "I already won."

There's a click as he disconnects the call.

I think I stand there for several minutes, adrift in the middle of my bedroom, wondering what the hell just happened. I've never understood Brett. Even when I thought we were playing the same game, he always went further than I expected a sane person would go. So I can't rule out that threat of him disclosing the whereabouts of my mother.

I need to talk to her. That's definitely a priority. But I can't call her yet until I process this. I can't be a panicked voice on the line, at least until I figure out whether it's the right time to panic. Who can look at this parole notification and tell me if it's real?

Carl Bayer. That's who. So after I spend one more minute on deep breathing, I call him.

He answers on the second ring. "Hey there, kid! I thought I might hear from you."

"Why?" My voice sounds strained.

"Because I sent your girl some security company names."

"Oh." *Your girl.* I feel a pain in my chest just thinking about her. "Thank you. But that's not what I'm calling about. I just had the weirdest run-in with her ex. I think I have a problem."

A beat of silence passes by. "How do you feel about a burger at Peter Luger's?"

"What?" I'm not even sure if he's talking to me right now.

"They have the best burger in Brooklyn. It's a half a pound of prime beef on a bun. And they only serve it at lunch. Go downstairs, get into a cab, and meet me over there in fifteen."

He hangs up.

Once again I stand there, contemplating all my life choices. I'm supposed to be heading to the airport right now. But I can't, because of Brett's highly specific threats. I can't stand to let that fucker win a round. Delilah is expecting me tonight, and now it looks like I'm not going to show.

That's exactly what Brett wants. I shouldn't give it to him. But the alternative is pretty terrible for two women I love.

I go downstairs and stick my arm in the air. A yellow cab

turns the corner and stops in front of me. "Peter Luger," I tell him as I slip into the back.

————

The largest burger I've ever seen in my life slowly disappears as I tell Carl the story.

He makes grumbling noises interspersed with chewing noises while I talk. "I don't know how the guy got your number," he grouses. "Team security and I are going to have to have a talk."

"That's the least of my problems," I tell him. "He threatened me, and I'm so angry I can't see straight."

"Yeah, I know," the older man says. "Take a breath and let me think this through."

There aren't enough deep breaths in the world to calm me down right now. Now that I've had a while to get over my shock, the solution seems no clearer. Meanwhile, I'm missing my flight. I haven't said a word to Delilah, but I'm itching to apologize. It would kill me to stand her up.

"Okay, we have to tackle this stepwise," Carl says. "First, I'm going to verify whether your father was actually released from prison. If he was, then we're going to think about his access to your mother."

"She legally changed both our names," I point out. Kelly is a name she chose out of the clear blue sky when I was three years old, and we moved from Florida to California. "Does that help?"

"It helps some, depending on how smart your father is, and whether your mother took advantage of special provisions that help the victims of crimes."

"We weren't officially the victims of any of his crimes. So that probably wasn't an option." Although my mother was so afraid of my father that we left in the night, driving cross country to avoid him. She never reported his abuse. He went to prison for different crimes.

"The fact that she moved is more useful than the name change," Carl says. "Parolees don't have resources to travel. They're required to stay in town and find a job, or risk going back to jail. A dumb man will ignore his parole officer. And a desperate man can hitchhike to California. But he'd have to be highly motivated to settle that old score."

That's what I can't predict. "I don't know my father at all. I don't know if he terrorized my mother out of a deep-seated obsession, or merely because she was convenient."

Carl nods, patting his mouth with the linen napkin. "So we'll get a Florida PI to check in on your father's situation."

"*Subtly,*" I add. "He can't know who's interested."

"What do you take me for?" The older man snorts. "I've been gathering intel since before you were born."

"Sorry," I say quickly.

He only laughs. "Don't be. It's okay to be worried about your mom. You and Brett Ferris aren't cut from the same cloth. That's why he's got you so riled up. It says a lot about you that you don't understand his methods."

"Which are?"

"When shit gets real, fear and intimidation are his go-to weapons. I need you to walk me back even further, here. When does the history between you two start? High school?"

"Exactly. Tennis team rivalry."

Carl Bayer nearly loses control over a sip of his beer and has to clamp a hand over his mouth while he laughs. "Tennis team?" he sputters eventually. "Rough sport."

"I know." I crack a smile, because it does sound ridiculous. "But we hated each other. He was slick and obnoxious, and he drove me crazy. I was scrappy and desperate and gave him hell. It was ugly."

"How ugly?"

"We both cheated. I'm not proud of it. He was really slimy with the line calls. In tennis you police yourself. So I sunk to his level. And I think it surprised him that I would do that."

"Hmm." Carl strokes his chin. "I think this guy has an entitlement complex. He probably assumed he earned those wins, even when he cheated. A guy who thinks the world owes him a victory always excuses his own behavior."

"That does sound like him." But I thought I deserved to win, too. Nobody worked harder than I did. I wanted the town's tennis scholarship so fucking bad. "It didn't matter, anyway. He outsmarted me. He asked me to meet him in a deserted location after a big tournament I'd just won. He said he had something to tell me."

"And you went?"

"Of course I did." I sigh. The teenaged Silas was too cocky to anticipate disaster. "I get there, and it takes him about two minutes to unhinge me. He tells me, 'I really think the scholarship committee should know that you're the son of a murderer. I'm gonna make sure they hear about it.'"

I put my fork down and sigh. I remember with perfect clarity how hot my anger ran at that moment. "I punched him."

"And that's what did you in, right?" Carl asks. Because the cues I missed in high school are already brutally obvious to him.

"Yes. There was a security camera. For the price of a broken nose, he eliminated me as a rival."

Carl shakes his head. "You weren't the first teenager to let your emotions get the better of you."

"I don't want to do it again. Help me see what the hell he's doing right now. I can pay whatever it costs..."

Carl holds up a hand. "Let's worry about that later. I'll find a smart guy in Florida to check on your father. I'll bill you for his hours. But I'm gonna take a look at Brett, too. We need to know why he's desperate enough to threaten you. There's a story there, and we don't know what it is."

"He's obsessed with Delilah."

"Possibly. But it might be a business issue, too. He needs her more than she needs him, and we want to know why. Threatening you is risky, right? Not to mention illegal. Your phone logged the call. No chance you recorded it?"

I shake my head. Will I ever stop getting played by this guy?

Carl takes out his trusty notebook, flips to a fresh page, and starts making notes. "I'll see what I can dig up about his business and run a credit check."

"That family is loaded," I point out.

"There's a lot of ways to be loaded. Brett might have leveraged himself. Or maybe he leveraged his pride instead of his cash. He lost his girlfriend, but also his star talent, right? Although if he's short on cash, it would explain a lot."

"If he's short on cash he could just release Delilah's album," I point out. "Problem solved."

"Maybe." Carl keeps scribbling. "When a man acts crazy, there's often a very sane reason. Desperation makes people ugly. Let's find out what he's so desperate for."

"Delilah. He lost her. Now he wants her back."

Carl stops writing and looks up at me. "Let's hope it's not that simple. She's safer if this is just about money."

Shit. "I can't just stand her up, Carl. I have to go to California."

He puts down the pen. "Give me twenty-four hours to do some research. If your girl loves you, she'll listen when you explain it all later. And give Brett a minute to think that he's won. It'll calm him down."

"So right now I should just…"

"Do nothing. Say nothing. Her security team is spying, right? They might be reading her texts. I know this will hurt worse than a bee sting on your ballsack. But I need twenty-four or forty-eight hours of your silence to figure out how big a threat this guy is."

I hate everything about this. "When she starts texting me, what the hell am I going to say?"

"You're going to tell her that Coach changed his mind. It's not even much of a stretch. Now eat that." He points at my burger. "And let me get to work."

DELILAH

I'm sitting at the bar at Roadie Joe's. The place looks exactly the same, except for the most important detail. Silas isn't here. He stood me up tonight. My only date is Mr. Muscles.

I take another swig of beer, and I still can't believe that Silas stood me up.

His text didn't even roll in until I'd sat down at a table outside, wearing a low-cut dress and a flower in my hair. A goddamn flower, like somebody's prom date.

I feel so stupid right now.

Sorry, something's come up. Coach needs me here. My apologies.

That was it.

I'd read it three times, looking for a real explanation. Then —even though only assholes make phone calls from the middle of a crowded restaurant—I'd tried his number.

No pickup.

Trying not to panic, I'd ordered food just to give the hovering waitress something to do. And while I ate, I'd sent Silas a barrage of texts.

It isn't like you to cancel with a text.

What is going on?
Is this really about hockey?
If something is wrong. I need to know.
And, finally, *Is it something I said?*

When I'd read back through my texts, I'd wanted to throw up. If they were song lyrics, I'd be panned for writing the most overused clichés on the planet.

My heartache is so very unoriginal. But that doesn't make it hurt any less.

And while I ate food I could barely taste and sat there quietly freaking out, people kept stopping on the sidewalk to point at me and whisper to their friends.

I can't even have my heart broken in private.

Eventually I'd paid the bill. There was still no word from Silas. But instead of letting Mr. Muscles steer me into the car, I'd paused on the threshold to the inside bar. The same dim room looked back at me, mostly empty. Just like the olden days.

I knew I should have gone back to my empty hotel room. But I couldn't face it. There's even a freaking candle on the bedside table, because I'd discovered my inner romantic just hours before Silas decided I'm not worth the trouble.

So I took a barstool instead, ordering a third beer that I'd opened myself. And wondered what the hell was really happening tonight.

It's so tempting to leap to the worst conclusion. *He changed his mind. I'm too much trouble. I didn't respond enthusiastically about the idea of living in Brooklyn.*

But it's too soon to beat myself up like this. The last time I thought Silas stood me up on purpose, I was wrong. And I don't want to be that girl anymore—the frightened one who always assumes the worst. For once I can just take a fucking breath and give the man more than two hours to explain himself.

"Can I get you anything else?"

I look up into the somewhat familiar eyes of the guy behind

the bar. His name tag says Danny. "Have you heard from Ralph?" I blurt out. They were friends. I'm sure of it.

Danny's eyes widen. "He doesn't work here anymore."

"I get that," I say quietly. "But we were supposed to meet here tonight."

"Oh," he says slowly. "I didn't know that. He hasn't been in here since last summer."

"Right. Okay." I feel like an idiot now.

"Funny thing, though? It was me who was supposed to tell you that the surfing lesson was canceled. Three years ago? I'm the one he sent to tell you. But I was too late."

"Oh." It comes out sounding as wounded as one syllable can. "But I waited."

"Yeah, we got slammed and my dad was yellin' away in the kitchen." He hooks a thumb toward the open window to the kitchen. "I didn't get to you in time. I'm sorry."

"It's fine," I say quickly. Although there's no telling what would have happened if I got that message. Or if I'd given my favorite bartender my phone number in the first place.

Maybe everything. Or maybe nothing. We might have flamed out a long time ago.

I'm so confused right now. And heartsick. I want to go home to L.A. where my bunny slippers are waiting. I'd bail on this concert if it wouldn't make Brett irate. I can't afford that right now.

I'm worried about Silas. I'm worried about my career. But I'm smart enough now to realize nothing will be settled tonight. "Can I have the check?" I ask.

"For a beer?" Danny waves a hand. "It's on me, Delilah. And if I see Ralph, I'll tell him he's an asshole." Danny smiles, like we're sharing a joke.

If I'm lucky, we are.

An hour later I'm sitting on the hotel bed, eating overpriced mini bar snacks like they're going out of style. There's a candle in the trashcan in the bathroom.

This is what wallowing looks like—peanut M&M wrappers and bad TV.

My phone rings, and I grab it with the desperation of a Titanic passenger diving for a life preserver.

But the call is not from Silas. It's from Brett. I drop it on the silky white hotel comforter and let it go to voicemail.

He leaves a message. I manage to ignore it for a few minutes. But I'm a girl who's desperately in need of some distraction. And it's not like he can ruin my night. That's already been accomplished. So I mute the TV and play the message.

"Hey Delilah," he says as a breeze scrapes past the microphone. *"I'm on the beach, looking at the stars. And I have regrets. Big ones. I know you're not very happy with me. Losing you is something that I haven't handled very well. I know that's all my fault."*

He heaves a sigh that's very unlike him.

"But I'm standing on the beach where it all started, and I want you to know that I'm done trying to hold on to something I already wrecked. Let's release your album next month, okay? Meet me for a drink tomorrow and we'll pick a date. We'll put Becky on speakerphone so she can get all the details."

My mouth falls open. But the message isn't quite finished.

"I just want you to know that I'm sorry. And your new album is going to do amazing things. And I hope someday you can look back on this and remember some of the good times we had. Goodnight, Delilah. I'll see you tomorrow night."

The message ends. My heart is beating double speed. Brett is finally giving me the thing that I want most in the world.

Except it's no longer the thing that I want most, is it?

Only a diva would still be upset right now.

I guess I'm a diva.

SILAS

I end up flying to California one night later. But the thrill is gone, because Carl still hasn't given me the go-ahead to tell Brett to fuck off.

So instead of finding Delilah, I'm sitting at my mother's kitchen table, a glossy brochure spread out in front of us. "The security system works by registering the opening and shutting of doors and windows in your home. The contacts look like this." I point at a photo of a small device mounted in a doorjamb.

My mom wrinkles her nose.

"If you're home alone and a door opens, there's a little beep to alert you. If you think it's an intruder, you can hit the panic button, and the cops will be notified immediately. And if you're not home, you'll get an alert from an app on your phone. The system even has its own backup power source. So it works when the power goes out."

I'm sure my mom has seen the same movies I have. Everyone knows the bad guys always cut the power first.

Mom reaches out and folds the pamphlet closed again.

"Sweetheart, I really don't think this is necessary. I don't want to live like a prisoner in my own home."

"You won't be a prisoner," I argue. "And hopefully none of this is necessary. But I would feel better if you were protected."

"Because then you're going to tell Brett Ferris where he can shove it, right?"

Have I mentioned that my mom is awesome?

"I haven't decided what I'm doing yet." Not that a second punch to Brett's face isn't tempting. "Carl Bayer is still gathering information about Dad, and about Brett's rationale for threatening me."

She gives me a sad smile. "Brett Ferris and your father have a lot in common."

"What? How do you figure?" One of them is an ex-con with violent tendencies. The other one is a rich snake in preppy clothing. I really don't see the resemblance.

"They've both got us sitting here, looking at overpriced home-security systems, trying to stay out of their way. And you and I have done nothing wrong."

She has a point. But that doesn't make this easier.

"Go find your girl," Mom says, covering my hand. "It's not like you to back down from a fight."

"Oh, I'm not," I promise her. Although I've learned to pick my moments. "But I can't go in with guns blazing. Last time I lost my cool at Ferris, it changed everything."

"For the better, maybe," Mom says. "You love hockey, and you love Brooklyn. Tennis was such a lonely sport. All that pressure and nobody at your back."

"Who's side are you on here?" I joke.

"Yours, baby boy." She beams at me. "But you were *born* a goalie—always the responsible one, making sure everyone else is okay." She gives the security-system pamphlet a shove. "You're allowed to look out for your own needs, you know. Be selfish. Take more than your share. Your mother will be just fine. I still keep a baseball bat under my bed. And I'm not afraid to use it."

The idea of my mom fighting off an attacker with a baseball bat makes me want to hurl. She and I are definitely going to talk about that security system again soon.

"Now go find your girl. Or go see Danny at the bar. He's a co-owner of the place now. He and his dad are in business together."

"That's cool. I guess I could go see Danny. Maybe it will take my mind off everything." I can't deny that I'm drawn to the idea of visiting Roadie Joe's again. It was in that bar that I fell in love for the first time, even if I never called it that.

My heart knew, though.

"You want a ride?" my mom asks. "I assume you'll have a few beers. You could Uber home. It's pricey."

I'm sure I could afford it. But if my mom wants to give me a ride into Darlington Beach? I'm not turning that down. "You're the best. Let me just change my shirt."

———

By the time I order my mojito, it's already nine thirty. The young stranger behind the bar reaches for the superfine sugar and the pile of mint leaves without looking at me.

"Sorry, man," I say. "I know there are easier drinks to make. I used to have your job."

He looks up. "Really? You don't mean here."

"That's exactly what he means!" booms my friend Danny's voice. He comes up behind me to clap me on the shoulder. "The famous one returns to visit the little people he left behind."

"Oh, please." I roll my eyes. But I don't mind his humor. Walking in here tonight felt like walking into my past. I was so angry at the world last time I worked behind that bar.

My mom might be right about a couple of things. Hockey —

after a rough start—has been good to me. And I need to lighten up a little.

"Tell me everything," Danny says. "What was up with that first-round elimination? What was up with your patchy playoffs beard? I have so many questions."

The kid behind the bar is looking at me differently now. I'm no longer the guy who ordered a time-consuming cocktail, but rather someone he ought to recognize.

Sorry, kid. I'm not really that interesting.

"Enough about me," I say, patting the bar stool next to me. "I hear you're a businessman now. Did drink prices go up? Do people have to kiss your ass now?"

The bartender snickers.

"Yes, and yes." He sits down next to me. "Life is good, Ralph. But I never wanted out of Darlington Beach, like some people." He nudges me in the elbow. "I like it here. My hours kind of suck, but it's like hosting a party all year long. And I don't have to cook my own food."

"Unless the chef calls in sick, and then you have to cook everyone's food," says the kid. His name tag reads: *Dick*.

"Let me take a wild guess, here," I say. "Your name isn't really Dick."

The kid grins as he squeezes limes into my drink. "So you really did work here."

"Absolutely."

"You're the hockey player, right? I heard about you. Quit before the dinner rush one night because you got called up to play."

I let out a bark of laughter. "That's what I'm famous for? Leaving the bar unattended? I suppose it could be worse."

"Yeah," Danny agrees. "But we're going to have to revisit that summer in a second, okay? Let me just make sure the kitchen is still on top of things, and I'll be right back. Pour me a beer, Dickie." He zips away, the way a restaurateur having a good night should do.

As my drink lands in front of me, I pull out my phone to check my email. There's a new message from Carl waiting, so I open that sucker right up.

He's a man who says a lot in few words.

Daddy is now a holy roller. Clean prison record the last ten years. Started their prayer group. Joined a megachurch in Florida the day he got out. Bags groceries for minimum wage. Living with his sister. That's all we can learn from afar. I don't rate him as a big threat.

But Brett is a mess. His business unit is failing. He's in default on the loans he took out to partner with MetroPlex. His other artists aren't bringing in cash. Delilah is all he's got. The guy can't afford to sit on D's album. Don't know why he's still doing that, unless he thinks she'll blink first.

I'm doing a little more digging. Hang tight for tonight.

"Hey."

I look up as Danny sits down beside me again and takes a swig of beer. "Hey yourself. Crazy night? The music festival is kicking in already?"

"Yeah. These next six weeks are going to make my year, though." He beats on his chest with one fist. "I'm ready! Bring it, drunk music lovers! I am here for you!"

I laugh, because Danny hasn't changed since our high school days.

"You could put on an apron, you know," he says. "Stop drinking sissy drinks and help a guy out. I think you still owe us at least a shift."

"I'm on vacation. I'm supposed to be having fun."

As if I could, though. Delilah is somewhere in this town right now, and I'm supposed to be beside her.

"Here's what I need to know, then." Danny sets his beer down on a cocktail napkin. "Why was Delilah Spark sitting right where you are and asking me about you last night?"

I actually stab myself in the chin with my straw as I lift my drink. "What? Really?"

Danny gives me a look that suggests I'm as pathetic as I feel right now. "I must have looked familiar to her, because she asked me point blank if I'd heard from you."

My flinch is swift. "Yeah, that's a long story I'm still trying to sort out. We're kind of a thing. Or I hope we're a thing."

"*Dude.*" The young bartender gapes at me. "That's even cooler than being a hockey player. She's *hawt*. Little weird to order your beers unopened, but…" He shrugs. "Stars gotta be a little eccentric, right?"

I sigh.

Danny clicks his tongue. "Somebody looks bummed. Did you two fight?"

"Like I said, it's complicated. And it's been that way since I met her three years ago right here." I pat the glossy wood surface of the bar.

"Nothing comes easy to you," Dicky says. "And I mean you specifically. Always gotta fail spectacularly before things start looking up."

That sounds accurate.

"Gotta say, she looked pretty sad, too," the chatty bartender offers. "Her bodyguard kept trying to get her to leave, but she stayed a while before settling up. Good tipper, though."

Goddamn it. I hate the image of her sitting here alone, wondering why I stood her up.

"Does this have anything to do with Brett Ferris?" my oldest friend asks. "I heard they broke up, and he's not happy about it."

"Sort of," I admit, looking over my shoulder just in case. Darlington Beach is a really small town.

"Now that dude is *not* a good tipper." The bartender grins. "Not a half hour after Delilah Spark left with her bodyguard, that asshole comes in. Sits down right there." He points at a barstool. "Orders a club soda." He rolls his eyes. "Leaves me fifty cents because he's too lazy to pick up his change. And then? He takes a stack of cocktail napkins and tucks them into his pocket, like somebody's grandma." The kid mimes this part. "Like he's too cheap to buy his own. Rich people are the weirdest."

Danny chuckles, and I sort of chime in. But my mind is stuck on something he just said. *Cocktail napkins.* They're pretty much useless, unless you want to advertise your bar, and catch the condensation that rolls off your beer glass.

Or if you want to be a creepy stalker and terrify someone.

My body goes totally cold. I set my half-full cocktail down carefully. "Did he leave after that?" I ask, and my voice sounds tinny.

"Yup." The kid mops the bar. "Good riddance."

I've heard enough. "Danny, I think I have to go find my girl."

"Aw." He claps me on the back. "Would you please come in for lunch tomorrow, though? I can take an hour off to hang with you."

"Sure," I say absently. "Sounds great." I pull my wallet out as I get to my feet.

"Your money is no good here," Danny says.

I toss a twenty onto the bar. "That's for Dick-who-isn't-really-a-Dick, then. See you boys tomorrow."

And I run out of there and into the salty air of Darlington Beach. I need to find Delilah. Right away. I know which hotel she's staying at, of course. It's about a half mile away.

I break into a jog.

DELILAH

"Charla is not going to like this," Becky points out as I slip on my shoes. "She wouldn't want you to negotiate anything without her."

"I won't," I insist. "And I'll use her as an excuse if he pressures me." I tuck my hotel key into my clutch. "But I think Brett *needs* to release *Lucky Hearts*. Maybe he can't afford to wait any longer. And if he can save face by meeting with me in person instead of dealing with a snarling manager, then I will throw him this bone."

Becky flops backward on my hotel bed. "He wants to throw you a bone, all right. His."

"Not happening." I run a Chapstick over my lips. "Doesn't this outfit say, 'casual but not offering anything'?" I look down at my plain black top and unassuming jeans.

"Sure. But that man doesn't read signals very well. Please text me if you need backup of any kind."

"Don't worry so much. I can handle myself, you know."

"Call me when you're back. We can watch some bad TV together and not think about tomorrow at all."

My stomach dips at the thought of opening the music

festival without Silas. I want him in the first row, and I want my surfing lesson.

There's a tap on the door. "Car is downstairs, miss."

For fuck's sake, we could just walk. Everything in Darlington Beach is walkable. I miss walking places without the hulk in the hallway. "Coming," I say, because you have to choose your battles. "Bye, Beck. Find us a movie."

"Will do," she says with a sigh.

———

Five minutes later we pull up at the Ferris beach mansion. My phone has buzzed twice during the short ride. But I don't check it. Not yet. I want those calls to be from Silas. And if they're not, I'll be heartbroken all over again.

I don't have time to be heartbroken. I need to focus. So the calls can wait.

Mr. Muscles opens the car door for me, even though I could do it myself. "I'll wait outside, miss."

"Thank you. This shouldn't take all that long." I walk up to the big oak door and knock, hoping that Brett's parents aren't around. They never liked me very much, and I'm sure they like me even less now.

When the door opens, it's just Brett standing there, looking a little sheepish. It may be the only time I've ever seen him without a perfectly confident expression on his face, honestly.

I square my shoulders. This bodes well for me. "Hi," I say in as friendly a voice as I can summon.

"Hi, sweetheart. It's good of you to show up. I know I haven't been easy lately."

Somehow I rein in my desire to agree with him. "I'm not always the easiest, either. But I'm excited to talk about the release."

"I'll bet you are." He runs a hand through his hair, and it

sticks up on top when he's done. It makes him look like a little kid and oddly vulnerable. "Come through to the sunroom and we'll compare calendars. How does your September look?"

"It looks great if we're going to release an album. I was going to do some more collaborating, but that can all be pushed back. I can make myself available for promo."

"Good, good," he says, leading me into his parents' sunroom. The last streaks of pink light the sky. If it were still daylight, I would be able to see their million-dollar views of the beach from here.

I used to be so intimidated by this house and this family. That must be part of why I let Brett snow me for so long. I believed the lie that says rich people have the most value.

But it isn't true. I've been dirt poor and filthy rich. And I've been the same person the whole time.

We sit down on different parts of the L-shaped sofa. I take out my notepad and a pen, but then rest it on my lap. "How've you been?" I ask, playing nice.

"All right. Can't complain." He clears his throat. "You?"

"Working. Busy. You know me, I'd rather write songs in my bunny slippers than do practically anything else." I'm a liar, though. I've spent the whole summer believing that there was something bigger on the horizon for me. Something better than just success.

Brett doesn't need to know that, though. Tonight I'm all business.

He pulls out his phone. "I'll want to know what Becky thinks of a Thursday release. It will hurt your first week's Billboard ranking. But we'll get a lot of attention for jumping out ahead of everyone else."

I jot *Thursday release?* on my notepad. This is so civilized.

"If we launch next month, we'll use the short timeframe to our advantage," Brett says. "We'll play it up as a surprise release. And we'll just squeak into the Grammy eligibility year."

My heart flutters just hearing the word *Grammy*. "Who are we competing against in September? There must be a bunch of people pushing out albums in front of the cutoff."

"I made a list." He offers me his phone.

Each week in September is listed with new music launches tallied underneath. "The second week would be best, right? I'd rather go up against a big hip-hop album than those solo artists."

"Agreed," Brett says, retrieving his phone. "So we're looking at Thursday the thirteenth, or Friday the fourteenth."

I scribble that down, too. It's only a month away! I'm getting happy chills just thinking about it. A new single, out in the world. It's terrifying and wonderful all at the same time.

"Our in-house publicist will get a lot of inquiries," he says. "Those will be referred to Becky. Is there any new media on your no-fly list?"

I shake my head. "Bring it. I won't enjoy doing interviews, but I know it's important." I need him to know that I'm willing to be a team player for this release. It's crucial to both of us, no matter how awkward our history makes this.

He sits back on the sofa and gives me a sad smile. "Okay. I guess there weren't that many details after all. The grunts are going to handle the rest."

That's what Brett calls everyone who isn't a CEO or a star. A *grunt*. I hate that term. And I hate how revealing it is about him. This man has more red flags than a communist-party parade, and I ignored them all.

But now I plaster a smile on my face, anyway. I've just got to get through this meeting.

"There's only one more detail," he says.

"Hmm?" My phone vibrates again with an incoming call, distracting me. I'm not going to look.

"I really need you to sign this."

When I look up, he's placing a file folder on the coffee table. He flips open the cover. It's a contract.

My heart drops with a thunk that's probably audible. "Brett, don't do this. We're not having this fight again."

"I never wanted to fight," he says in a low voice. "So let's not. But I need your third album."

"Why would I ever—"

"Just read it, Delilah. I put in a reversion clause. The language won't allow us to hold back the third album. Or it's automatically yours. There's no way for you to lose out."

Suddenly I'm blinking back hot tears. "But you already did that to me on *this* album! Why would I *ever* trust you?"

"It was a mistake," he says. "I apologize. I was so upset at losing you, Dee. I went a little crazy."

"You know I can't sign this," I say as calmly as I can possibly muster. "Charla Harris will have to do a full contract review. And my second album needs to be out before I'll even consider it."

Brett drops his head. It's the first time I've ever seen him look beaten. "Okay," he says simply. "Okay."

Nearly sagging with relief, I close the folder and rest a palm on it. "I'll FedEx this to Charla first thing tomorrow." As if I'd ever sign it.

Brett stands up with a sigh. "Something to drink?" He paces toward the mini fridge in the corner. That's another thing I learned from Brett's family—that rich people like their beverages to be available anywhere. "I got a couple of those Mexican sodas you like."

"Thank you," I say automatically. I'm doing the math on how many more minutes I have to pretend we're still friendly.

He brings me the bottle, unopened of course. Then he opens a beer for himself. "To *Lucky Hearts*," he says. "May it top the charts for weeks." He raises his beer, as if to make a toast.

I hastily twist the top of my soda bottle. It doesn't quite hiss as loudly as a soda should, but the familiar scent of watermelon is appealing. I stopped drinking these because they reminded me of Brett.

He's waiting. I touch the bottle to his and fake one more smile. "To *Lucky Hearts*."

Brett holds my eyes as he takes a swig. So I do the polite thing and mirror him. As I swallow, though, I know that something is wrong. The taste is wrong. Salty and strong. I set the bottle down with a thunk on the coffee table.

Oh shit. I need to get out of here.

SILAS

Delilah does not answer her phone. I waste precious time hitting redial. And when I inquire at the hotel desk, I'm told Delilah isn't registered.

Of course she's not. They would have used someone else's name.

It's only then that I wise up and call Becky. She answers on the first ring. "Silas? You have some nerve."

"I know. But where is she? It's important."

Becky grumbles, "She went to the jerk's house to talk about her album launch. That's what happens when you cancel on her—"

"Got to go," I interrupt. "Talk later." After disconnecting, I shove the phone in my pocket and hightail it out of the hotel, heading down toward the water.

I reach the sandy beach and keep on going. It isn't far to the Ferris house, and this is the most direct route. How many times did I do this run in high school? Hundreds? Running in the sand is great resistance for the thighs and glutes. I have to stop and burn a few seconds kicking out of my shoes and socks, but then I'm tearing down the beach, past the mansions.

This was always my view of Darlington Beach—jogging past other peoples' dreamhouses. Beautiful, but so out of reach. When I met Delilah, I still had that chip on my shoulder. I still felt like an outsider, even though I'd lived here most of my life.

None of that matters anymore. There's just the cool sand and my pounding heart. I need to see her. I need to know she's okay. And then I need to tell her my new theory about her stalker.

Maybe I'm wrong, but I can't afford to be cautious anymore. I'll hire a bodyguard for my mom if I have to. Tonight Delilah will know how much I care.

So will Brett Ferris. But that can't be helped.

The Ferris house comes into view, lit up and beautiful. It has a privacy hedge, but beach houses aren't fortresses, no matter how ritzy. Nobody wants to spoil the ocean view.

As I approach the hedge, I look up at the glassed walls of what must be an impressive, elevated sitting room. There's movement, and I realize it's the vertical blinds. They're moving around a mechanized track, slowly closing off the view into the house. In seconds I won't be able to see inside. So I jump straight up for a desperate glimpse before it's all closed off.

My view lasts only a split second. Delilah is sitting on a sofa, her head in her hands, dark hair cascading over her shoulders. And Brett is leaning over her, holding a pen.

What the actual fuck?

Seconds later, I'm testing sections of the hedge, looking for a way in. I get impatient and force the stiff branches apart, hurling my body at the narrow opening until I fall clumsily onto the patio on the other side.

It hurts, but I'm a hockey player, so I don't really care. Lurching to my feet, I look up at the windows. The blinds are closed, swinging gently. I creep sideways toward a planter at the patio's edge. Would it hold my weight?

A hand clamps over my mouth. "Don't scream," whispers a male voice. "I'll get her for you."

Shock makes me immobile for a split second. I jerk violently around, elbow first, intending to catch my assailant in the face.

He anticipates me, dodging the blow. I get a glimpse of his face—it's the bodyguard, the one Delilah calls Mr. Muscles. "What the—"

"Hush!" he hisses. "I'm going inside to get her. Where's your car?"

"Don't have a car."

He pulls a key fob out of his pocket and thrusts it into my hand. "You're taking her to the E.R."

"And you?" My brain is still playing catch-up.

"Waiting with *him*. For the police. I think he *drugged* her." The look of revulsion on the big man's face probably matches my own. "Come on."

I follow him around the side of the house to a door. He pushes me aside, out of sight, then knocks loudly. "Delilah!" he yells. "We got a situation."

Nothing happens. I count out far too many of my rapid heartbeats, and still there's no movement on the other side of the door. "I'm breaking a window," I announce.

"No," he whispers. "You're invisible, you hear me? He won't let you in. But he'll open the door for me." He pounds on the door again. "If you guys don't respond, I gotta call the cops," he yells.

Hurried footsteps are the immediate response. Just before the door opens, Mr. Muscles levels me with a glare that says, *Don't move yet or I'll snap you in half.*

"What's the matter?" Brett's voice demands. "You're interrupting a meeting."

"Emergency," the bodyguard says, pushing his way inside. "Gotta see my girl."

"She's not *your* girl," Brett snarls.

There's a crash, followed by a shout and a thunk—as if something is hitting the floor. I think it might be Brett.

That's all the invitation I need. I yank the door open again and charge inside. The bodyguard is standing over Brett, who's sprawled on the floor. "Don't move, fucker," he growls down at him. "Or I *will* kill you."

I'm already past them both, heading for the front of the house. My heart is in my mouth as I reach the bright room where Delilah is slumped sideways on the couch.

"Jesus, baby," I whisper as I scoop her up into my arms. "I'm so sorry. But we're out of here now."

Her eyes flicker open, but they don't seem to register much before closing again.

I carry her into the kitchen, where the bodyguard is now sitting on Brett's back, dialing his phone. "Go," he says. "The hospital is—"

"I know where the hospital is." I'm already carrying her out the door and toward the shiny rental sedan in the driveway. Delilah's head lolls against my shoulder, and her eyes are slits. But she's not all the way unconscious. So I don't panic. Much.

"It's...a drug," she slurs.

"I know," I say, lifting her higher onto my body as I approach the car. I brace my hip against the vehicle and awkwardly fumble for the door handle on the passenger side. "You'll feel better soon," I promise both of us.

"Don't let me go to sleep," she begs. "Don't want to lose time."

"Okay," I babble. "I promise. I'm going to buckle you in, okay?"

"Don't leave me here."

"I won't. Never again. We're going to drive away now." I kick the door open and slide her onto the seat, buckling her in. Then I stand back to shut the door.

Her eyes open all the way, and they're filled with terror. "Wait!"

"I'm not leaving you. Just jumping in on the other side." I close the door, run around the front of the car, and slide into the driver's seat. A tear tracks down her cheek.

My thumb swipes it away. "I'm not leaving you, okay?"

"You did."

"Big mistake," I say, pressing the car's start button. "Never again."

I drive like an asshole to the medical center. Good thing it's only a few miles down the highway. I park in front and run through the doors marked EMERGENCY with Delilah in my arms. This guarantees that I have everyone's attention. Nurses come running, and someone finds a gurney.

"Don't leave me," she mumbles, eyes closed.

"Still here," I promise, and I don't let up even when the nurse asks me to leave the exam cubicle. "No can do," I say, holding Delilah's hand.

The medical team asks a whole lot of questions, not many of which I can answer. Did I see the drug? No. Was it a powder or a liquid? No idea.

They do some tests. Apparently, the available antidotes are almost as unpleasant as the drug itself, so the protocol is to monitor Delilah's heart rate and breathing.

There are machines for this, but I'm their backup. I watch each of her slow breaths and hold her hand.

Becky arrives next, summoned by Mr. Muscles. "Omigod!" she wails when she sees Delilah stretched out on the E.R. bed. "I knew something was off. I feel terrible."

That pretty much sums me up, too.

Eventually, the cops arrive. I don't have any idea how much time has passed. Becky takes my place beside Delilah, and I let the cops interrogate me in an office down the hall.

"Tell us everything that happened at the Ferris residence," they say.

It doesn't take long, since I didn't see much.

"I think he wanted her to sign something," I tell them at the end. "He was trying to give her a pen."

They can't give me any information, so I give them all my contact details and go back to Delilah's side. She hasn't spoken in a while. All I can do is sit and hold her hand, watching her chest rise and fall slowly. She seems to fade in and out of consciousness. But her pulse monitor gives a steady rhythm, so the nurse says I'm not allowed to panic.

"We're going to admit her for observation," a doctor says at some point.

"He stays," Delilah says, even though I thought she was asleep.

"Okay, honey," a nurse agrees. "Let's get you upstairs."

When I stand up to accompany them, my body is as stiff as a ninety-year-old's. I groan, and the nurse clucks her tongue. "Are you going to let me look at all those scratches now? There's one nasty one over your eye."

Delilah's eyes pop open suddenly. "Who hurt you?"

"The shrubbery," I admit. "I kinda dove through the privacy hedge. If there are security cameras, the police are probably laughing their asses off right now."

She actually gives me a faint smile as the gurney rolls toward the elevators. But I don't deserve it. Not after leaving her to fend for herself with Brett Ferris.

It's going to be a long time until I get over this.

DELILAH

When I wake up, I'm in a strange room, staring at a strange ceiling. It's late morning, judging from the bright sunlight coming through the window.

I have no memory at all of how I got here. Yet the creep-tastic sensation of having lost time clings to me like a bad dream.

"Holy shit," I rasp, with a voice that sounds like I haven't used it for a year. "Not again. Fuck my life."

"Sweetheart," says a calm voice. "You're fine. Everything is okay."

I turn my head, and the room spins. A woman sits in the chair beside me. She's knitting a sock with yarn the color of a tropical sea.

Weirdly enough, the sight of her calms me right down. In the first place, knitting ladies are a benevolent force in the universe. And there's something in her steady gaze that's familiar to me. "Who...are you?"

"Marie Kelly. My son refused to go and lie down for a few hours until I promised to sit here with you."

My son. "You're Silas's mom?" I blink. She looks too young to be his mother. But now I realize why she's so familiar. Those kind eyes.

She nods.

Several things fall into place for me. First, I just cursed up a storm in front of Silas's mom. Second, it's Silas who deserves all my cursing. That man stood me up, and I'm not over it.

Except... Something tickles the back of my disoriented consciousness. He was here with me. At this hospital, I think? I remember strong arms circling me. No—*carrying* me. But where? The last thing I remember clearly is...

Brett's house.

"Omigod." A shiver runs through me. "He *drugged* me. That bastard." My voice is an angry scrape. My memory is like a kaleidoscope. Colorful but fractured. Silas carried me out of Brett's house. I have no idea how he got there, or why he showed up. But I do remember demanding that he never leave me again.

Hi, subconscious. Nice of you to speak up when I'm drugged.

"How can I help you, honey?" Mrs. Kelly asks. "Would you like a drink of water?"

"F—heck yes," I say, nearly dropping another f-bomb. I'm so thirsty.

She lifts a small bottle of water out of her bag. "Silas said you would need to open this yourself." She shows me the top. The seal is unbroken.

Silas left me an unopened bottle of water and instructions for his mom?

My heart melts a little. I'm very eager to hear why Silas disappointed me earlier this week. And maybe I'm insane for having romantic thoughts about him while recovering in a hospital room from *a poisoning by my ex-lover.*

But none of that matters to my heart. I still trust Silas. I don't know if that's a good thing or not, but it's true.

She hands me the water, and I twist the top. Or I try to. But

—good lord—I have no grip strength. I let out a little squeak of dismay as the water bottle remains stubbornly closed. "Could you..." I stop. I haven't let anyone open a bottle for me in so very long.

Yet Ms. Kelly reaches over and gives it a quick twist. I hear the snap of the plastic seal. And I don't even have the energy to feel phobic about it. I remove the cap and lift that bottle to my parched lips. I drink so quickly that I end up coughing.

"Oh dear," Silas's mom says. She steadies the bottle in my hand while I lean forward like a geriatric patient and try to expel the water droplets from my trachea.

A man runs into the room so fast that he's a blur. He skates to a stop beside my bed. I open watery eyes and look up to find Silas. "Are you choking? Is she okay?" he barks.

"She's fine," his mother says calmly. "As fine as someone can be who tries to drink water lying down." She hits a button somewhere and the back of my hospital bed slowly begins to elevate. I get control over my lungs, slowly.

Becky is the next person to dart into my room. "Omigod are you okay?"

"Yup," I cough. "Never better."

Silas flinches and his mom laughs. Then Mrs. Kelly stands up. "I think I'll let you all take it from here. Nice meeting you, Delilah. Let's do this again when you're feeling a little better."

"Sounds like a plan," I rasp. "My voice is so shot." And then it hits me. The concert! I'm supposed to sing tonight. "Holy shit, it's Friday!" I wheeze.

"Easy," Silas says, his warm hand on my bare arm. "The concert is postponed."

"Until when?" I croak.

"Whenever," Becky says with a wave of her hand. "The music festival lasts through next month. If you want to play the show, they'll find you another night."

I relax against the pillows and sigh. "Okay." I want to ask

about Brett, but I'm a little afraid to. Silas moves his hand to my hair, which is reassuring. He takes a sip from a Starbucks cup in his hand, and strokes my head.

"Is that coffee?" I squeak. He nods, and I can smell it now — rich and dark. Because of my phobia, I haven't had a cup of Starbucks coffee in years.

But there's something about waking up in a hospital room that makes things very plain. The very event I've been dreading for years finally happened. It sucked, but I'm still here. "Can I have a sip?" I ask.

Silas's hand goes still on my hair. "Of course." He removes the lid and offers me the cup. "You can have a sip of my drink anytime, anywhere."

I take it and sip without stopping to think about it. The coffee is hot and bitter and feels great against my parched throat. Even better — Silas wraps an arm around my shoulders. I hand back the cup, then lean my head against his solid bulk. "Okay. Tell me the truth. Where is Brett right now?"

"Probably at his bail hearing," Silas says. "There are multiple charges. Possession of a controlled substance and assault in the second degree."

"Bail hearing," I repeat slowly. "This probably isn't the first time he's done it."

Silas rubs my back. "Probably not," he agrees. And he's holding back from saying more. I can feel it.

"What? Tell me all of it. I'm not scared." That's a lie, but it sounds good out loud.

"It's possible that the first time you were drugged, he was the culprit. You told me once that he was there to help you afterward."

Another shiver hits me. "That is just twisted. But it makes sense. He didn't want me to call the police after it happened." God, I'd trusted him even when I knew I shouldn't. I wanted Brett to be my savior. I wanted him to launch my career.

And he did.

"Here's the part I'm not sure about," Silas says. "My friends at Roadie Joe's say he came in, ordered a drink, tucked a stack of cocktail napkins in his pocket, and then left again five minutes later."

"Cocktail napkins?" It takes a moment for that to sink in. "You think he's my stalker, too?"

"I do. The motive seems pretty clear. He would do anything to keep you under his thumb. You were afraid to change security companies, right? He liked it that way. And mailing napkins to you didn't require a lot of skill or daring."

Wrapping both arms around him, I plaster my face to his T-shirt. "I don't ever want to see his face again. I will knee him right in the balls."

"You and me both."

———

The rest of the day is sort of a groggy blur. Doctors poke at me a little while, but it's clear that I'm going to be fine. When I'm cleared to leave, Becky and Silas try to sneak me out of the hospital via the back entrance. I hear only a few cameras click as Silas tucks me into his mother's car.

There will be some scary photos of me out in the world before nightfall. Becky won't show them to me, though. She knows better.

Silas sees us to the hotel elevator but doesn't come upstairs. "Get some rest," he says. "I'm going home to shower. Can I bring you dinner later?"

"Are you going to explain why you went MIA this week?"

"That's the plan."

"Make it good, Ralph. I can't wait to hear this later."

He gives me a sad smile and leaves.

I'm pretty happy about getting a shower, too. Becky clucks

over me like a mother duck the whole time. "I should have known something terrible would happen," she keeps saying. "I didn't trust my gut."

My gut is on probation these days, too. I was never smart when it came to Brett. My gut always knew there was something sour where his heart belonged. But I thought I could handle him.

I was wrong.

I pull on my most comfortable yoga pants and a tank top and wonder how long it will be until Silas is back.

Unfortunately, he isn't my next visitor. There's a loud knock on the door, and when Becky answers it, Charla Harris sweeps in, looking fierce. "I will fucking kill him. No—I will sue him for every penny and *then* kill him. When I'm finished with his bloody corpse, I will then spank you for going over to his house alone to negotiate with that violent freak."

I blink. "It's lovely to see you, too, Charla. But it's unexpected. Don't you have a dinner or a spa appointment scheduled somewhere?"

She rolls her eyes. "It takes a lot for me to cancel appointments, as you well know. But one or two things are motivating. Such as your near death."

"I'm fine. I swear. I'll be okay."

"Of course you will be. But now we have paperwork to sign, girl." She snaps her fingers. "Pay attention."

Wait, what? "How'd you get in here, anyway?" I have to ask. Security is a little more important to me than usual today. "You weren't on the list."

"Oh." She smacks her forehead. "I was recognized by your giant bodyguard. And he wants a word. He's in the hallway."

"Mr. Muscles?" I hadn't seen him at the hospital. One of the other guys was on duty outside my room last I checked. I cross the room and peer through the peephole.

Sure enough, Mr. Muscles is there.

"Miss," he whispers when I open the door, clasping his hands together like an old woman in church. "I'm so sorry. Terribly sorry. I never liked that guy, and I had a suspicion that he wasn't all right up here." He points at his broad skull. "But I listened to my boss and I just..." He takes a deep breath. "I wanted to apologize. I was watchin' through the window, and when you drank that soda and then got woozy—" He shudders. "I should'na ever let you go in there alone."

I shiver too. And it's going to be a while before I can think about last night without getting freaked out. Now that I'm less woozy, it all seems more real.

"Anyway." He sighs. "I turned in my resignation today. I gotta take some time off and evaluate my skills."

"What? No!" I yelp. "It's not your fault that Brett's a sociopath. And I guess your gut told you to look through the window..." I realize I don't quite have the whole story yet. "What happened after that?"

He shrugs his mountainous shoulders. "I saw you sort of slump forward. Ferris was trying to get you to sign something. Then I had to waste a few seconds calming down your boyfriend, who was climbin' through a shrubbery. I parked him outta sight while I knocked on the door. When the Prepmonster answered—"

"Prepmonster?" I shriek in tandem with Becky. And maybe Charla, too.

Another shrug. "That's what I call 'im in my head. Anywhos, when he answered the door, I forced my way inside and drop-kicked him while the boyfriend carried you out."

He dropkicked Brett? And I missed it?

I leap forward, and my hug catches Mr. Muscles by surprise. And I swear it's like hugging a tank. "Thank you for doing that for me. And please don't worry. I'm fine."

"Know you don't like me much," he whispers. "I tried to do a good job."

"It wasn't personal. I was pretty sure that Brett was keeping tabs on me and using you to do it."

"He was," the big man says. "I knew it. But it wasn't like I ratted you out after every shift, okay? There were these logs I was required to fill out—who you were with and where we went. They told me it was all because of that stalker. But I could tell Brett is a jealous fucker."

"Jealous fucker," Charla says. "Good name, but I like Prep-monster better."

"Same," Becky agrees.

"Sorry just the same," he says. "And I should go and let you rest."

I pat the tank on his giant arm. "You take care of yourself, okay? Don't make any rash decisions on my account. You can stay on my security team as long as you like."

"Okay, miss. But I 'spect you won't be on the West Coast much longer, anyway."

"Why not?" That's news to me.

"The boyfriend," he says simply. "Guy like that you hang onto. I would if he was mine. Hot and super nice. If he's also good in bed, that's like a unicorn right there."

The three of us stare up at him in stunned silence. The *depths* Mr. Muscles has revealed tonight! I'm almost too fascinated to remember how shitty the last twenty-four hours have been.

Eventually, Becky clears her throat. "Good advice."

"Right!" I say brightly. "You have a good night. Take it easy. All is well here."

He nods his giant head and then leaves us.

"Can't believe we missed the drop-kick," Becky says, sighing.

"I'd pay cash money to see that," Charla agrees. "And speaking of cash money…"

"It must be a lot of coin if you flew up here to talk about it." I sit down on the sofa and stare out at the ocean. The beach is always beautiful. Too bad I hate this town. My gut was right about Darlington Beach, at least.

"So, listen. MetroPlex is afraid you'll sue." Charla plops her body into a chair. "And if you want to, I'll hire you the lawyers to do that. But there's an alternative. They'll hand you a better offer for *Lucky Hearts*."

"Wait." I'm already under contract with them on that album and have been for nearly three years. "I don't understand."

"I did a little renegotiating." She smiles evilly. "I said we *might* not sue if they improve your terms and then launch the sucker. You're getting a little better royalty rate and a guaranteed release within five weeks. They are suddenly *very* eager to launch the record."

"But…why?" They didn't care before.

"Your old contract has something called a fiduciary duty clause. It means that the record label is supposed to do everything they can to increase your income. Even with them sitting on your album it was going to be —"

" —too hard to prove they mishandled me. I remember."

"But when the head of your label is arrested for poisoning your fucking drink, it's suddenly *really* easy to prove that they're not looking after your best interests. If Brett is convicted, we'll win our suit with no problem. But it will still take a year or more in court."

Becky squeals. "That's why they're in a hurry to launch. This is good, right?"

"Exactly," Charla says. "Unless Delilah wants to sue the fuckers. It's really her call."

I consider my options for about a second and a half. "Let's launch the album and cash their checks," I say. "The music matters more than my anger. They can't have album number three, though."

Charla waves a dismissive hand. "No shit, Sherlock. The

suitors are lining up already. I would never let you sign a contract that obligated you like that."

"Thank God for Charla," Becky whispers.

Indeed.

I look out at the ocean again, and marvel at the twisty path that's led me here. "I want to sign the renegotiation with Metro-Plex," I say. "Let's just end this."

"Smart girl. And I didn't even have to drug you." She pulls a folder out of her bag. "Too soon for that joke?"

"Too soon," Becky agrees quickly.

SILAS

"What's with the long face?" Danny asks as he hands my takeout order over the counter. "Your girl is recovering, right? And now the whole world knows what we've always known."

"That Oakland is an under-appreciated baseball team?"

Danny smirks. "That Brett Ferris is a weasel, a cheat, and a psychopath."

"Yeah, but he's already out on bail. She needs an order of protection against him. And I'm supposed to get on a plane tomorrow morning." Leaving Delilah again? I don't know if I can do that right now.

"Ah. No wonder you look so unhappy." He hands me my credit card slip. "Hang in there. You exposed that fucker this time. The whole town is talking about him. He can't show his face in town soon."

I sign my name and hand back the receipt. Everything Danny says is true, but it doesn't make me rest any easier. "See you around?"

"A guy can hope. You playing the Sharks anytime soon? I'll hit up StubHub."

"I'll find you some tickets, I promise. It's good to see you."

"You too, man. Take it easy."

As if I knew how.

I'm brooding as I carry our dinner to the hotel. The night-time air is California-sweet with a salty taste, but I can't enjoy it. Halfway there, I stop and pull out my phone to text Bess, my agent. *What happens if I don't get on that plane tomorrow?*

Her response is a phone call about thirty seconds later. "Silas, you have to get on that plane. The organization will fine you."

"Money doesn't matter to me right now."

She makes an impatient noise. "You know it's not right to do that to your team. It's bad for morale. Buddy, if someone died, they'd give you a little time…"

"Bess! Jesus." My stomach rolls.

"She didn't," Bess says softly. "Everything is going to be fine. And that's why your butt needs to be on that flight tomorrow. Don't even push your flight back, okay? Not even a few hours. She's not the only one who's depending on you. It's too early in your career to be a diva."

I know she's right. And I don't want to let anybody down. But after we hang up, I don't feel any better. When I reach the hotel, I ride the elevator to the penthouse floor. In the hallway outside Delilah's suite, there's a new beefy bodyguard on duty. I don't recognize him.

"ID, please," he says.

I hand it over, happy to know they're being cagey about who gets in to see her.

"Ah. Hello, Silas. This is for you." He returns my ID along with a hotel keycard. "She may be napping. You're supposed to wake her up."

"Okay. Thanks, man."

He actually salutes me. I hope he's ex-military. I hope he's a goddamn Navy SEAL. "You know what Brett Ferris looks like, right?"

"Like this?" He pulls something out of his back pocket, which proves to be a deck of photos, all of them of Brett in different settings, wearing different clothes.

"Yeah. I guess you got that covered. Later."

He salutes again.

I let myself in to what must be the most beautiful hotel suite in Darlington Beach. Floor-to-ceiling windows look out over the darkening ocean. Across a generous living room, big double doors open to reveal a spacious white bed. And Delilah sleeps peacefully on it, her hair spread out on one of the many pillows.

My heart breaks a little bit at the sight of her. It doesn't matter how strong she is. There will always be someone willing to hurt her. Nobody is unreachable, and her job makes her a target.

I set the food down on the coffee table and toe out of my shoes. In the bedroom, I perch on the edge of the bed and lay a hand on her head. She doesn't stir. So I strip off my T-shirt and lie down next to her.

My intention is to let her sleep. But I can't lie this close to her and not bury my nose in her hair, kiss her forehead.

"Silas," she whispers. Or maybe it's just a sigh. But I put an arm around her and pull her against my bare chest. Without opening her eyes, she makes herself more comfortable against my body as her breathing evens out again.

This is exactly what I need. She's safe, and she's in my arms. I might not get on that plane tomorrow, even if it costs me my job. Because if I'm feeling a little traumatized, Delilah might be a wreck tomorrow. She has every right to be.

And that's partly my fault. I can't walk away now.

We lie there awhile, my mind spinning. I stroke her hair and run a hand down the soft skin of her arm. The heat of her body soaks into mine, and our heartbeats find an even rhythm.

She stirs after a time, stroking my bare waist with her thumb, pressing a kiss to my chest. I lie comfortably still, wondering if she needs more sleep. But she nuzzles me with her lips, her tongue finding my nipple and pressing flat against it.

My blood stirs. Of course it does. The thrum of desire I feel for her never goes away. But I didn't come here to ravage her. So I run a patient hand down her silken hair, and tell my body to relax.

Delilah, though. She's not on the same page. She makes a trail of kisses across my chest before continuing the path up to my neck. I turn my head on instinct, granting her better access. Her kisses give me goosebumps, and I can't hold out any longer. "Come here," I rasp, capturing her face in my hands. I pull her up for a kiss.

We're nose to nose as our lips meet for the first time in way too long. I hold her brown-eyed gaze as I kiss her gently. The kiss flips a switch inside my worried soul, and the taste of her lips is what finally convinces me that she'll be okay.

"Dee," I whisper up at her. "I missed you. I'm sorry I —"

She presses a finger to my lips. "Did you have a really good reason not to show up the other night?"

"Yeah," I say against her finger.

"Then you can tell me later."

She replaces that finger with her mouth. I groan as she deepens the kiss, her body spread out on mine. And we ignite faster than tiki torches on the beach. My hands wander down her back and under her shirt, my palms skimming over warm skin, then down to cup her ass. I roll my hips up off the bed, and she moans into my mouth.

A second later she sits up, moves off me and unzips my shorts. I lift my hips again to help her out, and she tugs off everything at once. Freed of my clothing, my hard cock slaps me in the belly. Delilah pulls her shirt off, too, and throws it across the room.

"Jesus," I say as her breasts bounce free. I try to sit up, drawn like a beacon to her body.

"Nope," she says, pushing me down again. "Not yet."

I fall back on my elbows, smiling. "Feeling bossy?"

She doesn't answer me. Not in words, anyway. Instead, she straddles my thighs and takes me in hand.

"Unngh," I say as she strokes my shaft with a firm grip. "Okay. Your way is fun, too. In fact—"

I don't even remember how that sentence was supposed to end, because she leans down and takes me into her mouth.

Whoa. It's just a little more difficult to worry about the future when her tongue is stroking me and those smoldering brown eyes look up just as she gives me a good, tight suck. "Jesus, girly," I grunt, stroking her hair with shaking fingers.

She keeps up with her exquisite torture until I'm trembling. "Wait," I beg. "I'm not ready for this to end."

Thankfully, she releases me. As she sits up again, I take a deep breath to try to calm down.

But oxygen can only go so far. I'm rock-hard and desperate. And it's a shock when Delilah kicks off her yoga pants, then throws a leg over me. She lines me up beneath her body and *sinks down on my bare cock.*

I let out a shout as she sheathes me in silky, clenching heat. All my muscles clench involuntarily as I try to get a hold of myself. "Hey," I gasp. "Condom."

"No need." The vixen gives her head a quick shake. "I came prepared."

"Day-amn." I sit up, and we're nose to nose again. "You feel incredible. I'm probably going to disgrace myself."

She shakes her head. "I really need to be this close to you right now."

"You got it." I wrap both arms around her and take another deep breath. She's right, too. "There is nowhere I'd rather be." I tug her hips closer, and we're chest to chest *and* nose to nose.

Then tongue to tongue. It's physically impossible to be any closer than we are right now.

Delilah shows me some mercy by moving slowly at first. Gripping my shoulders, she rides me like we have all week. But it isn't long until we're both too wound up to go slow. And every time I jack my hips off the bed, she lets out an earthy, helpless sound. I break out in a sweat as we pick up the pace. I'm aching and desperate and yet so, so happy.

"Jesus," Delilah pants, throwing her head back. "You really want to roll me over and go into beast mode, don't you?"

"Maybe," I gasp, thrusting again. "Now that you mention it."

She gives a throaty laugh, and I need to hear that sound almost as much as I need to come. She puts her hands to my face. "Do it, then."

About two seconds later she's flat on her back, and I'm going hard and fast. Her knees hug my sides for dear life, and her breasts bounce with every snap of my hips. "Now, honey," I beg.

"*Yes*," she cries, or at least I think she does. All I can hear are my own moans and hers answering me back as we lose ourselves in the release we both need so badly.

When my brain comes back online, we're side by side on the bed, hand in hand, still breathing hard. After another minute of trying to get my heart rate down, I open my mouth to tell her something important. "I—"

But she speaks at the same time "So—"

We both pause to let the other speak.

"You first," she says.

I laugh, because timing never was easy for us. "I love you," I say and then laugh again. "How about that?"

She sits up and looks down at me. "Oh! God." She leans over and kisses me. "I love you too! Thank you for making me say it."

"I didn't make you."

She shrugs her naked shoulders. "Sometimes I need a push. But I'm trying."

"What were you going to say, though?" I reach up a hand and cup her sweet face. "Just now?"

"Oh. Well this is embarrassing." She gives me a nervous smile. "I was just going to ask if you brought food."

I cover my face with both hands and crack up. "Of course I did."

❀ ❀ ❀

We eat in our underwear on the bed. We don't bother with plates from the kitchenette or good silverware. I've brought a pasta with salmon and an order of avocado sliders. We trade the containers back and forth while we talk.

And I finally get my chance to explain why I stood her up the other night. "It wasn't because I had cold feet, or didn't want to come. Brett threatened us."

"*What?*" The fork pauses on its way to her mouth. "That asshole is always coming between us."

"Because we let him," I point out. "I let him just this week."

"Never again," she grumbles. "I want to hear the whole story."

That requires going back in time and filling her in on all the parts I'd skipped before.

"He got you *arrested* in high school? Then he threatens your *mom?*" Delilah is horrified when it all comes out. "*What* an asshole. I had the worst taste in men."

I laugh. "Well…"

"*Had,*" she says. "Past tense."

"Still."

She sets down the food and grips my knee. "I'm still not

used to you. Part of me doesn't quite believe that I deserve you."

"Shit. I'm the same."

"*Why?*"

"Because I didn't level with you before. If I'd told you what Brett did to ruin my chances, you might have understood how calculating he really is. You could have avoided every single awful thing that's happened to you in three years."

She blinks. "I don't know if it would even matter. We could both go insane trying to second guess ourselves."

"I suppose." I clear my throat. "You're probably right. And maybe I'll stop feeling so responsible if they convict him. Still. I *really* don't want to get on a plane tomorrow."

She swallows. "Do you have to?"

No.

Yes.

"That's not an easy question. If I want to keep my place on the team, then I have to leave. They could fine me just for missing today's practice. It's not just the coach I'm letting down. It's two dozen guys who need to get the season off to the right start."

"Shit."

I pick up our empty food containers and put them back into the bag. I carry the whole thing out to the kitchen.

When I come back, Delilah is sitting very straight on the bed watching me. "I don't want you to go. But I know you need to."

"I sure don't want to go. What would you say to coming home with me for a little while?"

"How would that work?"

"You'd think of it as a vacation. No—a retreat." I gather her hair in one hand and lift her chin with the other. "It's a selfish request. I don't think I can go back home and keep my head in the game while I'm so worried about you."

"I'm okay, Silas."

"Yeah, I can see that. But I'm not over it yet. And you've had a really rough time. I just want you around. And I want you safe. I want to be able to climb into bed beside you at night and be totally sure you're all right."

"Okay."

"Okay?"

"I'll go on retreat to Brooklyn." She smiles at me. "The schedule Charla set up for me is about to get the ax anyway. We have to shift gears and go into launch mode."

"Is that stressful?"

"Sure, sort of. There will be interviews and appearances, late-night TV. Stylists and crap."

"Do you feel up to that?"

"Well, I *never* feel up to that. But it's for something I really want. So it'll be all right." She reaches up and puts a hand on my face. "You look so worried."

I'm sure I do. Twenty-four hours ago I was carrying her limp body into the E.R. But I don't want to talk about it. "Want to go for a walk on the beach?"

"Yes!" She slides off the bed. "Let me grab a sweatshirt."

We both get dressed. When she comes back, I'm tapping on my phone.

"Who are you talking to?"

"Nobody yet. But would you mind if I asked Becky to find you a seat on my flight tomorrow. Is that okay?"

She stops. Then opens her mouth. Then closes it again. And then? Her eyes get wet, and she covers her face with her hands.

For a second I'm so stunned I don't move. But then I cross the room to her in two quick strides. "Hey! Easy." I wrap my arms around her. "I have no idea what I did. But I'll undo it."

"No!" She sniffs, clinging to me. "I'm sorry. I *never* cry."

"It's okay."

"I mean *never*." She wipes her eyes on the sleeve of her sweatshirt.

"Shh." I rub her back slowly. "Deep breaths. Want to fill me in?"

"It won't make any sense."

"Try me."

"I don't trust myself. The first thing I told you when you showed up in my New York hotel room is that I didn't want a man to complicate my life."

Uh-oh. "I remember."

"Because I fucked things up so badly before. I let him control me, because I was overwhelmed. He managed my career, and he managed my life. I was swept under."

"Okay." I've got her tucked against my chest, exactly where I like her to be.

"And I swear it's the only reason I'm hesitant about going to New York. Because it's your turf, and you'll have to help me manage. Again. I'll feel like I never learned how to adult."

"But—"

"—hang on, I'm not done. Just now you were thinking about plane tickets and how we needed one. And you didn't just buy it. And you didn't just ask Becky. You asked me first." She pulls back and looks at me with red eyes. "Just keep doing that. I want to go to Brooklyn with you so badly. But I can't let anyone *handle* me for a while."

I wipe her tears with my thumbs. "Okay."

"Okay?"

"I never wanted to manage you. I just want your company. I want to ask about your day, and hear about all the weird parts of your career. And I want you to sing to me."

"I could do that." She sniffs.

"See? We got this. In fact, there's something I want to show you on our way out." I take her by the hand to the living room, where I left my shoes and my gym bag earlier. From the bag I pull the T-shirt I had made a week ago.

"Oh my GOD!" she shrieks when I hand it over. "That's hilarious."

"I thought so. And thank you for validating my world view. But it's a joke, okay? That's how I see my role here. A good listener, followed by comic relief."

Her eyes well up again. "Thank you. I love it so much."

"You're welcome." I step closer and give her a squeeze. "Are you sure you're okay?"

"I think I'm...a total wreck!" She pushes her face into my shoulder and sobs. "He *drugged* me."

"I know," I whisper.

"I *let* him."

"Shh. Okay." Her body shakes with sobs, and I hate that so much. But trauma doesn't ask permission. And there's nowhere else I'd rather be right now. Nowhere at all.

✳ ✳ ✳

Eventually, we do take that walk on the beach. Delilah's bodyguard follows us at a discreet distance, while we walk barefoot through the sand.

I squeeze her hand as the waves crash onto the beach. The tide is coming in. We walk mostly in silence, because Delilah is emotionally drained. My heart is full, though. Things aren't settled between us, and they sure aren't easy. But I'm here, and we're together. It's all I ever wanted.

She stops suddenly, looking straight ahead.

"What is it?" The beach is mostly empty. I see one guy riding his bike slowly down the path at the edge. But that's it.

"The lifeguard tower."

"Oh." There it is. The spot where I was supposed to meet her three years ago. "Come on, then."

Hand in hand, we walk to a spot of her choosing. "Right here. This is where I waited."

"For a guy who asked fifty times for your phone number and never got it."

She smiles up at the dark sky. "Huge mistake. One of many."

"We've both got those. But I think we need to let them go, if we're going to be happy."

"I suppose you're right." She twirls around in a circle, her arms out. "Here's the place where nothing started. And nothing ended. It's just a spot on the sand."

"For us, maybe. I'll bet it's an important spot for someone else's love story."

She drops her hands. "Someone else's love story. Hmm. That's kind of lyrical. It would make a good chorus."

"You can't shut it off, can you?" I ask with a smile.

"Nope. Occupational hazard." She takes my hand again and steers me back in the direction we came.

"You need your notebook now, right?"

"Just to scribble down those four words. I can't write music tonight. I'd rather just hang out with you."

Hearing that makes a warm place in my chest.

"What do I need to know about Brooklyn? Is this a bad time to mention that I've only been there once?"

I laugh out loud. "No, it's the perfect time. It's like Manhattan, but with slightly less traffic. And slightly less convenient subways. But the pizza is top-notch."

"Confession—I always thought it would be amazing to live someplace where cars are unnecessary."

"I walk to work every day. And so can you. Heidi told me there are recording studios in the Navy Yards development."

"Oh, yeah." She squeezes my hand. "That's where I was the one time I went to Brooklyn. Is that near your neighborhood?"

"It's a five-minute walk from my apartment, Dee."

She stops and turns to me. "You mean, I was only a five-minute walk away from you?"

"I guess so. Unless I was traveling."

"I hope you were. Because I hate to think that fate just decided I didn't need to run into you."

"Let's not let her do that again," I promise.

"Never again." She stands up on her tiptoes and kisses me.

DELILAH

"I need to just play with this bass line for a second. Hold, please."

I sit back and wait while Songwriter Sarah messes around on the keyboard. We're in another windowless room, of course. Since you can't see the sky, a recording studio can make you forget what time of day it is, the weather outside, and where you are.

As it happens, we're in Brooklyn, at the recording studio that's only a five-minute walk from Silas's building.

I've been in Brooklyn for about seven days, and it's been terrific. My days are filled with emails and Skype chats with Charla and Becky, as my album launch is hastily planned.

My "office" has been the large sectional sofa in the living room of Silas's apartment. I have the place to myself for large chunks of the day, so I don't feel like I'm in the way very often. In the evenings, we go out to dinner. Sometimes it's all four of us—with Jason and Heidi, too—and sometimes just Silas and I.

Last night we sat around on the sofa and watched a super-hero movie. Usually those bore me, but just listening to Jason and Silas pick it apart was entertaining in its own right.

I'm…happy. It's such a dull little word. Not one I'd try to put into a song lyric unless absolutely necessary. But that doesn't make it any less fulfilling.

A few days ago, I texted Songwriter Sarah to postpone our second recording session. Charla would have canceled for me, but I like Sarah so I'd wanted to tell her myself.

Oh no, she'd texted back. *Do you hate the songs? Do you want to destroy them with fire?*

I'd laughed out loud. *No, silly. Still love the songs. There's been some drama in my life and my whole schedule has changed. Right now I'm in Brooklyn for a couple of weeks with my boyfriend.*

That's when Sarah called to tell me that she lives in New York, making only sporadic trips to L.A. And that she was here right now.

"Oh! How convenient!" I'd said. So here we are in the studio, tinkering.

"Okay, I think I got it," she says. She plays the new bass line.

"Yes! That totally works." "Ask the Universe" is really coming along, but my head is in a few different places today. "You mind if we shut it down for today, though?"

"I don't mind." She scribbles a note onto the music in front of her. "Okay to turn off the recording?"

"Yeah." I stand up, look through the glass at the engineer, and make the universal sign for *cut*—a hand in front of the throat.

"This was fun!" she says, adjusting her big glasses. "As always. I know you have a launch coming up, but I hope it's not too ass-kissy to say that I am at your disposal. Generally." She gives me a nervous smile.

"We will definitely do this again. But could I show you something? It involves a five-minute walk."

"Sure!" She jumps up and starts shoving things into her canvas tote bag. "Where are we going?"

The walk takes ten minutes instead of five, because we stop for coffee. For myself I buy a bottled juice, because old habits die hard. Yesterday Charla Harris suggested—in that not-so-gentle way she has—that I could benefit from a therapist. "Someone to help you process the bullshit the Prepmonster fed you. Someone to help you order a fucking cup of coffee again. Say the word and I'll find you someone."

She probably isn't wrong. But there are a few other questions to answer first. And one of them is about five doors past the door to Silas's apartment. I pull out the keycard that Heidi slipped me this morning, and I let myself and Sarah into the nearly empty space.

"Wow," Sarah breathes. "Nice place."

"Isn't it pretty?" I've already spent a fair amount of time staring at the realtor's photographs and squinting at the floor plan, trying to imagine my life in this space.

It was surprisingly easy to do that, and it's even better in person. Golden light bounces off the exposed bricks and the honeyed wood floors. Big windows show Brooklyn to its best advantage.

"That *kitchen*," Sarah says with a sigh.

"I know!" I turn around and admire the sleek cabinets and high-tech faucet. "It almost makes me want to learn to cook. Do you cook?"

"Nope. I'm terrible. That's what takeout is for."

We both laugh.

"Okay," I say. "So here's my question. I've never had to build a home studio before. My L.A. studio was already done up when I rented the place. And even so, I've never recorded anything there that needed to sound great. So how do musicians do this in New York? Like, what if I buy this apartment, and it's an acoustic disaster?"

Sarah walks slowly across the space and peers into the bedrooms, one at a time. "Okay, in the first place, New York makes every musician a little bit crazy. I mean, it's the best place and the worst place in the world to be a musician. It's a great music town. But it's pricey as shit."

"So every musician has this problem?"

"Yup. And every apartment is potentially an acoustic disaster. You can't control everything. What if a tap dancer moves in above you?"

We both lift our chins and look up at the high plaster ceiling, as if there was something to be learned up there.

"The thing is, though, if you have a little money, you can solve any acoustical problem. It's really just about how you want to live in this space. You could hire somebody to cover over every surface of one of these bedrooms, and truly soundproof the whole place. But that seems like a shame, right? It's so attractive the way it is."

"Yeah."

"If it was me, I'd turn one room into an office-slash-composing space. And leave it looking like this. *Then* I'd install a prebuilt booth for those moments when you really need a good take."

"What do you mean?"

Her eyebrows disappear behind her glasses' frames. "Oh my gosh, let me show you. I look at these websites the way some people look at expensive shoes..." She taps her phone a few times and then hands it to me.

There's a photo of another beautiful apartment. In the corner, there's a bright orange recording booth—like an oversized phone booth with a handsome man playing a saxophone inside of it. "Oh. And these work?"

"They're amazing. But they're not cheap. I'd spend the money, but I don't own my apartment so..." She shrugs. "You can buy a really small one if you don't want to give up much of the room. Or some of them fit two or three musicians, if you want to work that way. See?"

The next photo is another stunning living space with a recording booth right off the kitchen. "Wow, okay." Maybe this isn't as complicated as I thought.

"How have you never seen this before? People have them in L.A."

"I told you I'm kind of a hermit, Sarah."

"And I thought you were exaggerating." She takes her phone back and taps the screen. "I'm sending you the link. But there are two or three companies who make these. I have mine all spec'ed out, of course, the way some people price out cars. It's a two-seater in lime green." Her smile is adorable.

"Thank you. I appreciate the help."

"Anytime!"

She leaves a few minutes later. But I don't. I spend a nice long time strolling around in the empty rooms, thinking.

SILAS

At about six o'clock I shoot a text to Delilah. *We're going to watch some film, and I'll be home by seven thirty. What do you want to do about dinner?*

She replies immediately. *Takeout! I'll handle it if you tell me what you want. And it's okay if you say pizza again. I won't judge.*

I laugh out loud. A week in Brooklyn, and she already knows which things my friends give me crap about. My pizza addiction and my musical habits. Although they don't tease me about listening to Delilah's music anymore now that they understand why I was her superfan.

Pizza, though. It's still a problem. *Since you brought it up, pizza sounds great. I'm in the mood for a meatball pie.*

Will do! See you at 7:30!

I'm the first guy out of the video room when our session is over. They guys will give me some shit about that, too. I don't care, because I get home right on time. But when I arrive at my apartment door, there's a sticky note on it.

I remove the sticky note and just stare at it for a second. *Silas—I'm in 309.* That's Dave's apartment—the empty one.

I've managed not to bring it up again—not since that one time I sent her the photograph. She's been enjoying herself this week, and I wasn't about to ruin it by pressuring her to stay.

Although I want that.

It's a short trip down the hall. I knock with the backs of my knuckles. Since the place is nearly empty, my knock echoes inside.

"Come in!" she calls. When I try the door handle, it's unlocked. Inside, I find Delilah seated on the sofa that Heidi and I put there a few weeks ago. She glances up at me, and I have to pause there a moment and take in the whole picture. She's wearing a black T-shirt, just like the first time I met her. Her hair is swept up in a loose bun, where a bitten pencil seems to hold it in place. Her face is bathed in candlelight and a shy smile.

I have never seen such a beautiful sight in my life. And I'm not just saying that because there's a Grimaldi's pizza box on the rented coffee table. Plus a bottle of wine and two of my own wine glasses.

"Well, *hello* there," I say as I close the door behind me. I drop my gym bag to the floor. "Did you decide we need some peace and quiet tonight?" I cross the room to sit down beside her.

"No, it's not like that. But there is something I wanted to talk to you about."

I glance around this gorgeous room. I wish this were our couch, in our place. But I keep that idea to myself for now. What I wouldn't give to come home to her like this on a regular basis. "What's up, buttercup?"

"You remember how I gave you that big speech in Darlington Beach? The one about needing you to check in with me instead of planning my life for me? And how much I appreciate that?"

"Yeah?" Have I overstepped? I wrack my brain, wondering what I did. "That does sound familiar."

"Well, today I didn't show you the same courtesy. And I'm feeling a little worried. I did a thing without asking."

Oh, phew. This isn't about me at all. "What thing? You changed my pizza order?"

She gives me a little poke in the ribs. "I made an offer on this apartment."

"You…" I play that back in my head a couple times just to make sure I heard correctly. "Really?"

"Yep. I made an offer at the new asking price. So I can't imagine your teammate will turn me down. And it's a cash offer, too, so…" She studies her fingernails.

I let out a genuine whoop of joy. "And you thought maybe I wouldn't *like* that?"

"Well, it is awful presumptuous of me. I've been visiting only a week. And I did it without us discussing it first. It does sound a little crazy."

Not to me. "If I recall, I put this bug in your ear in the first place. So you weren't exactly flying blind, here. But who says I care about crazy? You and I can be a little crazy. We're never going to be a normal couple—the kind who's introduced at a cocktail party. The kind who goes out on a few dates, then escalate smoothly, like a jet taking off. Sex on the third date. No psycho exes or missed chances on a beach…"

She's laughing, and I love that sound. "I guess that ship has sailed."

"Right? I mean, maybe someday we'll be guests at that kind of cocktail party. And some well-meaning person will ask—how did you two get together? And you'll turn to him and say, 'How much time do you have?'"

She's laughing so hard she leans against me and shakes.

I flip open the pizza box and grab a slice.

"So it's okay with you?" she gasps. "That I'm buying an apartment down the hall from yours?"

"It's more than okay with me. In fact, I hope that one of these days you'll invite me to move my stuff out of that one and into this one. But if you want to do this stepwise—dormitory style—I'm good with that."

She takes a slice of pizza, too. "If we don't work out, then I will have made things super awkward and sad."

"It would be sad. But it would be even sadder not to try," I say before cramming more pizza into my mouth. "That's what I think, anyway."

She covers my free hand with hers. "Thank you for just rolling with this."

"You're giving me exactly what I want," I admit. "So I'm not just rolling with anything." We chew our pizza while my head spins. "I do have questions."

"Hit me."

"What about Becky?" I hate to think of Delilah trying to settle in a town where she has nobody but me.

"Becky is ready for this. She's busy calling all her old friends who live anywhere remotely near Brooklyn and asking them if they know anyone who needs a roommate. Becky grew up in Connecticut. She's no stranger to these parts."

"Oh." Well, that's handy.

"Becky's been to more New York pizzerias than I have."

"Not like that's hard. We have to broaden your horizons. And what about security? Will you let me ask Carl to find you somebody?" When I start traveling in a few weeks, I'll worry.

"I already made that call. He said his firm could handle whatever I need, and he'd find me a daytime bodyguard that I like."

"That's really all my questions, then."

"I'll have to go home to L.A. for a while, anyway, and figure out my move. Besides, my offer hasn't been accepted yet. I might be rearranging your expectations for nothing."

"Oh, it will be. Any delay is because Dave is frolicking on a Vermont hillside somewhere, too busy to look at his phone." Absently, I grab the wine bottle and remove the foil. I pick up the corkscrew and start turning before I remember. "Whoops! Sorry. I'm going to let you do this." Delilah is back to drinking things that she unseals herself. Phobias can't always be vanquished by one bold sip of coffee in a hospital room and some positive thinking.

And I really don't blame her. I'm still having bad dreams about the night she was drugged. Sometimes in the dream, I can't reach her. And then I wake up in a cold sweat.

"You open it," she says.

"Yeah?" I finish the job, then pour her a glass and offer it to her.

With a look of determination, she takes it from my hand and immediately takes a sip.

"What, you couldn't wait for the toast?" I tease.

She frowns, and then notices my grin. "You asshole!"

I cackle. Then I lift my glass. "To new apartments and big risks."

We touch glasses, and I hold her eyes while we both take a sip. Then we sit back to admire the view. Outside, the sun is setting. The sky over Manhattan is streaked with orange.

"God, I fucking love this place," Delilah exclaims. She grabs her phone off the table and peeks at the lock screen. "No message yet. But the realtor seemed pretty excited to hear from me."

"It will come," I promise. I wrap an arm around her. "Nice kitchen, by the way. I like that it's open plan."

"I like it, too. I like everything about it. I want to furnish a condo, like grownups do. I moved into Brett's place with a suitcase, and moved out with barely more. I'm going to choose furniture, damn it."

A gurgle of laughter escapes me.

"I know I sound like a diva right now," she says, patting my knee. "I promise not to make everything pink and girly." She sets her wine glass down and turns to me.

"Like I'd care," I say. "I laughed because choosing furniture does not sound fun to me. I'll sit on whatever." Just to prove the point, I set my glass down, too. Then I move my ass onto her lap and gingerly sit down.

"Ralph!" she complains. "That's not funny."

"Switch with me, then?"

"Fine."

I move off of her, sitting on the couch. Then I put my hands on her waist and turn her around so that she's straddling me. "Hi."

"Hi," she breathes.

I run a hand up her black T-shirt. "This is almost what you were wearing when I met you."

"Almost?" she blinks, clearly having no memory of her clothing that fateful day.

"Your shirt said, *Kind of a Big Deal.*"

"Oh!" She grins. "I remember. That was my favorite shirt for a while."

"Not any longer?"

"I gave it away a long time ago. Anytime I wore that shirt I meant it as irony. But after you start selling out stadiums, it just makes you look like a diva."

"Just so you know? You were kind of a big deal to me then. And you still are now."

Her face softens. "You say the nicest things."

"I mean them," I whisper.

"I know," she whispers back. "That's what makes it nice."

"Delilah—I love you, sweetheart. I know it's soon. And I don't want you to feel obligated to—"

"I love you, too," she says. "Even if my life is still a mess. You're just so easy to love."

My heart swells. "Kiss me?" I ask, lifting my chin. "I've been hungry for you all day."

With a smile, she leans over to comply. I wrap my hand around her hair and take what I need. Her mouth is silk against mine. One kiss leads me right into another. I use my free hand to stroke down the smooth skin of her arm and tug her closer.

Pretty soon we're hardcore making out on a rented couch, half our pizza forgotten. And my heart isn't the only thing swelling. "Delilah," I whisper.

"Yes?" she breathes into my mouth.

"We could christen this place tonight. Break it in. Try it out."

"Is that good luck?" she asks, her smile rubbing mine.

"Totally," I say, and she laughs. "Couch or kitchen counter?" I murmur as I slide her T-shirt up.

"Both," she says, removing my shirt and then wrapping her arms around me. We're skin to skin. "We've earned it."

She's right. We have.

EIGHT MONTHS LATER

SILAS

I'm face down in our bed, Delilah's naked body pressed against mine. Sunlight is streaming through the window, and my alarm is sounding. I reach out a hand and fumble around until I silence it. Then I push my face into my pillow again and sigh.

It's April, and we've already clinched a playoffs spot. So that's awesome. And today's my birthday, which is nice too, I guess. Delilah and I had very energetic sex until two in the morning in celebration.

I do not want to wake up, though. Because we're leaving on the last road trip of the season this morning. It's been a great season. An *epic* season. But I don't want to leave. Not when the bed is this comfortable, and the girl beside me so warm and naked.

We lasted until Christmas in separate apartments. When Jason and Heidi got engaged, I started paying attention to the real estate listings, just in case something in our building came open. Or something across the street. I didn't want to rush Delilah, but I didn't want to stay forever as a third wheel in the apartment down the hall.

Then Delilah caught me reading a message from the building administrator on my phone, and she immediately asked me to move in for real.

"Are you sure?" I'd asked. "I'd never rush you."

"I know that," she'd promised. "And I really needed to at least pretend to sort out my own life for a little while. But you're part of my life, and you're the reason I'm in New York. And I don't feel so fearful anymore."

So I'd moved in the next day, only to find that Delilah had left half the closet empty this whole time.

"For you, obviously. I always intended to live here with you. I just needed to do it stepwise."

Now I slip out of our bed, careful not to wake her. I pull on some boxers and shuffle into the kitchen, where Delilah's coffee machine waits. She chose everything with quiet deliberation, sometimes asking my advice or Becky's, or Heidi's.

I hit the button on the machine that starts the whole process —grinding the beans, and brewing the coffee. From the cabinet, I pull two Brooklyn Bruisers mugs. Her selection, again. But they're a choice made because of me.

When I moved in, Delilah apologized for keeping me waiting and for setting up the whole place before she installed me in it, too. "You're not unimportant to the equation; in fact, you're the *most* important," she'd said the first night we lay together in what was not yet our bed. "But—"

"I get it," I'd promised her. And I do. Standing in the well-appointed kitchen is like living with Delilah's most high-functioning, happiest self.

This place is home, and it's been amazing to watch Delilah find her groove. She has friends here. There's Becky, and Songwriter Sarah. And various music people at her new record label, which is part of her old record label in a way that I don't completely understand. But after *Lucky Hearts* went platinum,

Delilah and Charla decided to stick with one of the executives they knew for album number three.

Delilah is in a good place. And I'm the lucky guy who comes home to her whenever neither of us is traveling. She's going on tour this summer, and whenever my team is done with the post-season (and please let that not be too soon) I'll be joining her for the European part of that tour. Paris. Rome. Berlin. I can't wait.

Meanwhile, she's writing new music in her home studio—the room formerly known as Dave's extra bedroom. Where my retired teammate used to keep his exercise equipment, Delilah has guitars, comfortable chairs, and a soundproof recording booth that looks a little like something from a Dr. Who episode.

The alcove den is all mine, though. It's the only space she didn't furnish. "I think it's been waiting for you," she said.

That's our TV room now. And—as Heidi suggested all those months ago—I put in a pull-out couch for when my mom comes to visit.

We have a great life. It could only be made greater if I didn't have to get on a plane in two hours.

When the coffee is done brewing, I pour a splash of milk into each mug and carry them both into the bedroom. Delilah has to get up soon, too. It's a weekday, and Becky will turn up for whatever business appointments they've got planned.

"Hi, sleepy," I say, sitting down on the bed. "I made coffee."

Delilah sits up fast, clutching the sheet to her bosom. "Omigod, is it late?"

"No," I chuckle at the pillow marks on her face and her wild hair. "Becky isn't here yet." I offer her the mug.

She takes it from me. And as I watch, she takes a sip. And then another. Delilah is seeing a therapist. They're working on aversion therapy. These days, Delilah drinks cups of coffee that either Becky or I bring her. It's just the two of us for now, and it still isn't easy. But she does it every day.

Her eyes lift, and she catches me watching her. "Thank you."

"You're welcome."

"But now I have to hand this back to you, and not because I'm flunking coffee drinking."

"Okay?" I take the mug.

"I have a present for you."

"Oh! I thought I got my present last night." I give her a sleazy wink, and she laughs.

"But I believe in lots of presents. Hang on." She leans over, plucking her silk bathrobe off the floor where we tossed it last night. "Drink that coffee and don't go anywhere."

She disappears in the bathroom. Water runs, and so I prop myself up against our headboard and relax. My mind wanders to hockey, as it often does. We're going to play Toronto and Ottawa, before returning home to get ready to face whomever our first round of playoffs competition is. Coach will probably play me for both of those games. I'm still the number two goalie, but I played a third of our games this season. And sportswriters keep praising "Brooklyn's deep bench of goalie talent," which always makes my heart go pitter-patter.

The other thing that makes my heart go pitter-patter emerges from our bathroom a minute later, her smooth legs tempting me beneath that silky robe.

"Eyes up here, Ralph," she says, teasing me.

"Oh, they were headed there, too," I promise, taking a pointed look at her cleavage. "I don't know what else you got me for my birthday, but I liked the first present a whole lot. Just saying."

"Good to know. Since my other presents are a little…" She frowns. "Irregular. Especially the last thing. I'm out on a limb, here." Now my curiosity is piqued. She sets a wrapped box down on the bed and then sits cross-legged in front of me.

I put a hand onto one smooth knee. "You know I'll love it. Whatever it is."

Her smile is nervous. "Open it before I lose my nerve."

The box doesn't weigh much. It only takes me a few seconds to tear off the wrapping paper. When I lift off the top, there's a black T-shirt in my size. I unfold it and find that it says, *Kind of a Big Deal*. I laugh, of course. "For me?"

"I saw it in a Brooklyn window," she explains. "And you are a pretty big deal to me, so…" She clears her throat. "I wrote a song with that title. For you. But it's not finished yet."

"Can I hear it?"

"Of course." She hops up and fetches one of her acoustic guitars from the top of her dresser. Then she sits down opposite me and checks the tuning.

Goosebumps rise on my body immediately. I always have this reaction when she plays something for me, and I always will.

Her fingers begin to pluck the strings, picking out a smooth, upbeat rhythm. And my chills only multiply as she starts to sing.

It was a day just like any other day
In a town somewhere far away
I wasn't looking for everything to change
I didn't know we'd come all this way

But you're kind of a big deal
Ask anyone
It's the way that I feel
Ask anyone
There's nothing so real
When you hold me close…

My eyes are wet and I don't know why. And then the second chorus stops me in my tracks.

But you're kind of a big deal
Ask anyone
It's the way that I feel
Ask anyone
There's nothing so real
Will you marry me...?

"Really?"

The song ends abruptly as she silences the guitar strings with one hand.

My startled gaze collides with Delilah's. "You want to get married?"

She swallows. "I really do. And I know I was probably supposed to wait until you asked, but..."

I get up on my knees so fast that they crack, and I lean over and kiss her. "Let's get married. I didn't know you wanted to."

She wraps one arm around me and buries her face in my neck. "I'm sorry. I needed to say it first. So you'd know you didn't have to hold back."

"I *was* holding back." Christ, I think I've been holding back since the first day I saw her.

"After I wrote this, I almost chickened out," she whispers. "But you've been so patient with me. You're my rock, okay? I needed a big, important way to tell you."

"Uh, I'm pretty sure you nailed it." I sit back and look at her, my eyes still wet. "Even if I didn't let you finish. Set your guitar down for a second, okay? There's something I need to show you."

I open the drawer in the bedside table and fish out a box I've been keeping there. It's the kind of little box that's for only one thing.

"Oh!" She claps a hand over her mouth. "I can't believe it! You beat me to it?"

"No way. It's a good thing we're on the same page. After all this time."

Now her eyes are damp, too. She takes the box and opens it. "Omigod, Silas!" She looks up and laughs. "You're amazing."

The ring inside the box is a cushion-cut two-carat diamond in a classic style. The box is custom. The lid says, in careful embroidered letters, *Sparkle On... Your Finger.*

"I love it so much!" she says as tears break down her face.

"Will you marry me, too?" I ask. "Make me the happiest guy in Brooklyn?"

"I will," she says. "Any day of the week."

"Maybe..." My mind spins. "This summer. Between your tour and training camp. We could take a week on a beach for a honeymoon."

"Yes!" She's still holding the box as I pull her into my arms. "I can't wait."

"Me neither. And I can't *believe* I have to get on a plane right now."

"It totally sucks," she whispers. "No, it doesn't. I take it back. I regret nothing today."

I kiss her temple and sigh.

That's when the front door of the apartment opens. "Yoo-hoo! I'm here!" Becky calls out. "You kids probably aren't decent, are you? Happy birthday, Silas!"

"Thank you," I say in a thick voice, while Delilah wipes her eyes.

Reluctantly, I leave the bed and put on a clean white shirt and a suit for my trip. Delilah pulls herself together, too. We give each other a secretive smile while I collect our coffee cups and get ready to greet the team. *"Are you going to tell her?"* I mouth.

She holds up her hand to show me the ring sparkling from her finger.

This should be fun.

When I emerge from the bedroom, it isn't just Becky in the living room. Avivit is here, looking as badass as usual in her black pants and T-shirt. "Morning, sports guy," she says to me.

"Morning, soldier." She gives me a fractional smile. I think she's part robot.

When Carl Bayer told us that he had a bodyguard for us to meet, I'd expected someone like Mr. Muscles.

"Meet your new bodyguard, Delilah," the older man had said. "Avivit is ex-special forces in the Israeli military. And since your brand is all about girl power, I thought, why not add some real girl power to your team?"

Avivit and Delilah get along great. And I'm glad Delilah is safe. But Avivit has no time for me. "I'll bet you know seventeen different ways to kill me," I'd joked the first time she showed up for work in the morning.

"Eighteen," she'd said.

But Becky loves me, so at least I've got that. "How's the birthday boy?"

"Spectacular!" I say, because it's true. I still can't get my head around it.

Then Delilah comes out of the bedroom. "Morning, Becky. We're just having the usual Thursday, right? A few calls. A meeting. My new engagement ring." She holds up her hand.

And Becky *freaks*. My ears may never be the same. There's some hugging and screeching and then Becky attacks me, too. Even Avivit smiles.

"This is the best news ever!" Becky cries. "You deserve this. Both of you! When are you getting married?"

"Not sure," I say cheerfully.

"Where?" Becky tries.

"Don't know that either," Delilah adds.

"We'll figure it out," I say. "It's complicated. But we like it that way." And Delilah hugs me a little more tightly to tell me she agrees.

———

Thank you for reading Superfan! Grab the bonus epilogue at: SarinaBowen.com/bonus-bruisers

ALSO BY SARINA BOWEN

THE BROOKLYN BRUISERS

Rookie Move

Hard Hitter

Pipe Dreams

Brooklynaire

Overnight Sensation

Superfan

TRUE NORTH

Bittersweet

Steadfast

Keepsake

Bountiful

Speakeasy

Fireworks

THE IVY YEARS

The Year We Fell Down #1

The Year We Hid Away #2

The Understatement of the Year #3

The Shameless Hour #4

The Fifteenth Minute #5

Extra Credit #6

GRAVITY

Coming In From the Cold #1

Falling From the Sky #2

Shooting for the Stars #3

HELLO GOODBYE

Goodbye Paradise

Hello Forever

With Tanya Eby

Man Hands

Man Card

Boy Toy

With Elle Kennedy

GOOD BOY by Sarina Bowen & Elle Kennedy

STAY by Sarina Bowen & Elle Kennedy

HIM by Sarina Bowen & Elle Kennedy

US by Sarina Bowen & Elle Kennedy

Top Secret by Sarina Bowen & Elle Kennedy